D1563672

THE FALL

Other Books

THE

FALL

Book One

Connor Stevens
&
Brian Wiggins

This is a work of fiction. Names, characters, business, events and incidents are the products of the author's imagination. Any resemblance to actual persons, living or dead, or actual events is purely coincidental. Climate change, however, is very real. For the purposes of this story, we gamed out potential outcomes if nothing is done to fix the problem.

<u>An Important Message from The Authors</u>

We poured a lot of energy into writing this book and (hopefully) making it a good read. Before we get into the story, we have one simple request: Please do not forget to leave a review for this book. The value of book reviews – even just a single review consisting of a few words – can have a tremendous impact on the trajectory of books, the people who read them, and the authors who write them.

If you spend the next 30 seconds leaving a review for this book within the marketplace you purchased it, it will not only help us enormously, but it will also help readers like you who are looking for amazing stories like the one you're about to read.

Whether you choose to leave a review for this book now or later, by simply sharing one thing you learned or liked about this book, you will help support us in writing more books like this and more readers around the world who are seeking similar books.

We are grateful you have chosen to purchase this book and are taking the time to read it. You can find our other books at any Amazon or www.cb-books.com. You can also get updates through our mailing list.

Thank you,

- Connor and Brian

DEDICATIONS

Connor:
To Les.

Brian:
This is for Joanne. You're my favorite.

CHAPTER 1

Jason Thane took a deep breath of recycled air from his cycler[1] and cleared the fog from his goggles.

Three months of investigation, seventeen different search warrants, and six different informants working a whisper campaign to increase the pressure had finally paid off. Tommy Delucca was caught, flipped, and was going to get Jason access to what was rumored to be one of the largest splice stash houses in the Eastern Gaps.

He checked his watch. It read just before noon. He had been out of his usual police-issued UV gear and in civies for less than an hour. He didn't want to draw attention when they entered the basement bolt-hole and perpetual party where Delucca's contact was allegedly found. A film of sweat crawled on Jason's skin. He stretched as best he could in the confined space of the driver's seat for the hundredth time, trying to work the cramps out so he could run if he needed to.

All that was left now was for Delucca to lead him in, make the introduction, and hopefully sweet talk their way up to the top floor of the apartment building. The balding man with a rattail mullet and a hopeless combover trying to cover a losing battle with baldness sat in the back seat, muttering to himself. His eyes darted between staring at his shoes and out the window

---

[1] Apparatus that covers the mouth and nose and filters/recycles air

as he constantly wiped sweat from his brow with his sleeve.

Jason couldn't help but smile under his cycler. *Is that all?*

Jason scanned the block again. It was noon, and the street was practically empty, devoid of the usual bustle of people one would expect to see in a large city in the middle of the day, even in a less-affluent area like The Gaps, the places where the sun did actually shine to everyone's detriment there. The sporadically, and sometimes haphazardly, mounted bargain-bin and makeshift sun shields offered minimal protection at best.

A stark contrast to the streets of Center City, he noticed, where under the protection of the towering sky shields the upper-crust denizens were able to more freely go about their day, though still needing a degree of UV protection. He did note a few higher-quality shields being installed around the neighborhood. *Maybe that's a good sign. Maybe these landlords are finally putting some money into these properties.*

He saw a group of kids roofing, hopping over and rolling under the ventilation pipes and utility boxes, leaping the short alleys between buildings, sometimes even braving the long, thin stretches of support beams and breezeways crisscrossing the streets with their arms outstretched for balance. Part of him wanted to warn the kids off, to shout at them to play somewhere safer; another part of him warmed with the memory of doing the same thing with his friends when he was that age, racing to see who could reach the sunset first.

Jason signaled silently for the interdiction team, hidden up and down the block in unmarked patrollers or disguised as civilians on the street, to ready and hold.

His partner in the passenger seat, Les, grunted, the sound muted and distorted by his cycler's intercom. "*Estas seguro²?*"

Jason gave a stiff nod as he gave his UV gear a final check. "Don't want to spook the neighbors—no sense in going loud unless we have to. And we've got kids on the roofs. Don't want to create a bad situation."

Les returned the nod, his expression unreadable under his cycler and UV glasses, but Jason saw the faint tension in his partner's shoulders, a stiffness in his back. He wasn't happy about this. "You've seen this new splice. Makes PCP look like kids' cereal."

Sending in the entire team was the safer option; Jason knew this, but he also knew that sending an entire tactical team into a neighborhood watering hole, where the biggest crime was not paying for a liquor license, would not endear him or the 15th Squad to the community. And if the community wasn't in sync with the police on at least the issue of Splice overrunning the streets, then one arrest wouldn't make a lick of difference.

"You go in with an army, they'll be gone before you get to the second floor," Delucca said from the back seat.

"I've got this," Jason said, hoping his partner was reassured. He turned on his comm to communicate with the rest of the team. "Belford, you're on the back door just in case." There was no response. "Belford, respond." More silence. "Belford-"

---

² "You sure?"

"I'm on it," Derrick Belford finally responded. "Still should be me going in the front, though."

"Belford on the rear door, check," Jason responded and cleared the comms.

"How does one person get to be so entitled?" Les asked.

"It's a gift," Jason said. "He didn't even need to get a gene-mod. Just born with it."

"Well, good call. I can only imagine how it would go if he were first in." Les shook his head.

Jason smiled under his cycler and refocused his attention.

The anticipatory adrenaline spike flooded Jason's chest. It made his arms and legs tingle, and he closed his eyes and let the same feeling he got before every race, before every match, before every competition he had ever done, wash over him, embracing it rather than pushing it away. After a moment, he honed the sensation down to a razor edge and exited the car.

Even under his protective gear, the blast of heat was palpable, despite the sun hidden behind a blanket of gray clouds. He reflexively checked his civilian UV gear one more time, making sure no skin was exposed. The knot between his shoulders released a tiny bit when he confirmed everything was buttoned up properly.

Jason strode across the street with Delucca. They descended the stairs to the basement bar entrance. Jason noted it was less a bar and more an old storefront with thick brown paper taped over the windows. He could hear the muted music and conversation as he approached. He took one last deep breath, feeling his lungs expand, let it out, and pulled open the speakeasy door.

The sunlight cut a sharp silhouette on the floor that disappeared as the door swung shut. Jason's goggles adjusted to the low light almost instantly, and he could see the cast of characters around the makeshift bar. Third shifters a few hours into tying one on after work. Barflies just starting their day holding down a stool. A mix of shifty-eyed rabble side-eyed Jason with suspicion. A trio of college-aged kids, one with preternaturally blue eyes that only came from genetic modification, occupied a corner table, likely slumming it with some "dangerous Gappers" so they could brag to their friends.

"Lose the gear," Jason said so only Delucca could hear him.

"What? Why?" Delucca whispered back.

"Because I don't want you bolting the first chance you get."

Delucca hesitated a moment before slowly stripping off his headgear and UV coverings. He placed them in an available cubby near the entrance vestibule. "There, happy?"

"As a clam," Jason replied. "OK, where's the guy?"

"Patience, *mon frere*," Delucca said. "These things have a kind of ebb and flow, you know? I'm already putting my neck on the line. Don't rush it and make things worse." Then, almost to himself, Delucca muttered, "Can't believe I agreed to this."

"Me either," Jason said. "But here we are. Let's go."

Delucca meandered through the crowd. Jason stayed as close as he could, and the skin on the back of his neck itched. Too many people caught his attention, like the woman with a purple mohawk staring at him from the corner. Or the stoned guy with a scorpion tattoo on his arm sprawled out on a couch with two women, all of whom looked stoned out of their minds.

I'm starting to regret not coming in without someone to watch my back.

Delucca held up a hand. "One minute, there's my guy."

Jason moved to follow him.

"Are you nuts?" Delucca said in a harsh whisper. "These people don't know you. You trying to get me killed?"

"This doesn't work if I'm not with you," Jason whispered back. "No stash, no deal, and you do your dime."

"Just…just let me make the introduction, OK?" Delucca said. "This guy gets us in the door, but only if he trusts both of us. So just let me work, OK?" A flop sweat had broken out on Delucca's forehead.

"Fine," Jason replied. "Make it quick."

Delucca approached a tall man with a shaved head and tattoos on his scalp. The man did not appear happy to see Delucca, and from where Jason stood, it looked like tense words were exchanged, though he couldn't make out what was said through the crowd's jostling and murmured conversations that filled the air like white noise.

Finally, Delucca returned. "OK, we're in." His voice was tight.

"You sure?" Jason said. "You don't sound confident."

"No, I'm sure," Delucca said, but Jason didn't hear conviction behind his words. "That way, over in the back. Stairs will take us up to the top floor. They've got all the other entrances up there blocked."

Choke point. Good security. Makes this a nightmare if things go south and we have to go loud.

Delucca led Jason through the crowd. Jason noticed his guide glanced around more, almost twitching whenever someone bumped or brushed against him.

"Calm down," Jason said under his breath.

"Calm down," Delucca repeated with a rueful laugh. "These guys are nuts. They'll kill me, and after I'm dead, then they'll go to work on me."

"I already told you that we'd protect you," Jason said, grabbing Delucca's elbow and steering him forward. "That's the deal."

Delucca grumbled something unintelligible. "The way you protected Rusty when you flipped him?" he growled. Then he sighed. "You know what…screw it."

The telltale click and hiss of a splice ampule snapped Jason's attention to Delucca's thigh where he had jabbed the doser in.

Where did he get that?

The elbow that cracked Jason in the nose left him seeing stars and stumbling. Delucca darted to the rear entrance. The door slammed open with a loud bang and hung awkwardly on its hinges as he sprinted into the harsh light outside.

The starter pistol went off in his head, and Jason accelerated instantly.

"He's running, rear entrance." Jason's electronically distorted voice echoed in the small room. "In pursuit."

Jason was already out of the door when radioed acknowledgments and commands for redeployment came through his earpiece and his team moved to intercept. Jason felt the corner of his mouth twitch in a slight smile at how calm everyone sounded. No shouting, or cursing, or panic; just a team of professionals adapting to the situation. His team.

The back door opened into an alley littered with detritus from overflowing dumpsters and whatever crap the wind blew in. Jason didn't slow as his goggles adjusted back to being outside, and he grabbed the door frame to make the sharp turn to follow Delucca. The squat man was pumping his arms furiously and bounced off a parked car, using the vehicle to make the right turn without losing velocity, plowing through Belford and sending the larger cop sprawling on his back.

Why wasn't Belford on the back door? And how did Delucca get that far ahead? Jason willed himself to run faster, controlling his breathing as best he could to avoid overworking the cycler. A second later he was past the car and noted the dent in the door where Delucca had collided with it.

Now in a full run behind his quarry, Jason registered that Delucca wasn't wearing any protective gear, just the old, stained, sleeveless undershirt and jogging pants he had worn into the basement party. At virtually the same moment, Les' voice came over his earpiece. "Is he not wearing…?"

"Yeah," Jason replied, "no gear."

"Is he nuts?"

Nguyen's voice crackled over the comms. "Drone just spotted five runners on the roof right now. Came out of our building."

"Redeploy," Jason commanded between breaths. "Delucca must have warned them. Don't let them get away."

Officers radioed in their acknowledgments.

Delucca ran like a bear was chasing him, and he was pulling ahead. *I know he's spliced up, but I should have caught him by now. And the sun exposure alone should have dropped him. How is he…?*

Delucca leaped over a chain link fence with what looked like little effort.

"Delucca's spliced up, something new" Jason radioed to his team. "Anyone still in pursuit, approach with extreme caution."

More acknowledgments, but Jason barely registered them. He calmed his mind, stilled all other thoughts floating around in there, and focused on the target in front of him.

A deep breath in, hold, exhale.

A deep breath in, hold, exhale.

A deep breath in, hold, exhale.

He remembered playing Star Wars with Alexei outside in his front yard, imagining they were piloting the *Millennium Falcon* as they got ready to sprint down a hill together, his friend turning to him and saying in his twelve-year-old cracking voice, *"Punch it."*

Jason poured on the acceleration, willing each foot to launch him forward faster, to lift and fall quicker than the previous step, refining his form with each stride to maximize his power and speed.

They weaved in and out of alleyways. Delucca stopped gaining distance. Then the space between them started diminishing. One step at a time, Jason closed the distance.

They reached a parking structure. Delucca ran up through the exit ramp, vaulting the toll bar, and Jason pursued, curving around and around as they climbed higher and higher.

They reached the roof, an expanse of sunbaked blacktop with nothing above it but sky. Delucca skidded to a stop, turned, and swung a haymaker at Jason. He was quick, and the blow landed, sending Jason spinning to the ground. The overweight man moved in with the grace of someone who never learned how to fight properly, and with the speed of someone much lighter.

Jason was faster. He got to his feet and moved forward in an instant, closing the distance between them more quickly than Delucca had expected. Before the squat man could throw another punch, Jason was inside his reach, landing elbow after elbow squarely into Delucca's face and throat. Jason drove him back, but Delucca continued to swing wildly, occasionally landing a glancing blow.

The large man drove his head forward into Jason's face, and Jason saw a flash of white and then red at the impact, and then heard the crunch of his nose breaking. Jason clinched the back of Delucca's head and pulled down, ramming his knee up with as much force as possible. Bone connected with flesh, and Jason followed by driving the point of his elbow straight down into the back of Delucca's head.

Delucca was driven down to one knee, then rose to his feet again with a fire in his eye that said he wanted to continue the fight. But his pace slowed and stopped. Jason held his hands up, ready to defend against the next onslaught. He was tired, and he knew he would be sore later, but he also knew he outclassed Delucca in every way...he just had to outlast him.

"Tommy Delucca..." Jason started his arrest speech between heavy breaths, but Delucca wasn't looking at him. His cheeks pulled back in an almost rictus grin, and tendons strained in his neck.

The scream that followed was a sure sign that the splice had worn off. Delucca's skin began to turn bright red, blistering in a few spots. No longer protected by the temporary genetic modification that splice offered, the virtually unfiltered UV radiation instantly gave him the worst sunburn of his life. Jason had seen on more than one occasion, as a beat cop and a detective, what happened if exposure wasn't stopped: sun poisoning, then a high likelihood of multiple cancers in the following years. More prolonged exposure: death.

Splice cooker or not, Jason knew no one deserved that fate. He tackled Delucca to the ground and tried to interpose himself between his former quarry and the sun. He kept his voice calm as he pulled a reflective emergency blanket from a pocket on his jacket, though now the burst of speed he poured on was catching up and he felt out of breath. "Suspect down, repeat, suspect down. We need a bus on my position. Tell paramedics we need to treat for third-degree sun exposure."

He covered the writhing man with the blanket as best he could. Two of his team ran up and did the same with their own emergency blankets. "Make sure to replace those when we get back," Jason said between gasps. "Don't want to get caught without one."

Nguyen jammed an extractor against Delucca's arm and the vial filled with blood. She shook the sample and held it to the light.

Les jogged up. "Ambulance is on the way." Jason nodded to his partner as Delucca continued to writhe and whimper under the blankets.

Nguyen held the sample, now striated with different colors, alongside the color-coded testing card. "Looks like Delucca here had a little fast twitch muscle boost and an endurance boost…maybe a desensitizer, but it's pretty inconclusive."

Jason rubbed his jaw where Delucca had gotten a shot in. "Yeah, I picked up on that. I'll bet the exposure burned it out quicker than he expected."

Nguyen chuckled. "Guess he had a hot date planned. Don't think he was planning on it being you, Loo."

Belford finally came jogging up at a leisurely pace. "Need me?" He sounded bored.

"Why weren't you on the back door?" Jason demanded as he held his suspect down.

"I was," Belford said.

"No, you got blasted by Delucca at the end of the alley, not at the door."

"Same difference," Belford said with a dismissive wave.

"No, not the same," Les scolded. "You could have stopped or slowed him if you had been right on the back door like you were supposed to be. Instead, Delucca built up a head of steam and pancaked you."

"It's not my fault. You went in too early," Belford whined. "He took me by surprise. And I thought I would have a better angle on him from the street, so I made a judgment call."

"Didn't your parents pay for all of those gene mods when you were a kid?" Nguyen joked. "Faster reflexes, faster recovery, all that? And this guy still treated you like a bowling pin. Good thing the Lieutenant was here, huh?"

Belford's posture went stiff. "Kicked Thane's ass."

"Hey!" Jason shouted. "Both of you, knock it off. Nguyen, get that sample to the lab. Belford, the next time you're assigned to a position, you need to be on that position, not where you *think* you should be. It's the only way a team works. Got it?"

Belford somehow glared at Jason through his headgear and then felt around his belt. "Whatever."

Jason secured Delucca, who was finally settling down, and felt like his breath was getting under control. "OK," he sighed. "Now onto the next thing."

CHAPTER 2

Tommy Delucca was taken to the hospital under guard, and Jason's team, along with a phalanx of crime scene technicians, descended upon the speakeasy building. The chase was over, and the search for evidence and a lead to the next step of the investigation had begun.

The plan had been for Delucca to get them into the stash house, for Jason's team to finally arrest some people above the street-level dealers, and maybe, at long last, make a real dent in the illegal splice operations in that area.

The unending tsunami of the drug and related crime. The toll on the addicted from constantly mangling their DNA. The incalculable damage on the families on both sides. Jason felt the fatigue in his very marrow. The op was supposed to provide a short reprieve for the victims, the neighborhood, and his team.

Delucca's severe sun poisoning threw a significant wrench into that plan. It could be days, or even weeks before he'd be even able to speak to someone. Momentum was vital, Jason knew, and it was time to pivot to a new tactic.

Jason motioned over a group of uniformed officers sent to support the operation and led them inside the bar. As soon as he entered, he moved his goggles to rest on his forehead, released the clasp that held his cycler to his face, and let it dangle from the straps around his neck onto his chest. "Let's get a canvas going on the apartments upstairs. Murph, you and Park take two through four, Adesina and Santos, take five through eight. You three," he nodded to the uniformed officers, Ramirez, Geralt, and Novak, "take whatever's left. Anything anyone can tell us about who they've seen coming in and out, hanging with Delucca, giving the locals a hard time, you know the drill."

The officers responded in the affirmative in their muted, distorted tones through their headgear and turned to fulfill the assignment.

"Whoa, hold up a sec," Jason called. "Hold on. Do me a favor…when you start knocking on doors, make sure the headgear is off."

The officers looked at each other, their shoulders suddenly a shade tenser, heads cocked to one side a bit, unsure of the request. "Sir?" Geralt asked.

"Look, I know you're all used to wearing the gear full-time when you're on duty," Jason said, making eye contact as best he could through their polarized goggles, "but this isn't crowd control. These aren't hardened criminals or violent offenders. They're just people trying to get by. We need to connect with these folks, get them to trust us, share information with us. It's not going to happen if you look like you're ready to kick down their door. And let's face it…the masks were designed to be scary."

"But then…" Novak stammered, "…then they'll see our faces. They'll know who we are."

"Yeah," Jason nodded, "they will. And that's a good thing. If they know you, they're more likely to trust you. And a cop is only as good as their sources. This is how you do it. We're not at war with these people. We're supposed to protect them, not scare the crap out of them. So, masks off while you're inside canvassing. OK?"

Slowly, each nodded. Jason hoped he had gotten through to them and they would take the headgear off for their canvas.

He sat heavily in one of the well-worn booths and rubbed at his quads. He could feel the blood pooling and the post-race stiffness he was all-too-familiar with setting in. Les slid into the booth across from him, headgear and goggles still in place.

"You know I hate talking to you when you wear that inside," Jason said, half joking, half scolding his partner.

"I do. But I like to keep an air of mystery about me whenever I can," Les' distorted voice replied. "That it annoys you is a bonus." There was no hiding the humor in his voice. In a severe tone, Les continued, "What's next? Delucca's out for the time being."

"Yeah, I was not expecting that," Jason said, leaning back in the booth and kicking a leg up on the bench, and started idly playing with a coaster left on the table by the previous occupant. "I've seen gene juicers do some weird shit, but that was new."

"Guess he didn't get the half-life right."

"Guess so." Jason sighed. "So, we've got a canvas going, that might turn something up."

Les nodded. "Maybe. I sent a few uniforms up to the top floor to check the stash house. I'm guessing everyone bolted, but we'll see."

"Anything with our runners on the roof that Nguyen spotted?"

Les pulled a notebook out of a pocket and flipped it open. "Drone found one, died of exposure. Didn't wear any gear out, just booked it. Couple of our guys found another, same thing. Idiot not only went out with no gear and no mask, but somehow treed himself on a radio tower. Both made it about a mile, though, so that's impressive."

"The others? Didn't Nguyen say there were five?"

"You'll need to check with her. None of our guys caught them. Nguyen's trying to see what she can pull off the drone footage."

"Good call," Jason said. "How about any of the regulars in the bar?"

Les snorted, an odd sound coming through his comm. "No one saw anything, no surprise there. The scholastic crew over there might be worth looking at," he said, pointing at the college kids. "Blue Eyes was carrying weight."

"Really? How much?"

"Six grams."

Jason felt like his eyes were going to bug out of his head. "Shit. That's intent to distribute. OK, let's have a talk with the wayward youths."

Jason approached the table where three young adults wearing expensive-looking casual clothing sat, all with smirks on their faces, half-drunk beers in front of them. All of them shared a similar "processed" look; their noses and cheekbones and eyes almost too perfect, undoubtedly the result of getting gene jobs in their teens before puberty finished. Jason saw it more and more as parents with the means had their kids' genes "polished" to clean up any "impurities", even ones like normal physical development.

Gods forbid if their precious little angels didn't have everything perfectly laid out for them every step of the way.

The table was filled with half-drunk pints of beer and their clear face mask cyclers that would let the world see just how pretty they were.

"Name?" Jason asked the one with the overly-blue eyes.

All three of them ignored Jason.

"OK," Jason said. He scooped up the beer in front of Blue Eyes and swiped it for DNA.

"You can't do that without his permission," another one said, and he had the overly-sculpted look of someone who spent entirely too many hours in the gym, and just as many hours looking at themselves in the mirror.

"Actually, I can," Jason retorted.

"No, he can't," he said. "It's illegal search and seizure, moron. My dad's a lawyer and he told me-"

"Then your dad's a shitty lawyer," Les replied. "It's in plain sight, and you don't actually own the glasses, so you have no claim of personal property over it, ergo it's not subject to due process or the need for a warrant, which means we're allowed to pretty much do whatever we want with it."

The gym rat's mouth fell open, and no words followed.

"That's OK, while we wait for you to think of a comeback we'll talk with your friends here," Les said. "Don't hurt yourself."

Jason's phone pulsed with the result of the scan. "OK, Bertram Haverford-West. Want to tell me why you were carrying felony-weight of splice?"

Bertram finally made eye contact with Jason with his too-blue eyes, and Jason could feel the hate and condescension coming off of Bertram in waves. "Lawyer."

"Good call," Jason said, and pulled out zip tie cuffs. "Hope it's not your friend's dad. He doesn't sound like he's very good. Stand up, you're under arrest." Bertram didn't move. Jason leaned in close and got right next to Bertram's ear. "You can either stand up and do as you're told," Jason said quietly and slowly, "or I can spank you right here and embarrass you in front of your friends."

Jason backed away a step and locked eyes with Bertram.

Please give me a reason.

Bertram finally stood and held his hands out in front of him. Jason zipped the cuff on one wrist, spun him around, pulled the free hand behind Bertram's back, and finished securing the cuffs. "OK, you two are next."

There was a crash behind him, and Jason whipped his head around. Belford had one of the patrons, an older man, bent over a table, pressing their head into it. Les made a gesture with his head that said he would handle the rest of the *bogari*, and Jason strode over to the other cop.

"What's the issue?" Jason demanded.

"He blew over the limit," Belford said. "Give me some cuffs. I'm taking him in."

Jason sighed. "Sir, are you planning to drive?"

The older man shook his head as best he could with Belford shoving it into the table. "No, I live down the street."

"Let him up," Jason said.

Belford didn't move, and glared at Jason.

"Now, detective," Jason said.

Belford still didn't move. His glare intensified. "This *blister back* was mad dogging me-"

Jason glared at Belford. "With me. Now."

Before releasing the older man, Belford hesitated, and Jason walked briskly to an isolated corner. The two men stared at each other in silence for a moment.

Jason spoke once he felt like he wasn't going to shout. "I don't know how many times I need to have this conversation with you. Stop harassing people."

Belford gritted his teeth. "The same way you were harassing those kids?"

"They were carrying felony-weight. That man was drinking, which last I checked, was legal. Only difference I see is that he's a Gapper, and they are clearly *bogari*. Second, why did you need me to give you cuffs? Where are yours?"

Belford hesitated. "I forgot them."

"Again? This is the third time. You need to show up to work prepared." Jason brought his face close to Belford's. "Lastly...if I *ever* hear that term come out of your mouth again, you and I are going outside. Now get your shit together and go back to the office. Start your reports. We don't need you here."

Jason remained inches from Belford's face. Belford's jaw clenched and unclenched. He affixed his cycler and goggles and left without saying another word.

Jason realized the room had gotten very quiet, and most of the officers and patrons were staring at him.

"Back to work," Jason said loud enough for everyone to hear.

Les approached. "Well, that wasn't smart."

"Yeah, the mouth on him," Jason agreed.

Les shook his head. "No, I meant on your part. He's Chief Swan's pet, and *bogari* to boot. That's going to come back and bite you in the ass."

Jason knew Les was right. But he couldn't bring himself to admit it out loud to the veteran cop. "He's borderline incompetent and an overt bigot," Jason finally said, low enough that only Les could hear. "I don't care if he was born rich. He brings nothing to the team and if I had my wish, he would have never been forced on me."

"If wishes were horses, we'd be knee-deep in shit," Les retorted. "Just saying. Don't expect that to go unanswered."

The rapid thumping of multiple people running down old steps interrupted Jason's train of thought. Two uniformed officers burst out of the door leading to the stairwell into the main bar area. One ripped off his mask and vomited noisily and messily onto the floor, and the other leaned against the wall as their knees gave out and they slid to the floor. Their chest rose and fell in great gasps, audible through the cycler.

The fatigue of the chase and fight immediately left Jason and he was on his feet, rushing to the officers, Les at his side. "Hey, *estas bien*?" He began to loosen the cycler straps.

The officer reached up two shaky hands and pulled the mask off, but with a clumsy grip, like they weren't sure what her hands were for. "Holy shit," she repeated over and over between gasps of breath.

Jason gripped her upper arm in what he hoped was a reassuring manner. "Officer…" He looked at her nametag. "Gorsky. Hey, Gorsky, look at me. Just breathe. Look at me."

Gorsky took two more ragged breaths, then took one deep one, let it out, and turned to face Jason. Her eyes were wide and wild, and she still inhaled and exhaled unevenly. "I've never seen anything like that." Her voice was small.

"What? Seen what?" Jason gently prodded.

Gorsky only shook her head, her mouth open as if to speak, but no words came out. Her partner had finished emptying his stomach and was hugging his knees to his chest, gently banging the back of his head against the side of the bar as he rocked back and forth.

"Medic!" Les called out as Jason affixed his cycler and goggles in place. Whatever was up there, whatever they had seen, wasn't something that needed to be handled gently. And a part of him wanted the armor of anonymity the mask provided. The officers were terrified, and that alone gave him pause.

Without saying a word, Jason ascended the stairs, gun drawn, and Les and his team followed. They had been working together on the task force for over a year and knew each other's body language and tics like they knew their own. The efficiency and discipline calmed Jason's nerves, and he stepped more boldly with his team at his back.

Five flights of stairs later, they exited carefully into the hallway. The walls were exposed red brick occasionally covered with chipped and peeling plaster. The floor was covered with threadbare carpeting and looked wavy in places, like too much water damage had warped the wood underlayment. Jason was sure he would smell wet earth, dust, and mildew if his cycler wasn't on. Three bare bulbs provided the only light.

Jason cleared a doorway on his right, a laundry area with a washing machine that looked like it had seen better days, and a dryer of a comparable state.

They stopped at each doorway, one clearing the room, the rest watching the hall. It was slow going, and Jason felt his anxiety rising with each step, but he also didn't want to rush. Something had scared the crap out of the uniforms, and something like that wasn't to be taken lightly.

They finally reached the last door in the hallway. Rather than an open doorway or a cheap wooden door, this one was a thick metal fire door that was slightly ajar.

Jason's team stacked up at the door. He held his hand over his shoulder and counted down from three. He pushed the door open.

His goggles adjusted to the fluorescent lights that illuminated the area as he and his team entered.

The only sound was the gently humming commercial refrigerators, set to a cool 34 degrees. Jason counted six in his line of sight. The glass panels on the doors showed shelves filled to capacity with racks of glass vials.

Aside from overturned furniture and the general clutter that filled the room, nothing seemed out of sorts; nothing that would cause two officers to run panicked and render them virtually catatonic. He motioned to the team and they spread out to search, weapons at the ready, as they had many times before. Jason checked his breathing, consciously slowing it and calming himself, and stepped forward.

It only took a few steps before he first saw the blood spattered on the wall, and only a few more to see there was more, much more than those splatters indicated. He slowly maneuvered around a pony wall that separated the kitchen from the rest of the apartment, and found the source.

Bodies. How many, he couldn't tell. There were too many parts strewn about to do an accurate count, too many pieces ground into a paste to even fully identify them as individuals, but enough ragged meat to leave no doubt in Jason's mind that they were human.

He felt the heat of bile rising in the back of his throat, but he choked it down, and buried the gibbering part of his brain under a metric ton of detachment. There would be time to unpack what he was feeling later.

"On me," he called to his team, hoping his stoicism would come through. If he could stay calm, so could they.

They gathered around, and each one stopped dead in their tracks at the sight. Les removed his goggles, like the optics were lying to him. Nguyen stared stoically at the carnage. One of the uniformed officers who followed them up crossed himself and mouthed a silent prayer. But all stayed on their feet, and after their initial shock, all steeled themselves. There were bad guys to hunt.

He knelt near the pile and extended his phone towards it. The temperature of...Jason didn't know what to call it...read at 97 degrees. *Less than two hours...*

...we were downstairs while this was happening.

"Call the medical examiner, and get Crime Scene up here." Jason could hear how cold his voice was. He needed it to be. His lizard brain screamed at him to run away, but he couldn't listen. "Warn them first. And get the chief of detectives on the horn, I'll need to update her. This just got way more complicated."

Nguyen had re-affixed her headgear. "Did someone just do us a favor?" She sounded uncertain of her own comment, like it had surprised her.

"I don't know," Jason replied. "I don't know what this is." Bile rose in his throat, and he swallowed the rancid fluid. "OK, DNA scans on everything, I want to know who all these people were, every person who was ever in this room. Cameras," he said, and pointed to the devices mounted around the room, "probably nothing on them but check anyway, maybe we'll get lucky. Nguyen, can you pull up the drone footage over the area from the last two hours beyond what we already have? Maybe we got lucky and we caught the perp leaving."

His team silently fanned out and did their jobs. They swabbed surfaces for DNA retrieval, interfaced their phones with the cameras, and documented everything. Nguyen took out her portable screen and brought up the requested footage.

"Lieutenant?" Jason noticed a uniformed cop standing in the doorway, angled to avoid a direct line of sight on the meat pile. "Chief Swan wants to speak with you."

"Can you patch the call through to my phone?" Jason asked.

"She's uh…she's here, sir."

The entire team stopped what they were doing and looked at the officer. Jason didn't need to see their faces or any Gapper sign to know they all had the same expression stuck somewhere between shock and incredulity.

"Look who decided to get their UV gear faded for something," Les said, and a few chuckles from the others followed. Jason looked at his partner and said nothing, and after a moment, Les turned back to his task and said, "Sorry."

Jason nodded, and turned back to the officer in the doorway. "Lead the way."

CHAPTER 3

Jason made the trek back down to the basement, and pulled his gear off as he entered the bar proper. He saw the two officers who had made the discovery being seen to by medics, blankets draped over their shoulders to treat their shock and oxygen masks on their faces to help calm them down.

Chief of Detectives Alice Swan stood in the middle of the room, indifferent to the people attempting to work around her. Her UV gear was immaculate and polished, unsullied by frequent use and lacking the faded haze of direct sun exposure that marked every other officer's gear in the room. Her crystal-clear headgear dangled from a hook on a pristine belt.

Jason noted the contempt on her face as she scanned the room and pulled one of her gloves off one finger at a time. He guessed that she typically didn't frequent establishments such as this one. He couldn't even remember a time when she had been in the field, let alone in The Gaps.

Is this just another one of her drive-bys? Or did Belford already tattle?

He felt like he was mentally pulling on armor as he approached her.

"Chief," Jason said as he approached. He extended his hand.

She glanced at it, hesitated for the briefest of moments, and placed her uncalloused hand in his, shaking it once and withdrawing it quickly.

"Lieutenant," she said, regarding him with cold eyes. "Looks like you've found yet another way to bungle this investigation."

Jason ignored the comment. "I actually just put in the call request to bring you up to speed. We weren't expecting you on scene."

She continued to scan the room, looking over him, and Jason noted that she never made direct eye contact with him. "Yes, well, this was supposed to be a milestone operation, and quite frankly, I needed to see the results for myself. I see you didn't send a tac-team in?"

Jason knew she was trying to bait him into an argument, and bit back the first words that came to mind. "No, ma'am, I deemed it an unnecessary risk to the team and to the people here."

"You mean you made it all about you," she said.

"No, ma'am, I was thinking of the community and the safety of my team-"

"No, no," she said, waving a finger, "it wasn't a question. And the informant escaped?"

"Again, no, ma'am," Jason said, and he felt the edge of heat in his words. He battled back the anger in his tone. "The suspect attempted to escape and we apprehended him a few miles from here."

"So, you endangered the neighborhood by engaging in a pursuit with a dangerous criminal?"

Jason knew that no matter what he said, or what decisions he had made, Swan was going to continue to play contrarian with him. Jason felt a new wave of exhaustion wash over him at the thought of having to repeat this game again.

"The real concern," Jason said, changing the subject, "are the bodies we found in the lab."

Swan sniffed. "Why is that a concern? A few more dead blister back splice dealers makes the world safer."

Jason heard the brief pause in conversations around the room with the racial epithet thrown around as casually as Swan used it, like everyone collectively sucked in a breath and held it. The discomfort was palpable, but Swan showed no sign of noticing.

I shouldn't have to have this conversation again.

Jason tamed his initial reflex, Les' words ringing in his ears. He was pretty sure taking the same tact with Swan as with Belford would yield very different results, ones with zero chance of ending well for him or the team.

Jason stepped close so that only Swan could hear him. "Ma'am, please don't use that term."

"What term?" Jason saw her face become a picture of innocence.

"Ma'am, you know what term I'm talking about. Please don't use it. I just had to have a conversation with Belford about it."

She's going to find out anyway. Might as well get ahead of it.

Swan answered him in an equally quiet tone, almost whispering in his ear. "Or what?"

He stared straight ahead. "I'm not asking." He took a step back and stared directly into her eyes. She finally met his gaze, her eyes afire and defiant.

"The reason it's a concern," he said, turning the conversation back to the investigation, but not breaking eye contact, "is how they were killed. The bodies were completely dismembered and stacked in a pile. If you want, I can show you the scene."

Swan finally broke eye contact. She turned on her heel and started towards the door. "No, that won't be necessary. Just have your completed reports to my office by the end of the day."

"I'll bring Homicide up to speed as well and send you their initial thoughts," Jason said to her back.

Swan paused and looked over her shoulder. "Oh, no, that won't be necessary." Her thin lips contorted into a cruel, lopsided smile. "This is your crime scene, your investigation. The bodies are on your ledger, not Homicide's. This is on you to clear."

Jason felt his heart leap into his throat. "Ma'am, we're in the middle of a major investigation and if we have to clear a multiple-homicide on top of that, it will-"

Swan turned and was back in Jason's face with two quick strides. "...will give you enough rope to hang yourself," she hissed. "You were never qualified for this position, you were a diversity hire. Something to make the department look all nice and inclusive. '*Look, we have a Gapper in charge of clearing the Gaps of splice.*' You'll fail, and I'll finally be able to remove the task force from you and give it to someone better qualified. Someone with a more…desirable…background."

Jason felt the blood rush to his face, and could hear his heart pounding in his ears. He schooled his hands to remain unclenched.

"What?" Swan goaded. "Nothing?"

Jason bit back all the words he wanted to say, words he knew he would never be able to take back. He would be right, he knew at his core, but he also knew that winning the battle would have consequences. He visualized all of the outcomes of winning the confrontation in front of him, and all of them led to

Swan removing him from command, punishing everyone on the task force with career-ending assignments like the pawn shop unit and the morgue unit, and the investigation being mothballed. *You can't win if the fight is over. Stay in the war.*

She spun on her heel again and walked towards the door, pulling on her headgear. "Oh, there's a press conference in five days about the task force's investigation. No need for you to attend. I'll bring them up to speed with any...developments. I'll be sure to communicate your contributions."

The door swung shut behind Chief of Detectives Swan, and the room was left in impotent silence.

"Gods damned glasshead," Les said, startling Jason. He hadn't heard his partner approach.

Jason flinched. "You know how I feel about that term."

Les shrugged. "What's good for the goose is good for the gander."

"If we're trading old idioms, the problem with 'an eye for an eye' is that eventually everyone goes blind," Jason countered.

Les grunted. "Not to put more on your plate, but I've got someone you should speak with."

"Who?" Jason asked as he looked around the room. Amidst the uniformed cops and the bar patrons who were still giving statements, Jason clocked someone new, a woman with a tear-streaked face.

"You should talk to her," Les said.

"Les, Swan just dumped the homicides on us on top of everything else. I don't have time to deal with civilian complaints."

"Just…" Les didn't finish the sentence, but gestured toward the woman.

Jason sighed and approached the woman, dreading the conversation with each step. Public relations wasn't his thing.

The woman seemed to have picked up on his discomfort, and she raised her hands, palms out and crossed in front of their chest, the Gapper sign for *peace* or *peace upon you*, depending on the neighborhood. "Lieutenant Thane? Detective Caporelli told me you might be able to help me."

"Ok...may I have your name?"

"Jessica...Jessica Kline, sir. Jessie." Her voice trembled on the edge of tears.

Jason felt his resolve to extricate himself from the situation as quickly as possible quaver, and motioned to one of the bar stools. Jessie sat back down. Jason sat next to her, and finally got a good look at her. The woman was slight, on the side of gaunt, and looked tired, but pretty as well. She had fine lines around her eyes that made her appear older, but he figured she was somewhere in her early thirties.

"And how can I help?"

"It's my son, Markus," Jessie started, and choked back a sob. She took a slow breath and let it out. "Markus has gone missing."

Jason opened and closed his mouth a few times, trying to figure out where to start without insulting the woman. "I'm, uh...not sure how I can help with that...you'll want to file a report with Missing Persons..."

"We live upstairs," she said quickly, cutting him off. "And no one here ever gets help when they call, they just send one of those damned drones. I want to talk to a real person. This is my son, and I don't want this handled by some automated system."

Jason felt his stomach drop to his feet, and old memories tried to assert themselves. Jason tamped them back down to stay in the present. *That's why Les wanted me to talk to her.*

"Uh, OK...when did he go missing?" he asked.

"Today, this morning," she said, and started gaining momentum, her voice rising in pitch with each word. "I know, you're going to tell me that he's probably out with his friends or that he'll turn up, and that I need to wait twenty-four hours before I report him missing…"

"That's not true, ma'am," Jason interrupted. "You can report someone missing right away. But before you do…is it possible that he's just out with his friends?" Jason winced as he asked the question, hating it in equal measure that he had to ask it and that he actually did.

"No!" she snapped back. "I already asked all of his friends in the building, and they haven't seen him either! This is exactly why I didn't want to deal with a drone, because of stupid questions like this."

Jason held up his hands. "I'm sorry, I really am. I believe you, it's just that these are questions that we need to ask to eliminate the possibilities, OK? So, what happened? When did you notice he was gone?"

Jessie took a deep breath and let it out, and she seemed to calm down a notch. "I left for work at…7:30, I think, this morning…he leaves at eight and walks himself to school and texts me when he gets there. But he didn't this morning, and I called the school, and they said he didn't show. So, I left work, but my boss said if I didn't come back, he would fire me…oh, gods, I was supposed to be there thirty minutes ago…" Tears welled up in her eyes.

Jason put a hand on her shoulder and squeezed, hoping it was reassuring. "We'll send an officer with you to speak with your boss when we're done if you want, but I don't think you should go in tonight, OK? Take the night off. I'll give him a call tomorrow and see what I can do."

She breathed in a ragged breath and nodded.

"OK, so he didn't show up to school…then what?" Jason asked.

"Then…I called the police." The tears flowed anew onto her face. "One of those stupid drones showed up to ask questions. But then it just flew off, and I found a number for Missing Persons so I called them. But they said I couldn't do anything until he's been gone for 24 hours, and started going on about him probably having run away…but I know that's not what happened. I just…I just need someone to listen, someone to care."

A familiar pain struck Jason in the chest. The memory of him talking to a detective in a brown suit and mismatched socks, of the detective tapping on his notepad with his pencil but not writing anything down. The same explanations, the same tired responses to questions, the same inaction, and eventually, the news that no parent, or sibling, or best friend wants to hear from the same, disaffected lump of a man who never wrote a single note. A monotone speech given, and a family and friends left to pick up the pieces.

Jason pulled out his phone and opened up a new case file. "I don't know how much I can do," he said as he entered the details she had already supplied him with, "but whatever I can do, I will. Do you have a recent picture of him?"

Jessie nodded and pulled one up on her phone. Jason pulled the photo onto his, and put it in the file. He was making more notes when he noticed an officer standing in his peripheral, politely waiting but trying to get his attention.

"I'm sorry to interrupt, sir," the officer said. "The Medical unit just sent over a car…"

Jason nodded towards the door that led to the top floor. "Tell them it's down there, and give them a heads up about what they'll see."

The officer cleared their throat. "Uh, Lieutenant, they are here for you. Something about a mandatory physical for you to be cleared to be in the field?"

Jason caught himself grinding his teeth and willed himself to stop. "Right. Tell them I'll be there in a minute." He turned back to Jessie. "Ms. Kline, I'm going to get as much information as I can right now, and I'll follow up with you if I have any other questions, I promise. Here's my number in case you need to get in touch with me directly. OK?" He pushed his number to her phone.

Jessie nodded, wiping tears from her face. "Thank you."

Les escorted the woman out, and Jason signaled for Nguyen.

"Hey, first up, do we have anything from the birds that shows our perp getting away on the roofs?" he asked.

She queued up the footage from the raid. "This is what we got." The top-down video showed a clear view of the rooftops. After a moment of nothing moving, a fire door burst open and five men in various states of dress for being outside sprinted away in different directions.

Jason spotted the two not wearing any gear that he guessed were the ones that didn't make it. The others already had their masks up. The only identifying feature he could see was that one was wearing a red jacket with that looked to be some kind of design in black on the back, though he couldn't make out what it was from that angle.

Another moment later and all five were out of frame. Time passed, and no one else exited until a few uniformed officers stepped onto the roof in pursuit.

"Well, it's a start, I guess," he said. "So, random question…can you pull up the drone footage for this location from eight this morning?"

Nguyen pulled out her tablet and searched for the footage. A few taps later and a slowly panning overhead view of the building filled the screen.

"When is this?" Jason asked.

Nguyen checked the timestamp. "7:45 this morning."

"OK, move forward to 8:00," Jason said. He was welcoming the distraction from the carnage just a few floors above.

"What are we looking for?"

Jason showed Nguyen the picture of Markus Kline. "This kid. Leaves for school at eight, but he never showed up. I'm hoping we can pick him up on surveillance and see where he went."

Nguyen tapped on the screen, and the video moved into fast forward. The image circled around the building in a lazy loop, then veered off to the left and started tracking a different block.

"What was that?" Jason asked. "What happened there?"

Nguyen tapped on the screen some more. "Looks like it was diverted to an emergency call."

"I thought that drone was tasked to us," Jason said. "We were on an active op, it shouldn't have been in the queue for redivert."

Nguyen shrugged. "It was supposed to stay on the location, but I honestly don't know what happened there. Maybe too many calls came in? That could override the redivert status and requeue it."

Jason huffed. "Were there any other birds in the area that might have caught our scene?"

Nguyen searched through the drone listing and pulled up another. It took Jason a moment to recognize the location, despite the coordinates displayed on the heads-up display. It was one block over, but angled so it caught Jason's car parked in front of the bar in the corner of the screen.

"This is from about the same time," Nguyen said. "This is one that was in the area, not tasked to us." She touched the screen and fast-forwarded. The drone continued in its lazy circle, then veered off, the heads-up display showing an alert that it had been diverted for another emergency call.

"That one, too? What the hell happened?" Jason asked.

Nguyen continued to scroll through drone options. "Not sure, Loo. Looks like a bunch of calls came in, and all of the drones in the area were diverted for first response."

Jason shook his head. "So, there were no birds on this location at all when this kid went missing?"

"Looks that way. I'll keep looking, but I wouldn't hold out much hope on that end."

Jason cursed under his breath. *It can never be easy, can it?*

Try as he might, Jason couldn't keep his leg from bouncing. He couldn't contain the urge to move whenever he was in a doctor's office.

That his boss had just chewed him out didn't help.

I HATE HAVING TO DO THIS, he texted his wife.

I KNOW [HEART], Amira replied.

The analog clock on the wall ticked away the seconds, and Jason read the tired informational posters on the wall again as he idly scratched at the tape and gauze on his arm from the blood draw. He shifted and tried to draw the paper gown around him to reduce the draft raising goosebumps on his back, but he only succeeded in somehow making it cover even less.

WHY DO THEY KEEP THE OFFICE AT SUB-ARCTIC TEMPERATURES?!

The reply dots flashed on his screen and were replaced by BECAUSE THEY KNOW HOW MUCH IT BOTHERS YOU.

He heard footsteps approach and pause outside the exam room door, then a quiet knock before Dr. Misriak stepped in and shut the door behind her. Kind eyes peered at him through horn-rimmed glasses, and were it not for her steel-gray hair pulled up in a tight bun, Jason would have sworn she was no older than him.

"Back again?" she said with a smile and sat on the wheeled stool in front of the exam table.

"Yeah, you know the department," he said. "Always worried."

The doctor snorted. "About lawsuits. OK, so what is it this time? Exposure to drug manufacturing fumes? Stabbed in the ass by an amped up pimp?"

"That happened one time," Jason replied. "No, this time was just a mundane fight." The doctor looked at him over the rims of her glasses with a look he knew all too well. "A fight with someone spliced up on something new." She continued to stare. "And there was blood. From them. That got on me."

"There we go," she said and typed notes into his chart on her pad. She studied him in silence. "What's bothering you?"

A stack of bodies. "Nothing."

"Bullshit."

"Really, nothing," Jason said. "Today was just…a lot."

"Well, keeping it all bottled up is definitely the healthy way to deal with it."

"I'm fine," he said and realized too late that it came out too harshly. "I will be fine. I feel great. Just want to get this over with. No offense."

"Then this won't take long," she said. She put her pad down and pulled on exam gloves. "Can't be too careful, especially with someone with your condition."

Jason sighed. "I don't have a condition."

Dr. Misriak started palpating the glands around his neck and shoulders. "You understand that

Horkrim's Syndrome doesn't go away, right? It only goes into remission. If it were to flare back up…"

Jason remained as still as he could for the exam. "They cured me of that years ago, I told you that. I tell you that every time."

She took the orthoscope off the wall and examined his eyes. "And every time I tell you that it was an experimental gene therapy treatment that we *think* put your Horkrim's Syndrome into a permanent remission. We need to keep watch for any unknown side effects and to see what the long-term effects of said treatment are."

"I haven't had a flare-up since I was thirteen," Jason said. "I'm in the best shape of my life, and I feel great."

She peered up his nostrils with the device. "Absence of proof is not proof of absence. Open your mouth." Jason did as instructed, and she completed her exam.

"Well?" Jason asked.

"Based on your blood work and the exam, you're fine," Dr. Misriak said. "You're cleared to go back to work."

"Great," Jason said and hopped off the table. He grabbed his folded pants and pulled them on under the gown.

The doctor sighed as she typed more notes into her pad. "You never seem to grasp your import to medical research. The combination of Recombinex and gene therapies you went through was groundbreaking, but we still don't know the long-term outlook of the treatment. We don't completely understand the mechanism of how it worked, so that means we can't predict what will happen a year, or five years from now, or what outside factors could interact with your biology…"

Jason pulled on his shirt. "Yeah, I know, I know," he said, understanding where she was coming from. "It's just…I spent most of my childhood being poked and prodded. When I actually had the energy to play with other kids, it was a challenge just to keep up. Keeping my mind on a single task was near impossible, and I had to spend so much time just to keep up in school." He pulled on and laced up his boots. "I get that the science is important, and I want this opportunity for every kid that wasn't born perfect, but…"

"But you want to go outside and play." Dr. Misriak put her pad down. "I understand. You're still making up for lost time."

Jason immediately felt a pang of shame at the way she phrased it, even though he didn't detect any judgment in her tone. "Yeah, I guess. A little." He pulled on some of his UV gear. "Look I…yeah, I need to have a better attitude about this. You're right."

She looked over her rims again. "And no one is 'born perfect', don't ever think that."

A familiar knot in Jason's chest, one that crept in from time to time, lessened with the doctor's words. "You're right. Again."

"There you go," she said, punctuating the last word with a tap on her pad and she set it down. "Progress. Now get out. I have other patients to see."

Jason left the office with mixed emotions. The pangs of guilt over his selfishness of his time over a thirty-minute checkup mingled with the catharsis of knowing he was still healthy and the anticipation of getting back to the work of untangling the knot of

splice trafficking. Over all of it was the pall cast by
Swan and her impending press conference.

*Five days to wrap up an 18-month investigation and
multiple homicides. She really wants this to fail, wants me to fail.*

Despair tried to worm its way into Jason's
mood, but it was met with a wall of determination.

His train of thought carried him to the waiting
car without him realizing it, and he was jarred from his
contemplation when his phone rang. Nguyen's name
flashed on the screen. He tapped on his earpiece.
"Thane."

"Hey, Loo," Nguyen said, her excitement
evident in her first two words. "You better get back to
the bar, like pronto."

"Everything OK?"

"You have to see this for yourself. You're going
to love it."

"I'll be there in twenty."

The front of the bar was a sea of squad cars and
flashing lights. Yellow police tape cordoned off the
front facade. A few camera crews from the local news
piloted their drones around, trying to get a peek at
something they could report on the six o'clock news.

Les was waiting for Jason at the front door. He
opened the door and they both stepped inside.

Coolers were sitting on a rickety old table, filling
up every square inch of the tabletop.

"We found more," Nguyen said. "Hidden all
over the place up there."

Nguyen pulled one top off at a time and revealed the treasure within: each one was filled to the brim with splice ampules.

"*Verga*," Les said quietly.

Jason leaned over and tried to count how many doses of the golden liquid there were, but quickly lost count.

"This has got to be ten million dollars' worth," Jason said in the same reverent tone.

Nguyen awkwardly signed *ecstatic*. "Try closer to two hundred million, boss."

Jason felt his face go numb and gawked, forgetting completely that no one could see his expression. "How...how do you figure?"

"It's uncut, boss," Nguyen said, the ear-to-ear grin hidden under her gear plainly evident in her tone. "This is the pure, right out of the cooker shit. You just took down the motherlode."

Silence overtook the room, but Jason had zero doubt that all of them, every cop in the room, shared the same stupid grin.

Jason snapped himself back to reality but couldn't erase his smile. "OK, I want this inventoried and inventoried again. None of it goes unaccounted for. No one is left alone with it. Everything is aboveboard, start to finish. We need to pull every scrap of paper related to this property to determine who the actual owner is. Let's get to work."

CHAPTER 4

The Alexei Stone Foundation Gala was well underway. Months of meticulous planning had gone into it. Sponsors were courted, vendors were booked, and attendees with bottomless bank accounts were wooed. Every detail had been gone over with a fine-toothed comb via binders and spreadsheets that had taken over Jason and Amira's dining room table little by little, until they were eating their meals at the sink or hovering over the seating chart.

So, of course, the moment the doors opened for the big event, the wheels came off the wagon. Vendors were late. Sponsors had forgotten their banners. Attendees showed up early.

Years of being together meant he knew her ticks and tells, and stress was pouring off his wife through her body language. He ached to help her, to take on some of that burden, but this fundraiser, the Foundation, was her baby, and event planning was not his forte. If she needed his help, he knew she would ask.

But his thoughts drifted to his day. A man with no UV gear ran for two miles in direct sunlight. Swan's rampant bigotry and her ultimatum. The bodies stacked like ragged and bloody cordwood. A career-making splice seizure.

Jason resisted the urge to get another bourbon from the bar. He had seen what hiding problems at the bottom of a bottle did to his father-in-law. When they started getting serious, he swore that he wouldn't put his wife through the same thing. At the time, it seemed like an easy promise to make.

As best he could recall, it had been the most stressful day of his career. He started to understand the internal reasoning that could make it harder to keep that promise.

It was like poking an open wound, causing a shock of pain and involuntary recoil whenever touched. Generally, after work he would cook a meal for Amira and himself and go over the investigative details in his mind, mentally categorizing any new information, indexing it with what they already knew, and reviewing the big picture to see how the new information changed the landscape of the overall case, and start thinking about new deployments or investigative avenues that he would pitch to the team the following morning. It usually let him let go of the day and keep his work from invading his personal life. It was a challenge he saw other cops struggle with, but one he had felt he had mastered.

The same ritual that had brought him comfort and focus now only served to vividly revisit the scene in his mind. Every detail of the day was accompanied by a snapshot of butchery. Of a ticking clock.

He knew he needed time, time to come to terms with a level of savagery that he had never borne witness to before, that he didn't know was possible, time for his brain to process it to a point where it stopped babbling incoherently in terror and didn't send a shock of adrenaline through his system.

That time would need to be later, however. Tonight was Amira's night. Tonight was for Alexei's memory.

Jason saw that she had finally broken away from putting out fires and was getting a chance to network with the guests. He caught his wife's eye over the shoulder of one of the donors she was chatting up. She smiled slightly and brushed a lock of hair behind her ear without missing a beat in the conversation.

Jason put his drink down on one of the many high-top tables tastefully scattered about the museum lobby and wove in between the groups of donors and attendees, careful not to bump into anyone and jostle their drinks and canapes or accidentally knock over a server delivering pass hors d'oeuvres, and hovered just behind the donor to not interrupt the conversation.

"...and we're very excited to see the next steps," the donor said, gesturing with his half-filled glass.

"We are, too," Amira replied, pushing another lock of hair behind her ear. "We're hoping to finally expand the scholarship program into the entire school district this year and increase the number of recipients. The money we're raising tonight will go a long way to level the playing field for many kids."

The donor sipped his drink and clumsily signaled a waiter for a refill. "Yes, well, it's nice to see the money being put to such effective use. Which reminds me, I was meaning to ask you about the plans for future marketing efforts and how to best allocate funds for a more public reach..."

Jason stepped around the bespoke-suited man and sidled up to his wife. She slid her arm into Jason's, and he felt the familiar tingle of electricity from her touch, the same warm feeling in his chest from when she grabbed his hand for the first time in a darkened movie theater. "I'm so sorry, I meant to introduce you sooner. This is my husband, Jason."

"Ah, Jason, glad to finally put a face to the name. Bob Roberts with Hecht Trust." Bob smiled a practiced, if not entirely sincere smile, switched his glass to his left hand and extended his right towards Jason, who took it into his own. Bob's callous-free hand was cold and clammy from the drink, and it felt to Jason like gripping a damp, limp fish.

"Likewise," Jason said, returning the smile with the same sincerity. "Sorry to steal her away, but I have someone I need to introduce her to before they leave."

"Ah, of course," Bob replied, and turned back to Amira, his eyes wandering below her chin for slightly longer than Jason was comfortable with. "Let's get something on the calendar to continue the conversation?"

"I'll have someone reach out," Amira said.

Bob winced, and Jason realized he had locked down on his hand in a vice grip, Bob's knuckles turning white underneath, the insincere smile still plastered on Jason's face.

"Sorry," Jason said, releasing the man's hand.

"Quite the grip there," Bob said, a nervous twitter in his voice as he surreptitiously rubbed the circulation back into his fingers.

"Uh...yeah," Jason said, turning as Amira gently guided him away. "Too many years of jiu jitsu, I guess. Have a nice night." He leaned in close to Amira and whispered, "Sorry. You made the sign, I thought I was rescuing you."

Several paces later, she said in a low tone only for Jason's ears, "Is he still looking?"

Jason glanced nonchalantly over his shoulder. "Nope. He's already chewing someone else's ear off."

Amira's shoulders relaxed as they strolled through the room. "Thank god. They're new donors and I know I need to chat them up, and having them on board is a huge win for the foundation, but dear lord...I was giving you 'the sign' for like five minutes."

A humorous snort escaped Jason's nose. "Is his name really Bob Roberts? As in Robert Roberts?" he asked quietly, their conversation easily masked by the white noise of conversation and live music reverberating throughout the marble lobby.

"The man so nice they named him twice." She shrugged her pashmina over her shoulders. "And he definitely had a problem maintaining eye contact, and he wasn't even subtle about it. I thought assholes like that had died out."

"You want me to go talk to him?" Jason growled in a half-joking, half-not tone. "I mean, the dress is hot, but still..."

Amira rolled her eyes. "Great. 'Hot' is exactly what I'm going for at a charity fundraiser with the who's who of the city." She sighed and smiled. "I'm chalking it up to him having had too much to drink. If it's a chronic thing, I'll take care of it."

Jason chuckled. "Yeah, I don't want to be him. He'd have an easier time with me."

Amira feigned a look of ignorance and innocence. "I have no idea what you're talking about. I would just talk to him."

"I seem to remember you nearly twisting a guy's arm off for touching your butt at a bar."

Amira scoffed, again with an air of put-upon incredulity. "That was in college."

"I know," Jason said, putting his arm around her waist, pulling her close to him, and kissing her head. "You were more reasonable then."

She returned the gesture with an elbow to his ribs and a kiss on his cheek. She made eye contact and tilted her head. "Are you OK?"

"Yeah," he replied a little too quickly. "I mean, I will be. I'll be OK."

Her mouth pursed up to one side as she studied him. He knew this look. It was the look she gave him when she knew there was more to the story. It wasn't accusing him of anything, just a tic she had when she was concerned and frustrated.

"Seriously." He rubbed her arms.

She nodded slightly, satisfied.

"Amira, darling," a singsong voice called out. A lithe woman who looked to be entering her golden years, draped in an evening gown of expensive-looking fabrics, sauntered close with an amused smile.

"Lydia," Amira greeted, exchanging kisses on each other's cheeks.

"I'm so sorry that Leo couldn't make it in person tonight, he was called away unexpectedly to London," the woman said. "I hope the video message he sent over will suffice for tonight's keynote rather than him speaking in person."

"Yes, absolutely, and completely understandable," Amira said. "And thank you so much for finally agreeing to sit on our board. I'm so happy we'll see each other more often."

"It only took three years. And now our tea times are a tax write-off," Lydia joked.

Amira turned to Jason. "Jason, this is Lydia Lacroix, the COO of Majora Global."

Jason extended a hand. "I'm so glad we can finally meet. Leo talks about you all the time. It's nuts that we've never had the chance to meet in person."

Lydia returned the handshake, and Jason noted that her hands felt like someone who wasn't afraid to use them for something other than typing at a keyboard. Not a worker's hands, but hands that liked being useful. "The joys of busy people who are good at their jobs, I suppose. And I hear from more than just Amira that you are quite the detective…one of the best in the department, if the rumors are to be believed."

Jason felt himself blush. "Uh, thank you, ma'am."

Lydia gave him a playful scolding look. "None of this formal nonsense. I've written a sizable check, that should buy me some familiarity."

A young man in the wait staff livery approached Amira, tapped her on her arm, and whispered something in her ear; her face scrunched up for a quick moment, and Jason knew that was her "annoyed" look. "I'm so sorry, I need to see to something-"

"Go, go, take care of what you need to," Lydia said, and threaded her arm through Jason's. "I'm going to steal your husband for a drink and pretend he's my eye candy. We can finally get to know each other rather than hearing stories from other people."

Amira gave a coy smile and signed *laughing*. "He's only on loan. He's *my* eye candy."

Lydia returned the *laughing* sign and Amira melted into the crowd behind the staff member.

"You know Gapper signs?" Jason said, his eyebrows rising.

Lydia began to lead him towards the bar. "Why wouldn't I?"

Jason felt his blush return. "I didn't mean any insult by it, it's just that most people of, well…"

"Us rich folk don't usually speak the vernacular of the poor," Lydia said, her amused smile returning.

Jason's eyebrows tried to reach his hairline. "I'm just surprised you remember it."

"My brother and I both believe the only way you know where you're going is to remember where you started," she said, navigating them both through the crowd. "It's one of the reasons why we wanted to support your wife's foundation. We want to see more people have the opportunities that we did."

"It's a shame that Leo couldn't make it," Jason said. "I thought he was supposed to deliver the keynote speech. I was looking forward to finally sharing a drink with him."

"He was not happy about missing tonight," Lydia said. "But when you're the CEO of a company as large as Majora…well, even little fires are big. He was talking all week about how you two talk all the time but have never met in person, conflicting schedules, all that. Sometimes I think both of us wish that Majora didn't require as much attention from us as it does."

"Price of success, I suppose," Jason said.

"True. And a tale of 'be careful what you wish for, you just might get it'. So, Leo had to settle for another recorded speech rather than delivering it in person. They'll play it later tonight once everyone is good and liquored up. Speaking of which…" They had finally reached the bar, something that the catering company had wheeled in. "I'll have whatever you're having."

Jason signaled to the bartender and ordered two mezcals. Two glasses with the clear liquid arrived in short order; they toasted, and sipped their drinks.

"Why mezcal?" Lydia asked.

Jason was confused by the question. "Uh… because…I like it?"

"I think there is a lot to tell about a person by their preferred drink," she said. "For instance, there is a saying about mezcal. *Para todo mal, mezcal, y para todo bien, también; y si no hay remedio litro y medio.*" Jason heard the Spanish, but didn't understand enough of the words to make sense of it, which must have shown on his face. "For all bad, mezcal, and for all good, as well; and if there is no remedy, a liter and a half."

Jason shrugged and took another sip. "Sounds about right."

"Alexei must have been quite the person," Lydia said, changing the subject. "For Amira to go to this effort to start a foundation in his name and see it to such success."

Jason nodded, and didn't try to stop the smile that almost always followed thoughts of his childhood friend. "Yeah, he was. The best friend anyone could ask for."

"So, you were close with him as well?" Lydia asked. "You knew the twins growing up?"

"We were pretty inseparable. They were the only two who never treated me differently."

A curious frown formed on Lydia's face, and Jason could sense the question.

"I was born with Horkrim's Syndrome."

Lydia set down her drink and put a comforting hand on his arm. "Oh, dear, I'm so sorry…"

Jason smiled. "No, it's ok, it's been in remission for years. It's not something we usually bring up. There are new treatments out there that are showing a lot of promise. But growing up, most people, adults and kids, would either treat me like I was made of porcelain or like I wasn't there at all."

"But not Alexei?"

"Nope. He just treated me like a normal kid." Jason felt warm in his chest, and he wasn't sure if it was the liquor or the pleasant memory. "I could never keep up with him…he was a natural athlete, and really good at school, but he never wanted to leave me behind. He would always push me to run faster, to study harder, and he would be with me the entire time. Half the time I thought I was holding him back, but he insisted on sticking with me for some reason."

Lydia smiled, a smile that wrinkled her eyes. "That sounds like a wonderful friend. And it sounds like he would be very proud of you now." She downed her drink and signaled to the bartender. While they waited for their refills, she said, "OK, I need my sponsorship money's worth." Jason gave her a questioning look. "If I'm going to be on the board, I need to be able to bring in the money from other donors. To do that, people need to connect with the Foundation, and more specifically, to Alexei himself. People don't donate with their heads, they donate with their hearts, so give me something that will tug on the heartstrings."

Jason nodded along with her logic, and thought back. He had so many great memories with Alexei…

"OK," he said, settling on one. "So, Alexei and I were walking home from school one day, and I wanted to stop off and get some candy from the one corner store that had these peanut butter chocolate things that none of the other stores carried."

"Reese's?" Lydia asked with a smile. "I loved those."

Jason returned the smile. "Yeah, those, but there were these older kids that hung out front of this place that always gave little kids a hard time, and we were like eight or nine at the time, but I was like, 'We can outrun them,' or something stupid like that. So we go to the store, I get my candy, and on the way out, one of the older kids starts following us down the street, telling me I needed to give him my Reese's.

"So, we start running, but the kid catches up to us, and he grabs me by my jacket and tears my UV gear right off when he yanks me around. And then he smacks me in the face and my cycler goes flying off and hits the pavement and smashes to pieces."

He paused at the memory of how his skin immediately felt like it was on fire, and his lungs felt like he was inhaling broken glass.

"Next thing I know Alexei has tackled me to the ground and is covering me up as best he can, and he starts doing that buddy breathing that you learn in school, you know, where you take a breath and hold it and share your cycler. And he's doing this and kicking at the other kid, who's still trying to steal my candy or my change or whatever, just taking shots at his knees. I think one of them connected, 'cause that kid went down and was crawling away in tears.

"But Alexei stayed there, covering me and buddy breathing until someone called emergency services and they came and got us."

He remembered Alexei stopping by every day after school for the week he was at home recuperating from his sun poisoning, bringing Jason his schoolwork and helping him with it, and playing video games when they were done until dinner time.

Lydia tipped her glass to Jason. "That's perfect. We should all be lucky to have a friend half as good as that. I have zero doubt that he would be proud of what you've done with your life."

She finished her drink, and glanced over Jason's shoulder. He turned and saw Amira approaching, waylaid by another donor. "I've stolen you long enough. It looks like your wife needs a break." She swiped her phone by the payment terminal and keyed in a generous tip for the bartender. "Should I let Leo know you'll be calling tomorrow?"

Jason reflected on his day, and tried not to linger on the horror show of the lab or let his discomfort show on his face. He hoped he was successful. "Yeah, it'd be good to talk to him."

"Well, I'm glad we finally met face-to-face. Leo and Amira both speak so highly of you, I felt like I knew you already." She kissed him on the cheek. "Thank you for the drink and the company." Lydia patted him on the arm, and casually melted into the crowd.

Jason finally noticed the ring of people hanging in their periphery, no doubt curious as to what a titan of industry and a lowly police lieutenant would be discussing, and politely waiting their turn to curry favor with Ms. Lacroix.

With the distraction of her company gone, and left to his own devices, the earlier memories crept in from the margins. He quickly downed his drink and contemplated ordering another, but decided against it.

Amira sidled up next to him. "Hey there, cowboy. Talk about anything interesting?"

"You know, nothing much. I was telling her about Alexei."

She studied his face, the same lips-twisted-to-one-side look that said she knew he wasn't telling her everything. "That's it?"

"Yeah," he said.

Amira continued to study him. "Something's bothering you."

I had to see a murder scene where we can't even identify the bodies through DNA testing because the remains look like they were pushed through a meat grinder.

"It's nothing. Just work stuff."

"You know you can tell me about it, right?" Amira said, and rubbed his arm.

No, I can't.

"It was just...it was a rough day. Nothing I want to load you up with."

Amira held his gaze for another moment, then turned and leaned her back against the bar. "Good turnout tonight."

Jason grunted his agreement.

"This will go a long way to funding the Foundation's endowment," she continued. "And it's nice to know that there's a lot of generous people that believe in its mission."

Jason snorted before he could catch himself. Amira gave him a look.

"You have something to say?"

Jason pursed his lips. "Nope."

"You don't agree." She crossed her arms and stared straight ahead.

"I think their generosity is directly proportional to how much they can write off their taxes and assuage their guilt for being total assholes the rest of the year." The words poured out of him.

You moron. Way to ruin her night.

Amira shook her head. "You're just a cynic. You see so much bad every day that you can't see good when it's right in front of you."

Jason choked back a rueful laugh. "Are you kidding me?" He pointed to a man in a black suit. "That guy? He owns a laundry in the Eastern Gaps. We staked him out when the task force started because the business was used as a depot for moving the chemicals needed for splice manufacturing. His house is the size of an airplane hangar. Pays his workers a quarter over minimum wage. We busted him for trafficking, and he didn't spend a day in jail."

He pointed to an older woman in a red dress and an ostentatious scarf wrapped around her neck. "She's a partner in the accounting firm that does the books for at least a dozen different shell businesses used for money laundering. We got her dead to rights on at least twenty different tax and embezzlement charges, and what does she do? Liquidates the firm, declares bankruptcy, and testifies against the firm's supervisors, acting like they were the sole operators."

He subtly gestured to all the attendees as they continued drinking, laughing, and talking, seemingly without a care in the world. "I have zero doubt that I couldn't swing a dead cat in here without hitting someone who has committed fraud, or violated a half dozen federal trade and drug statutes, and not one of them has had to face the consequences other than a fine that they probably used as a tax write-off."

Amira nodded. "Maybe. Remember what my dad always said? You use the tools you have, even if they're rusty. These people may be privileged jackasses, but they also gave the foundation a ton of money. We can use it to maybe undo the damage and make things just a little fairer, just a little bit."

Jason nudged her with his elbow. "Looks like I'm not the only cynic."

Amira sighed. "I guess not. I just want to believe that people can be better."

"I get it. I do, too." Jason's shoulders slumped. "I just don't want to get caught up in the machine, you know? Everything is tilted in their favor, and a lot of that is because people let it be that way. Hell, sometimes with my work, I wonder if I'm a part of the problem."

Amira let go of Jason's hand and put both of hers under his jaw. "Hey, look at me," she insisted, and Jason looked into his wife's soft brown eyes. She lowered her voice. "You will never be like these people. Never."

Jason placed his hands over hers. "How are you so sure?"

"Because we've known each other since we were five. And I've never known you to not do the right thing. I don't know anyone who is as sure of who they are in the world as you are, even if you don't see it. Because you didn't grow up rich, or strong, or with any edge over anyone else...you have had to work for everything you have, harder than most, and you never take it for granted or miss an opportunity to offer a hand up to anyone else in the same position that you were." Amira smiled up at her husband. "Because I love you."

Jason smiled a crooked smile and kissed his wife. "Love you, too." He wrapped his arms around her. "Did you know I still get all warm and tingly when you're near me?"

"Oh really?" Amira said with a sly smirk.

"Yeah," he said. "Want to get out of here?"

CHAPTER 5

The blast of hot night air hit Jason in the face as he affixed his cycler, Amira doing the same. No sun meant no need for UV protection, but the air was still the equivalent of sucking on a car's tailpipe.

"Shall we?" he said through the external comm in a mock posh accent, and offered his arm to his wife.

"We shall," she replied in the same manner and laced her arm through his as they made their way down the museum steps.

While the day's heat still lingered, as it often did, a slight breeze carried through the tall canyons of glass and steel of Center City and down the long stretch of park and parkway that led to the Arts District. Jason's hair mostly stayed in place, but a lock of Amira's broke free and across her face. Jason gently moved it away as they strolled down the avenue towards their townhouse.

The city always seemed to come alive at night. The gargantuan sun squares glimmered far overhead in the moonlight, their flashing lights to warn off aircraft blended with the few stars visible in the near-constant haze that clung to the streets and buildings. More people filled the streets, unafraid of the oppressive sun now that it lay far beyond the horizon. Vendors with pushcarts filled with everything from food to tourist tchotchkes to daily sundries made their way up and down the streets hawking their wares, calling out to people as they passed. At the same time, musicians and dancers busked on street corners, filling the night with a chaotic, electronically-distorted soundtrack of life.

Jason recognized a few of the vendors and nodded greeting as they passed, the mobile shopkeepers returning the greeting with a nod or a doffed hat, twisting their finger and thumb into a signed smile.

The vendors hurried on their way, intent on making as much as they could in the limited hours they had in the City Center before having to return to the Gaps. Jason found it ironic and sad: Gappers were generally not allowed in the City Center during daylight hours, but once night fell, they were unofficially "welcomed" by the *bogari*. He had heard something about "culture" and "the heartbeat of the city" in a media feed, but Jason knew better. It was a safe version of poverty tourism that let the well-to-do of the city with their expensive clothing and transparent facemask cyclers feel like they were living dangerously while staying perfectly safe. It also gave them access to some harder-to-find items that the Gappers would bring, anything from knockoff handbags and fake IDs to drugs of every conceivable flavor.

Were any of those bodies people that were just trying to make a living any way they could?

Jason knew from experience that the players he came into contact with that were in the game weren't simple caricatures, that the morality of their decisions wasn't black and white. Extreme poverty meant people would find any way to get by, and sometimes those methods would get extreme.

There were undoubtedly bad people, like the one dealer he had busted who had been essentially holding an entire apartment building hostage as meat shields so that rival crews and even the police would think twice before going in guns blazing; Jason had felt a particular satisfaction slapping cuffs on that one.

Or the chemist known as "The Pharmacist" he had spent three months tracking who had been formulating a more addictive version of just about every drug imaginable to create a greater demand. In the process, he had left a trail of John and Jane Does that OD'd on his concoctions. When Jason busted him, the Pharmacist hadn't shown a bit of remorse. He even seemed a little impressed with himself. Another one Jason was happy to put away.

But then there were the kids that were acting as gofers for the corner kids, running the individual ampules of splice or tiny baggies of heroin from the stash to the customers, or some of the corner kids who were running the crews, or even the stickup boys who routinely robbed dealers...most of them were just trying to make a few bucks when no one else would hire them, either because they were too young or didn't have the skills, or didn't want to work the grueling hours for minimal pay that violated child labor laws left and right.

It didn't make it right, and Jason would still do his job, but he at least knew there was a difference between who someone was and what they did, especially when literal survival was on the line.

The thought returned to him: who were the people in that pile of bodies? Did he know them? Were they working in that stash house because they were just looking for a way to put money on the table, or were they more like the Pharmacist, callously trying to build a better mousetrap to ensnare more people into the cycle of drug abuse and addiction?

"You're doing it again," Amira said, bringing Jason out of his thoughts and back to reality. "That thing where you get that crinkle between your eyebrows."

"Am I?" Jason said. "Sorry, just...it's been a long day."

Amira looked ahead. "I know you're not all in on the idea of taking some time off," she started, and she paused to gauge Jason's response. He kept his face as neutral as possible, and nodded for her to continue. "But I think it would be a good thing. You've been carrying a lot more on your shoulders lately, and it's starting to show." She rubbed his arm. "Even you need a break. Maybe it's time to start looking for something else to do?"

Jason took a deep breath and let her words marinate. "Yeah," he finally said. "I know. Soon, I promise." Amira opened her mouth but Jason interrupted her. "I promise," he emphasized. "Things just got...complicated...today, and we have a limited time to act on it. But the task force is wrapping up, and as soon as it does, we'll have a serious talk about it."

Amira patted his arm. "Thank you, that's all I want."

Jason awoke to his phone ringing and a hangover. He blindly fumbled on his nightstand until his fingers found the phone and sat up in his bed. The space next to him was empty, and he smelled coffee brewing.

He squinted through the lingering sleep to see who was waking him up. The caller ID read "Leo Lacroix".

"Good morning, Super Cop," Leo's baritone said when the call connected.

"Good morning, Super Genius Doctor Guy," Jason replied, his voice hoarse from sleep and mezcal.

"Sounds like you had a good time last night," Leo said, and Jason could hear the smile in his voice. "Sorry I couldn't be there, I was really looking forward to finally having a drink with you."

"No worries," Jason said, and swung his feet out of the bed and onto the floor. "I think I did enough drinking for the both of us."

"What was your poison?"

"Mezcal," Jason said and squeezed his eyes shut to block out the light that set his head to pounding.

"I'm sending you something that will help with that," Leo said. Jason's phone pulsed and he looked at the message.

"A Bloody Mary recipe?"

"Everything you need, nothing you don't," Leo said. "Hydration, electrolytes, B-complex vitamins, and some spice to dilate the blood vessels in your head. And the capsaicin in the hot sauce is also an anti-inflammatory."

Jason chuckled. "Well, you're the doctor."

"So, hangover aside, how are you, my friend? I feel like I haven't spoken to you in months."

The thought of a Bloody Mary gave way to the memory of a bloody crime scene. "Rough, man. It's been rough."

"Everything OK?"

"Yeah, I don't want to bother you with work crap." Jason ran a hand through his hair and heaved himself to his feet. His head pounded again in protest.

"Jason, you can't carry these burdens alone," Leo said. "Believe me, I know. I mean, my burdens are nothing compared to what you must have to deal with every day, but carrying around that kind of weight…it keeps you from being your best self for you, the people you love, the people who rely on you…"

"Please, you run an international conglomerate. I'm just a cop."

"My biggest issues live on spreadsheets. Yours are in the real world. Don't ever doubt the impact that you have on the people around you."

Jason sighed. "We had a pretty bad crime scene yesterday," he finally said. "Just utter carnage. Like nothing I've ever seen before. I…I'm having a real hard time shaking the image."

"Hence the drinking last night? Because that isn't usually like you."

Jason nodded to no one in particular. "Yeah, maybe." He started pulling clothes out of his closet. "That, and Swan dumped the homicide on my ledger."

"On top of the anti-splice task force?"

"Yep."

He heard Leo sigh. "From what you've told me, this seems to be her MO, right? She's had it in for you since you were given the task force."

"I think she may get what she wants," Jason replied. "There's not a lot I can do."

Leo *tsk*ed. "You can't accept that. You're better than that."

"I'm just a guy working a job," Jason said. "She's got way more pull than I do, and she's not saddled with being from The Gaps. She gets to make the rules."

"The woman was born on third base and thinks she hit a triple," Leo said. "People like that think they are owed something, and yes, they have advantages. But they also don't know anything about sacrifice. That's your advantage." Leo paused. "If I've learned one thing about you over the years, Jason, it's that you're a fighter. Literally and figuratively. It's how you got yourself out of The Gaps, it's how you rose as high as you did as a professional fighter, it's how you've done as well as you have as a police officer."

"Did I ever tell you why my fight career ended?" Jason asked.

"I only know the story as I read it online," Leo said. "I don't think we ever spoke about it, however. Is there more to it than a simple injury?"

"Yeah," Jason said. "So, everyone knows Derrick Belford and I were scheduled to fight. I was undefeated at that point, I think he had maybe two wins, five or six losses. This was an exhibition fight for the IPFC. If I won and put on a good enough show, the possibility was there that they would offer me a contract."

"You were finally going to make it to The Show," Leo said. "How did Derrick get into that fight with that record? I'm not a huge fan of combat sports, but it doesn't sound like he was very good."

"He wasn't," Jason said. "But mommy and daddy had money, and as you know, money gets you many things. I think they sponsored another event and used that as leverage to get him in. But anyway, yeah, this was supposed to be the big break I had been working for. A way out of The Gaps, a way to secure Amira and my finances for the future."

"And then Derrick cheated," Leo said.

"Derrick cheated," Jason echoed. "But more than that. He already had gene treatments when he was younger. He was already strong and fast, even if he wasn't a good fighter. And I'd fought with people on splice before. It sucked, but I still handled myself. Whatever Belford was on that night…I don't think I've ever been hit that hard."

"If I remember, it was a new designer version of the drug," Leo said. "Everyone has tried to replicate the Recombinex formula I developed for years. Legitimate gene therapy is a booming market, but nothing works as well as my formula. All of the different versions of splice are just failed attempts, and I can't seem to do anything about them, no matter how much I try to shut things down from my end."

"Well, it keeps me employed," Jason said with a laugh. "But anyway, he wins the fight by tearing all of the ligaments in my knee."

"That would end just about anyone's career," Leo said.

"Yeah, but here's the thing…I healed up just fine. No lingering weakness or anything. I could have been cleared to fight within a year."

"Then why didn't you?" Leo asked, his voice dripping with curiosity.

"Because the rules were stacked against me," Jason replied. "We found out that Belford had popped on a drug test weeks before the fight, and the IPFC knew about it. They put the fight on anyway, knowing he was juiced up to the gills. And afterward there weren't any consequences for him. If any other fighter had been doing splice and injured someone that badly in a fight, they would have never gotten a fighting license again. But the IPFC signed him to a five-fight contract. All because his parents had the money to make it go away."

There was a long pause on Leo's end. "So, you walked away." Jason couldn't tell if his friend was disappointed or not.

"I walked away. I didn't want to have to take performance-enhancing drugs to be competitive, and even if I did, I didn't have the money to protect myself if I got caught." Jason took a deep breath. "I was screwed either way. So, I decided not to play the game. I filed the negligence suit, got paid, and gave up on that dream."

"The lesson you took from that was that the rules aren't fair, so why play?" Leo asked.

"Yeah."

Jason could almost hear Leo shaking his head. "I come to a different conclusion from that story. Remember what I said about sacrifice? Derrick Belford is a person who isn't willing to make sacrifices, whether to achieve something, or even to reconcile reality with their ego. For instance, what became of Derrick Belford after that incident?"

"He fought twice more," Jason said. "Lost both fights in the first round. Got his ass kicked. IPFC cut him, canceled the contract. Parents made more donations, eventually got him on the job on a career track. He's actually on the task force."

He heard Leo chuckle. "He works for you now?"

Jason couldn't help but echo his friend's laughter. "Yeah, yeah he does."

"You see? You're a fighter, through and through, and you've earned everything you have. That's worth more than being handed anything in this life.

And you're willing to make the sacrifices necessary to achieve what you want."

"Maybe," Jason said. "He's likely to be promoted ahead of me soon, especially the way Swan is constantly gunning for me. And this isn't the kind of fight where I can punch back. Literally or figuratively."

"Why not?"

"Because there are consequences," Jason said. "It's not like I can lodge a complaint, or hope to get by on my merits. Swan's basically aristocracy, same with Belford…and *bogari* play by a different set of rules, or at least, the rules don't apply to them the same way."

"I've found that once you've accepted the reality of the situation, what the 'facts on the ground' are, so to speak, that if the rules get in the way, you simply need to ignore them and make your own." Leo chucked. "But then, I'm also very rich, and I sometimes forget that not everyone has that luxury."

"Here's hoping that someone can change that one day," Jason said. "The rules thing, not you being rich."

Leo laughed. "Indeed. I quite enjoy it. Well, I should let you go. I'm sure you have to get to work."

"Yeah, probably," Jason said. He remembered his chase with Tommy Delucca. "Hey, before you go, quick question. We had a guy yesterday that was hepped up on some new strain of splice…dude ran outside with no protection, no mask for close to ten minutes before he started showing any signs of burning or anything."

"That's quite the adventure," Leo said.

"Any idea what could cause that? I've seen people on splice be outside and act like they didn't feel anything while their skin blistered up, but never where they didn't have a physical reaction."

There was a pause from Leo. "Theoretically, it could be possible," he finally said. "Biologically, we are supposed to be able to go outside and withstand a certain amount of ultraviolet radiation and impurities in the air. It wasn't so long ago, maybe two or three generations, that people just *went outside*. I suppose teaching the body to adapt to the current environment would be possible. Theoretically."

"Hmm," Jason said. "This is a new kind of splice, then."

"Without more data points, I couldn't say," Leo said. "But keep me in the loop, and I'll let you know if I come across any research from my competitors. As I said, gene therapy is an attractive field, plenty of people are playing in the market."

"Thanks, I appreciate it," Jason said. "And thanks for listening. Again."

"It's what friends are for," Leo replied, and Jason could hear that his smile was back. "Being rich has many advantages, but friendship isn't one of them. I truly treasure yours. Be safe, Jason."

The call disconnected. Jason wiped the layer of hangover sweat that had collected on his forehead, and decided that a hot shower was exactly what he needed.

That, and a Bloody Mary.

CHAPTER 6

Jason stared at the police tape-covered door that led into the stash house. He felt a churning in his stomach, and his arms felt like they were vibrating, a mix of apprehension and anticipation.

Alexei was at the forefront of his thoughts, a welcome reprieve from the memories of the horror show of the day before. Memories he hadn't visited in many years seemed to pop up in a strange word association game; snippets of conversations he heard or random objects or smells would tug at things he hadn't thought about in... he couldn't remember when.

Jason huffed out a sigh. "OK, ready?"

"No," Les said and pushed the door open and parted the warning tape.

He turned to the uniformed officer that was guarding the door. "Anyone else been in since we sealed it yesterday?"

The officer looked at his clipboard. "No, doesn't look that way. Looks like the ME was the last one here taking out the..." The officer's face began to get a green tinge to it. "Well...you know."

Jason nodded and stepped through the tape after his partner. The distracting memories were washed away with the jarring equivalent of a bucket of ice water on his face.

The apartment looked exactly the same as it had the day before, with the notable exception of no body parts. Nothing else had been cleaned or touched, preserving those moments of butchery. Jason was glad he didn't have to see the human meat pile again.

Jason and Les silently moved around the room, carefully stepping around any evidence marked with small numbered tripod placards. They fell into a rhythm they had perfected over the years, giving each other the time to process the scene individually without polluting each other's thought process with their own ideas, a habit that Les instilled in him on the first day they were partnered together. *"Never get blindly caught up in the other one's theory,"* he had said at that first crime scene, a robbery-homicide. *"Don't limit the possibilities with what someone else is thinking. Let the evidence do that. If you watch and listen to the scene, it will tell you what happened."*

"OK, what do you have to say?" Jason said under his breath. "Talk to me,"

At first glance, the room was chaos. Smashed bottles, overturned furniture, and blood. The blood was smeared haphazardly over every surface, creating a macabre Jackson Pollock painting. Jason looked past that and tried to envision the scene without it.

"Who benefits?" Jason murmured.

"Lieutenant?" the officer asked from the doorway.

"Huh?" Jason said, looking up.

"You said, 'Who benefits'...what do you mean?"

"Oh," Jason said, realizing he had said it louder than he thought. "Just a homicide thing. Murder always has a motivation, like jealousy, or rage, or hiding something, things like that. If we can figure out who benefits from the murder, we have a huge leg up on finding the murderer."

"I think I get it," the officer said. "Huh. Interesting."

Jason nodded towards Les. "Learned it from him."

Les didn't turn around from the blood spatter he was examining. "I learned it from Batman."

The officer looked confused. "Who, sir?"

"Batm-...are you kidding me?" Les looked over his shoulder with a look of pure incredulousness on his face. "You don't know who Batman is?"

"Uh...should I?"

"For the love of-," Les stood. "The Dark Knight? The Caped Crusader of Gotham? Founding member of the Justice League?"

The officer scrunched his face to one side in embarrassment. "Was he a professional wrestler or something?"

Les' mouth remained open in exasperation, and he slowly shook his head as he turned back to the blood splatter. "*Gilipollas³*, I can't, I just can't with these..."

The officer leaned towards Jason, still not entering the room, and whispered, "Did I offend him?"

Jason quietly laughed. "Yeah, a little." Jason couldn't help but smile. He felt some of the tension in his chest that had settled in as soon as they had entered the apartment dissipate, and he was grateful for the unintentional humor.

Les was muttering to himself when Jason reached his side, and Les rose again to standing. "I swear, if it's not in a game or a ten-second video, these kids..." He pulled out his notebook and started scribbling notes. Jason looked over his shoulder to see what he was writing, but he had long given up trying to

³ Dumbass

decode his partner's chicken scratch. Upon scrawling a final slash of something into the notes, Les looked up. "OK, what do you see?"

Jason turned and gestured to the shattered glass on the floor and tables on one side of the room. "OK, so the glass over here and here...I think this was from the beer bottles when that coffee table was knocked over, probably during the assault. Overturned table is there, and the glass is all under it and spreading away in the direction it tipped. But this glass over here," Jason said, motioning to the shattered pieces near the wall opposite the door, "I don't see any furniture nearby, so if I had to guess, someone threw it over here. Maybe at the perp, or maybe the perp threw it themselves?"

Les nodded in concurrence. "Means someone was standing over...there." He fished around in one of the pockets in his long coat and pulled out a small flashlight. He flipped it on and twisted the end until a bright blueish-purple light radiated from the diodes, and he shone it on the floor where the shards lay. "No blood." He twisted the light again until it shone yellow. He pulled down his goggles and made an adjustment to the settings. "Got a footprint."

Jason lowered his goggles and changed the setting to match the light, and the faint pattern of what looked to be a boot tread began to fluoresce subtly. He snapped a picture with his phone and added the new evidence to the log. "Looks like it's facing towards the door, not away, so they were facing whoever threw the bottle." He pulled an evidence marker from his pocket and placed it next to the print.

Les shut the light off and lifted his goggles. He pointed to some blood on the wall next to him. "Arterial spray." He gestured toward the wall, opening his closed fingers to demonstrate something exploding out. "Hits the wall here...so this victim was facing away."

He took two steps towards the next closest blood and traced a line in the air with his finger. "This one is coming towards the first one." He pointed to the glass on the ground to his left that Jason had just logged. "Bottle is thrown here." He pivoted his head to each of the blood stains that, while still chaotic and everywhere, Jason could now start seeing as discrete units. "Three more, all aimed towards the center of the room." He walked to the opposite side of the room with the overturned end table. "This one is aimed away."

Jason began to piece the timeline together. "So, victim one was...here," he said, moving to the first arterial spray Les pointed out. "Blitz attack, doesn't know what hit them. Perp moves to victim two," and he stepped toward the second spray. He made the sign for *kill*. "Boom, dropped. One of the others has the time to throw a bottle but doesn't hit the perp where there's any exposed skin...they still might be in UV gear. Then boom, boom, boom," Jason finished, gesturing towards the next three blood splatters.

"Last one tries to make it over the table," Les said. "Attacked from behind, and..." Les made the same sign for *kill*.

The partners stood silent for a moment, then another, processing their theory. Jason glanced around the room again, trying to see the big picture, ignoring the blood. The remaining scene looked like the room had been turned upside down: cabinets partially open, some hanging half off their hinges, drawers partially open, but the refrigerators containing ampules of splice remained untouched.

Les nodded to the untouched drugs. "Robbery? Couldn't find a key to open the fridge? There's at least thirty grand of splice in there, wholesale. Worth two to three times as much on the street. Definitely worth dropping six bodies."

"Maybe," Jason muttered. The drawers kept pulling his attention. Something about them… "No, not a robbery. Look here." He pointed at the column of drawers that were partially shut. "All of the drawers aren't open."

Les signed *I don't understand.*

"If this were a stickup boy or someone who knew what they were doing…and let's face it, whoever did this, they knew what they were doing…they wouldn't take the time to open a drawer and then close it." Jason opened the top drawer. "Blocks all of the other drawers, takes more time." He closed the drawer and opened the one on the bottom, then the one over it. "They would have started at the bottom and worked their way up, leaving all the drawers open."

Les nodded. "Good eye."

"This wasn't a robbery," Jason continued. "This was a hit made to look like a robbery." He pulled up his phone to make a note to follow up on his thought later and saw the picture of the glowing footprint.

"Got something?" Les asked.

"Not sure," Jason said. He glanced back at where they found it. "Hold on," he said and walked back to the evidence marker. "Vic one was here, right?" Les nodded. "We're both in agreement, it started here, couldn't have gone down any other way?"

Les closed his eyes in thought, then shook his head. "Nope, I don't see any other way. Unless we're missing something major, that's how this went down." He narrowed his eyes. "Because if it did..." They glanced back at the door on the opposite side of the room.

"...it means they were already in the room when they hit vic one, yeah," Jason finished. "And if it were a robbery, they wouldn't have started here, they would have started with vic six. Smash and grab."

"Inside job," they both said together.

"And no one saw someone covered head to toe in blood leave," Jason said. "Nothing on the drones, either, and we had our people on the roof. So how did they get out?"

Les got a sour look on his face. "Secret door?"

They both turned slowly, re-examining the scene. The room was filled with the silence of buzzing fluorescent lights and the low whisper of the vents.

The vents... "Where's the mechanical room?" Jason said, quickly looking for a door. Two doors led to closets with benign storage, but the third he pulled open led to a small room with utility meters and a quietly humming HVAC system. It took up most of the space.

"That thing is huge," Les said. "Way bigger than is needed for an apartment of this size."

"It's for the refrigerator units," Jason said. "They need to vent the heat shed. Otherwise, it shows up on infrared."

Jason banged and pulled on the ducts leading out from it...*bang*, nothing, *bang*, still nothing, *bang*...the sheet metal slightly separated from the vent. Jason and Les pulled at it, and an entire section pulled free, revealing access to the duct as it climbed up into the ceiling.

"Well, dollars to donuts, that's how they got in and out," Les said. "You want to see where that goes?"

Jason was already climbing into the vent before Les finished his sentence. He reached up, pulled himself in, and snapped on his pocket flashlight. The duct turned up towards the ceiling at a sharp angle. He noisily backed out. "Think it goes to the roof."

As his flashlight tracked across the apartment, a tiny glint in the corner caught his eye. He approached and saw it was partially jammed under the baseboard heater, all but hidden from view except from where he had been standing. He picked up a small piece of metal and turned it in his hand under the flashlight.

"Find something?" Les asked.

"Yeah," Jason said. "Looks like a pin with two lacrosse sticks on it." He held it closer to his face. "Looks like it says 'BYC Lax'. Any idea what BYC is?"

Les was silent for a moment. "Maybe...Burton Youth Center? Local sports program. I think they have lacrosse."

"Burton..." Jason mumbled to himself. Then his heart sank into his guts.

"What is it?" Les called.

"I think things just got complicated," Jason replied.

Les approached and took the pin into his hand. "Could be the kid's." He held it up to the light and examined it closer. "Could also belong to anyone from that rec center, and it's right down the road. Would be a pretty big coincidence."

"Coincidences mean you're on the right path," Jason replied. He held his flashlight in his mouth and hauled himself back into the duct, pulling himself further into where it made a sharp turn upward. He saw injected putty where whoever built the system had tied it into the apartment building's ducts. He shimmied around the tight turn, stood with his shoulders hunched, and shone his light upward. Where he expected to see a clear path to the roof, he saw only a few floors up, and the duct abruptly turned again. No light shone through.

He braced his hands and boots against the galvanized steel and pushed himself upwards, wedging himself into the space as he inched his way through. His foot slipped, and he braced himself to keep from sliding back down but lost his grip on the light. It bounced off his leg and clattered down to the bottom of the shaft.

Jason knew the vent should go all the way up. He also knew that sometimes dealers would use HVAC ducts to stash drugs, money, guns, and other contraband.

His gloved hand pushed into something tacky on the metal. He peeled his hand off the surface but couldn't see what it was in the darkness. He felt and groped above him, sure he was close to the blockage. He shimmied up a few more inches, and fished again. This time his hand felt something. It didn't feel like any fabric or plastic for a bag...it had a little give to it.

He found purchase on something and gave it a little tug to pull it free. It budged a fraction of an inch. He tugged again, and he felt something slip and release. Something much heavier than he was anticipating collapsed on him. He felt his breath evacuate his body as he lost his purchase on the duct and slipped, crashing at the bottom with whatever it was on top of him.

"*Estás bien?*" Les called from the end of the vent.

"Yeah," Jason said, feeling embarrassed. He felt his flashlight digging into his back and maneuvered to retrieve it. He clicked it on to see what had fallen on him.

He shouted something incomprehensible when the light revealed the lifeless eyes of a naked Office Novak folded into an inhuman position.

"I want a complete recanvas of the entire building," Jason told his team. "We are looking for any information about Markus Kline or who Novak last had contact with. A recent photo of Markus has been sent to your phones."

"The kid connected to the stash house?" Nguyen asked while looking at the photo on her phone.

"We have reason to believe that he's a material witness," Jason replied. "But let's keep that quiet. Don't need to cause any more trouble for the family or him. As far as anyone knows, we're just looking for a missing kid. Do not let on that we've got a dead cop. Our best guess is that's how our perp got out of the building." He nodded at the team. "Remember, headgear off when inside. Go."

The task force scattered into the apartment building, and Jason turned to the gaggle of uniformed officers who had responded to the backup call he put out a few minutes earlier. "Everyone else, I want a hard target search of every nook, cranny, alley, and bolt hole in a six-block radius from here. Same deal, as far as anyone knows, we're just looking for a missing kid who may be in danger. Don't spook anyone, but make sure anyone you speak with knows the gravity of the situation."

Les stepped up next to Jason. "As unlikely as it is, if you should find Markus Kline in the company of anyone who is not an immediate family member or an officer, maintain distance. Given what we know, any adult he's with is likely very dangerous. Wait for backup, and call us. Do not approach. Understood?" A round of affirmations returned.

"Ramirez, Geralt," Jason called out, "you two hang back. Everyone else, good hunting."

The briefing broke up, and the officers began fanning down the street. Les looked up and down the block.

"Don't take us off this, Loo." Ramirez said.

"Not going to," Jason said. "But you two were the last ones to see Novak. Anything grab your attention? Anyone that you saw, or something they said that stood out?"

Geralt and Ramirez looked at each other through their tinted goggles, then turned back to Jason. "About the kid, you mean?" Ramirez asked, her voice going up at the end in uncertainty towards his questions.

"Anything," Les said. "We weren't looking for Markus yesterday, but sometimes looking for one thing can lead to the other."

"I mean, not really," Geralt said. "It didn't seem like anyone had anything really concrete to go on, just normal neighbor stuff. They were complaining about the noise from the sun shield installations on the building, how it was screwing with their internet, that's it. Nothing I would want to bet on."

Jason and Les looked at each other. "OK," Jason said. "If you think of anything, let me know. All right, hit the streets."

"Is it a good idea to have them out there?" Les asked when the officers were out of earshot. "They're pretty charged up right now."

"We all are," Jason replied, watching the officers as they walked away. "But benching them won't help them. They need to stay busy."

CHAPTER 7

Jason spun his phone on his desk, trying to decide whether to call Jessie Kline or not.

The calls to Markus' teachers had gone as expected: good kid, good grades, never really in trouble other than the usual, innocent kind most kids his age got into. Nothing to suggest that anything was going on at home. He wasn't surprised but was glad he could officially cross Jessie off the suspect list. He was sure he'd be crossing Markus' estranged father off the list as well, but until he did, Jason maintained a healthy suspicion.

The stack of files on his desk reminded him of the sheer tonnage of work that sat squarely on his shoulders between the outcome of multiple murder investigations, the flow of splice into The Gaps, and the responsibility of a dead officer that was all going to be laid at his feet when Swan had her press conference. Les was right, there were only so many hours in the day, and he could only take on so much.

But he also knew that his father-in-law had been right: follow the evidence, no matter where it leads. Swan might be trying to put his balls in a vice, but Jordan Stone had shown him what it was to be a cop, a detective, and an overall honorable and good person, even when Jason's own father had seemed utterly disinterested in him.

He saw his face reflected on the phone's surface. *Oh, yeah, and then there's that guy.*

Alexei had never let him win a race, or let Jason tap him out in jiu jitsu class. He was never mean about it and never took advantage of the fact that Jason physically couldn't keep up. It never felt like bullying to Jason; it also didn't keep him from seething with frustration, either. He couldn't keep up, and sometimes, just sometimes, he hated Alexei for it.

Jason swallowed a pang of guilt when a memory popped up unbidden. Jason had just come home from his first round of treatments at the hospital and was feeling achy deep in his bones when his parents told him that Alexei was missing. For just a second, just a fraction of a fraction of a second, a thought materialized that Jason retracted immediately: *Maybe I can finally win one.*

His phone ringing yanked him out of his nostalgia. He felt his chair tilt dangerously backward before wresting all four feet back to the ground.

"Thane," he answered into the receiver.

"Hey Loo," Nguyen's voice came from the other end. "Better get down to Castor and Sedgley. We've got another body."

Jason and Les pulled up on a block blanketed in controlled chaos. Lights flashed everywhere in a cacophony of strobes.

Passersby stopped and rubbernecked at the police tape that had been hastily set up around the nondescript warehouse. Jason could see uniformed officers from at least three different departments that milled around the scene if they weren't involved in work that required immediate attention.

Drones whirred overhead, and several news crews were trying to get the best footage they could for their broadcasts, while reporters spoke into microphones with somber expressions visible through their transparent facemasks.

The locals were out and about as well, huddled under tarps and detritus precariously stacked and stretched over cellarways and whatever else they could find to support the makeshift protection. Some had cyclers, or things that resembled cyclers, but as to whether they functioned or not, Jason couldn't tell. As often as not, old pieces like that were completely shot and did nothing about the constant particulate count in the air. Others simply wheezed weakly, with no protection from the noxious air. Jason knew it wouldn't kill them immediately but could feel the burn in his own lungs just from thinking about it. Theirs was a slow death, one that was only delayed by the shots of relief from amping on splice whenever they could get their hands on it, but it was an inevitable spiral, inescapable.

Jason's heart hurt for them.

"Anyone you know?" Les asked.

"No," Jason replied, hoping to see at least one face he recognized, hoping when he didn't it was because they had finally gotten out, or at least survived a few more months and were hiding out somewhere else.

Les clapped him on the shoulder. "They made their choice."

Jason side-eyed his partner. "You know it isn't that simple. Most of the time they start amping just to get through the day as they go into their third shift in a row. I guarantee none of them would have wanted to end up here."

"It's not like they didn't know what the stuff was."

"Not saying they didn't. But we also don't give the rich kids shit when they start amping to be better at sports, get higher grades, or eke a few more dollars out of the stock market." He signed *disgust*. "Things go tits up for them, and they just check into rehab. Any consequences are bought off and buried. These folks out here never had the money for that kind of treatment, and they can never escape the consequences. Not saying that they should have started using, but why do the rich pricks get a pass when they already started with all of the advantages?"

Les returned Jason's point with silence.

"Exactly," Jason said. "Not saying there aren't problems here, lord knows there are, but how much of it could be solved if the playing field was just a little more level?"

"*Buena suerte*, kid," Les retorted.

Jason lifted the yellow tape, and he and his partner ducked under, wading into the chaos. Nguyen spotted them, waived them to a propped open fire door, and led them inside.

"How is it that Homicide isn't taking this?" Jason asked the junior detective.

"The body looks like the ones from before," Nguyen said once they were out of earshot from any reporters or civilians. Jason felt his intestines turn into a knot. "Sounds like they'll take it, but they also wanted us to take a look just in case it's connected to our investigations."

"And do we have a timeline?"

"Morning crew found the body when they opened up this morning." Jason glanced over at the detective, who quickly added, "We've got them isolated, don't worry." She led them through a maze of small rooms and tight corridors that belied the size of the building. "Best guess is that it happened a few hours ago, sometime overnight."

"Any ID yet?" Les asked.

Nguyen shook her head. "We're still...well, we're still looking for all of...the body. No DNA hits, however. Might be that they were never in the system."

"How is that even possible?" Jason asked. "Everyone is in the system."

Nguyen shrugged. "People slip through. But we did find this." She rooted around in her satchel and pulled out a clear evidence bag. Inside was a red jacket with a dragon embroidered in black on the back.

The jacket one of the escapees from the raid was wearing.

Jason and Les looked at each other and continued being led down the hall in silence.

Two uniformed officers stood guard by a thick metal door. Nguyen motioned to it, and Jason took a deep breath and let it out before going in, steeling himself for what he expected the scene to look like.

The room looked like a giant version of the prep kitchen Jason had worked in for a while in college to help pay his tuition, with stainless steel tables and surfaces everywhere. In the middle of the floor was a pile of meat. Jason breathed slowly and walked around the room. Les began circling the corpse, jotting notes on his notepad.

"This is the same guy, right?" Nguyen asked.

Jason ignored the question. "Walk me through it."

Nguyen pulled out her phone and began scrolling through her notes. "OK, this is a commercial bakery, they make...looks like mostly cakes and cheesecakes for local restaurants and grocery stores and the like. Last shift clocks out at eleven at night, first shift clocks in at seven in the morning."

Jason leaned over one of the prep tables to peer between it and the wall. "Eight hours with no one else here. That's a pretty big window." He checked his watch. "When did the call come in?"

"Looks like...eight this morning."

Les looked up at Nguyen. "They clocked in at seven and didn't call until eight? Why the delay?"

"They were cleaning," Jason said and pulled one of the tables away from the wall. "The floor back here? You could eat off it."

Nguyen's face contorted in confusion. "Uh, shouldn't...shouldn't that be normal in a kitchen?"

Les coughed a single chuckle. "Never worked in a kitchen before, did you?"

Jason pointed around the room. "None of these tables are on wheels, and there's no scratches on the floor, so they don't make it a habit of pulling them out to clean underneath." He gestured towards the hallway they had entered from. "The hallways are mopped on the regular, but there's still dirt where the floor meets the wall, and scuff marks above the baseboards. Means that they usually give the place a precursory cleaning to avoid getting dinged by the health department, but not a very thorough one."

"Might have something here," Les called and gestured to the pile. Jason approached, the whole while shouting down his brain as it babbled in a panic at the sight of the body. Les held up a hand with torn and ragged flesh at the wrist where it had been wrenched off the arm. "See the nails? That greenish-yellow?"

"Phenol oxidation," Nguyen said. "Yeah, it's one of the ways we teach drug stores to spot splice cooks."

Jason had a theory but wanted to test his younger co-worker. "So, what do you think happened? Why did they clean before calling?"

Nguyen turned in a slow circle and took in the room. "My first guess would be that they were trying to hide evidence of the murder, but why call us and leave the body? It's not the murder, it's that they were hiding something else." Jason nodded for her to continue. "My next guess would be that they were hiding drugs and didn't want any chemical evidence left behind. Most folks here are working for minimum wage, no drug or background checks needed and given the neighborhood...most places like this know who they're hiring."

"You're going with drugs," Jason said in a neutral tone.

Nguyen shook her head. "No, because why clean this thoroughly? And it's a murder, so most people would know we wouldn't care if someone was blowing lines of coke or dipping amps of splice..." She scanned the room again and then at the hand that Les was still holding. "This was a lab, but only in the off hours. They knew that would shut the whole place down for days, if not weeks, and they didn't want to lose out on the work. Morning crew comes in, sees the body, knows about the extracurricular activities that happen overnight, and cleans up as best they can."

Jason gave a half-smile. "We'll turn you into a decent detective yet."

"Look at this bruising," Les said, pointing to another disembodied limb. There were very clear hand-shaped bruises on whichever appendage it had been. "That's perimortem. The bodies at the lab didn't have those."

Jason's moment of pride in the younger detective was doused in the freezing water of the moment. "They took their time." The thought did not bring him comfort. "Psychopath? Or interrogation?"

Les shrugged. "I think that Venn diagram has some significant overlap. But if I had to guess..." Les dug through the meat pile and pulled what looked to be a finger from deep underneath. "Neither scene was frenzied. They're brutal, and disturbing, and there is unavoidable cruelty in both, but I'm not getting the vibe that this was for fun."

"How do you figure?" Jason asked.

"Look at the spray patterns. Pretty localized. And at both scenes, the bodies' parts were piled up, not thrown around the room. No evidence that anything was done with them once they were removed...more like what someone would do when demolishing a porch when they rip an old piece of lumber free." Les rose from his squat, and his knees cracked and popped. "This isn't someone who relishes their work, just someone good at ripping people apart. And given the general order that the parts are stacked, I'd have to say that this was a very crude and violent interrogation."

Jason wanted nothing more than to leave the room. He started going over the leads he had for Markus Kline in his head as a distraction...but then realized there weren't many.

I should look into that some more. Not getting anywhere fast on that.

"Oh ho," the veteran detective said and held up another disembodied hand. Part of a monstrous scorpion tail was tattooed on the back of it. "That's *kardeşlik* ink," Les said. "Bad news."

The name didn't ring a bell for Jason. "They new?"

Les shook his head. "Opposite. Very, very old. Very low-key. International without any specific country of origin. Name means "brotherhood" in Turkish, but I don't even think they originated there. Honestly, I didn't think they were even operating anymore. But that ink..." Les paused. "That's not something you get done for fun. Most tattoo artists won't even do it…kind of like giving a non-yakuza an *irezumi*."

"What are they into?" Jason asked. "Drugs? Human trafficking?"

"All of it," Les replied. "And they are very good at hiding."

Jason pulled out his phone. "OK, Les, seal off the whole building, and if there are any other employees around, let's get them separated so we can start questioning them. Nguyen, have one of the uniforms start pulling any old employee files. Then I need you to bring up the birds so we can see if they caught anything. I'll get the rest of the team here along with Crime Scene so we can start processing the scene. And remember, no word to the press about any details. Let's move."

Dark clouds threatened to open up at any moment, but that didn't seem to deter any of the reporters or locals that were still milling about in front of the bakery-cum-splice lab, both painting a study of stark contrast to each other; the reporters in nice, tailored UV suits that could have passed as normal indoor evening wear, and the locals in hand-me-down gear at best, improvised and potentially next-to-useless materials at worst.

Curiosity appeared to be the common denominator, though; no matter how many times they were all asked to leave, the requests didn't seem to faze them. Some of both groups stood at rapt attention at the police line. In contrast, others attempted to lounge in the meager protection provided by makeshift sun shields of blankets, trash bags, or reclaimed sheet metal precariously bolted to the sides and roofs of nearby buildings. Others were huddled under the limited space under a newly-installed high-end shield over a building down the block. In the distance, the towering sun shields that protected Center City almost gleamed against an angry sky.

"Hey! Why don' you look atcher own for this?" Jason snapped his head around and saw a woman made of sinew and bone, wrapped in a patchwork of emergency blankets and regular blankets, a mask that easily could have been older than him, and goggles that were little more than sunglasses. She was slightly hunched, and gnarled old knuckles held her "coat" closed around her. Her free hand signed something rather insulting at him, but had the tremor of a lifelong splice user. The toll of constantly mangling her DNA was finally resulting in the telltale signs of delirium tremens.

"Ma'am?" Jason asked.

"Y'all don't do nuthin' bout that rathole until one y'all cops drops a body in there, now yous are all up in here," she yelled, the cheap speakers in her cycler doing nothing to mask the sound of decades of heavy smoking.

"It wasn't us, ma'am," Jason replied as politely as possible.

"Yeah, that's what you'd say," she said as she began to shuffle away, signing some more vulgarities. "I seen it, but yous sonsabitches ain't gonna indict one ya own. Thin blue line bullshit."

An older-looking man with thick grey dreadlocks rolled over in one of the tent shelters next to Jason. "Wa'nt no cop did this. Was The Bear."

"Shut it, Freddy," the woman scolded. "You were tweakin' las' night, you didn't see shit. I seen it."

"Hold on," Jason said, taking a few steps after her. "What do you mean that you saw it? Did you see something?"

The woman paused for a moment and looked over her shoulder at him. "Saw one o' them cops go in there last night. Few minutes later, the screaming starts, then it stops just like that."

Jason's stomach dropped to his knees. "You saw a police officer enter the building last night? You're sure?" He had his doubts...the drone footage hadn't seen anything for most of the night, and he knew if she had the DTs she could also be suffering from hallucinations. But she also sounded sure of herself.

"S'what I just said," she cawed back at him. "Big boy, too." Her head cocked to one side.

Jason pulled out his phone and began taking notes. "What's your name, ma'am?"

"Nah, that's how they gitcha. I ain't tellin' you shit. You'll just lock me up and steal my stuff. Nope."

Jason decided to take a different approach. "OK, then, how about this...no names...what did the mask look like?"

"I dunno, diff'rent," she said. "Like tubes coming outta it. Kinda rattled when he breathed."

"Ok...about what time was this?"

The older woman scratched at her head through the bonnet that covered a nest of brownish-gray hair. "Lessee...the workers had left...maybe an hour, maybe two?" She waived her wrists in his face. "Don' gotta watch."

Jason furiously typed notes into his phone. "Where were you? And what did the officer look like?"

She gestured to a collection of dumpsters and refuse piled up into an ersatz shelter that looked like it could house a half dozen people. "He was tall, real tall. Big boy. Couldn't see much else."

"So, you see him enter the building...how long before you hear the noises?"

She signed *disturbed*. "Not noises. Screams. Like when a cat gets run over, only worse. Like almost right away. And they jus' kep' goin' and goin' and goin' an..." Her voice trailed off, repeating the last phrase over and over, repeating *disturbed* with her bony fingers each time, and Jason knew he was losing her.

"You sure I can't convince you to come in with me? We can get you a dry place while the storm blows through, get you a good meal..."

The old lady's goggled eyes snapped to Jason's face, and her DTs increased. "What? No, I ain't comin' wiff you! I ain't seen shit, leave me alone!" She began hobbling away towards the building with the newly-installed sun shield, and Jason knew that was the end of the interview for the moment.

"Give her a few," Freddy said. "She get like that. But mark my words...the Bear gonna gitcha."

"How about you?" Jason asked the older man. "You see anything?"

Freddy shook his head vigorously. "Naw, I ain't gettin' involved."

"You think she's being straight with me?" Jason asked, nodding towards the older woman as she teetered down the street, scratching at her arm.

"She said she seen it, she seen it," Freddy replied.

"Yeah, I just wish the drones could back her up," Jason murmured.

Freddy let out a wheezing laugh. "Boy, you new, ain't cha?"

Jason signed that he didn't understand.

Freddy's laughing continued, and devolved into a coughing fit. Once he finally caught his breath, he said, "Gene Bankers call 911 with fake calls and..." Freddy flitted with his hand, like a bug flying away. "Do it whenever they don' wan' no poh-lice lookin' over their shoulder."

Jason gave Freddy the side-eye from under his headgear. "That doesn't sound right, Freddy."

"OK, young bull, don' no one listen to ole Freddy no mo'...but maybe you could spare a few bucks for my time?"

Jason ignored the older man and tapped another note into his phone, but felt the impulse to look back after the older woman. She had joined a group of other indigents gathering under the eaves of a building with a brand-new sun shield, likely, he thought, in anticipation of the approaching storm. The rain carried just as much toxin as the air, but at least under the shield it would be dryer, and any watershed would be filtered.

The building itself was old and run down, Jason noticed, not some new tenement or gentrification project. He walked down the street towards it, his curiosity piqued. He knew it wasn't uncommon for businesses to install better shields when moving into a new location, usually at the behest of the city to help improve the neighborhood, but this didn't look like anyone was moving in. Some of the windows were boarded over, others simply empty eye sockets staring out of the bones of the abandoned building. Graffiti marked up most of the walls. More than likely, if Jason guessed correctly, there would be more than a dozen people flopped out inside, either squatting or using it as a bolt hole while their high ran its course. Not a real estate developer's dream scenario.

Some of the gathered, huddled masses there made a point to look away when he approached; others' vacant begoggled stares followed him as he walked by. He found a stanchion holding part of the shield up and looked for the installation placard, and found it bolted on at eye level, right where it was supposed to be, with the installer code and relevant data stamped into it. *Up to code...so whoever was hired to do the install is aboveboard.*

He tapped the number into his phone, and a moment later a name popped up on his screen: Greenway Protectives. He opened up the details to quickly scroll through but stopped when his radio crackled to life.

"Hey, Loo," Les' voice came over the radio, interrupting Jason's train of thought. "What's your twenty?"

Jason snapped a photo of the placard and answered the call. "About two blocks south on Kensington. What's up?"

"We're getting ready to wrap up here, not sure what you wanted to do with the witnesses."

"Hang on, I'll be right there."

In the short time it took Jason to walk back to his new crime scene, fat drops of water began to spatter on the pavement. He ducked into the bakery just as the sky opened up and sheets of rain poured down in a torrent. He shook his jacket to shed some of the dampness and navigated through the mess of rooms to the break room where they had been sequestering the staff all day. Les was leaning against the door frame reading through his notepad.

"So, what do we do with them?" Les said without looking up, gesturing with his head towards the half dozen workers gathered around some beat-up folding tables.

"We get anything useful?"

Les shook his head. "Nothing we hadn't worked out for ourselves. Most of them admitted to knowing about the lab, but it doesn't look like any of them actually operated it. Just working stiffs trying to make it another day. Biggest concern is them talking, I figure. I'm sure if we looked into it, we could find some outstanding warrants, keep 'em locked up for a day or two."

"Not sure I like that," Jason said. "Unless one of them has something major outstanding, let's cut them loose. They've been through enough, and we may need them to be cooperative later. Just make sure that they know they can't talk to anyone about what they saw...say it's an open investigation and it would be a felony, something like that."

Les cocked an eyebrow and got a bemused expression on his face. "Telling me to lie, kid? That's not like you."

Jason smirked. "Guess you're rubbing off on me. But we really can't have them talking, and if it's the only way..."

Les held up his hands defensively. "Hey, no judgment here. By your command."

"The tattoo is something, though, right?" Jason said. "That can't be a coincidence, *kardeşlik* tat on someone found at a splice lab who also ran from a stash house with a record haul of the stuff and where a missing kid was."

"Coincidence means you're on the right path," Les said, echoing Jason's words.

CHAPTER 8

Jason marveled, not for the first time, at the glass-walled municipal services building. He remembered practically choking on the cost of shielded glass when he and Amira had to replace the windows in their bedroom. He couldn't imagine the price tag that came with a five-story facility made out of the stuff.

The cavernous lobby was awash in a facsimile of natural sunlight, a trick, Jason had learned, of tinted glass and strategically-placed LEDs. As he strode to the elevator bank through a sea of people in fashionable business suits and expensive haircuts, he tried to ignore the eyes he imagined were following him, silently judging him and his off-the-rack ensemble.

"Always feel like I'm walking through a pack of starving hyenas when I come here," Jason murmured to Les.

"I always think of them as platypuses on dating apps," Les replied, staring straight ahead as he waited for the elevator to arrive. Jason felt his eyebrows trying to climb into his hairline. "Interesting to look at, but ultimately pointless."

The two cops stifled their laughter as their elevator arrived.

Moments later, they were deposited on the third floor. They padded silently down a lushly-carpeted hall, following the signs for the Organized Crime Unit.

"You sure you want to talk to these mooks?" Les said. "They couldn't find their asses with two hands and a map."

Jason shrugged. "Worth at least asking the question, right?"

Les made a non-committal face. "If you say so."

They pushed through double glass doors with "*Organized Crime Unit*" etched into them, and into a spacious bullpen. A cylinder of monitors displaying live drone footage from around the city dominated the center of the room, and floor-to-ceiling windows acted as office walls, and lined the perimeter, offering views of the downtown district that would have any realtor salivating. The air was thick with a rich coffee aroma, and the room was silent.

Or rather, Jason realized, it had gone silent when they entered. All eyes in the office, of more than a dozen cops he counted, were on him and his partner.

"Did I fart?" Les said under his breath.

A man in a well-fitting three-piece suit stood from an office and strode across the floor towards them. He stopped two paces from Jason and Les, and clasped his hands behind his back. Jason immediately smelled talcum powder and pomade emanating from him.

"May I help you?" he said in enunciated, proper tones.

"I'm Lieutenant Thane, this is Detective Caporelli," Jason said, extending his hand. "We're with narcotics."

"I'm aware of who you are," the man said, keeping his hands clasped behind him.

Jason cleared his throat and lowered his hand. "Well, we're working an investigation that's taken a few twists on us, and I wanted to see if I could pick your brains for a few minutes, see if you can't point us in the right direction."

The man snorted almost imperceptibly, a small thing that Jason almost thought he imagined. But the way the man held his head, almost as if he was literally looking down his nose at Jason, confirmed that he didn't.

"Sure," the man finally said. "I have a few minutes." He turned on his heel and strode back towards the office he had emerged from. Jason looked at Les, who shrugged, and Jason took it as an invitation to follow. He felt a shiver up his spine as he crossed the bullpen and past the bank of monitors from the surreptitious glances from the other cops that seemed to go back to look at something *very important* on their desks whenever Jason looked their way.

The man stepped into his office and took a seat behind a Brobdingnagian dark wood desk; Jason saw that "Captain R. Haldeman" was etched into the glass next to the door.

Guess his job's pretty secure.

Upon entering, Jason noted that there weren't any other chairs in the office for Jason or Les to sit in, meaning that anyone would have to remain standing for whatever business they had with the Captain.

"Speak," Captain Haldeman said.

Jason cleared his throat again and attempted to ignore the dog-like command, focusing instead on the case at hand. He pulled out his phone. "We've had a couple of murders with the same MO that have shown up during the course of our investigation," he said and brought up the photo of the scorpion tattoo from the severed hand. He looked at it as little as possible. *I'm tired of seeing body parts every time I close my eyes.* "We've seen some commonalities in the ink that some of the subjects have had, and we wanted to see if there was anything anyone in your unit could share with us." He placed the phone on the captain's desk so he could see the photo.

Captain Haldeman folded his hands on his desk and leaned forward, never looking at the phone. "You came down here to ask about a tattoo?"

"Yeah," Jason said slowly. "Is that a problem?"

The captain snorted again and didn't attempt to hide it. "Cute." He spun the phone to face him and glanced at the picture. "Doesn't look at all familiar."

Jason's brow furrowed. "Sir, with all due respect, can we talk to some of your detectives? We have multiple homicides and a missing child, and the tattoo is the best lead we have on both right now."

"Oh, yes, detective, by all means, which of my men would you like to speak with?" Haldeman's voice dripped with honey and venom as he dramatically gestured to the bullpen. "We're here to serve, after all."

Jason was perplexed. "I thought we were all on the same team, sir," he said. "I'm not asking anyone to 'serve', just to give us some insight. And it's lieutenant, sir, not 'detective'."

"Well, let me be clear, *Lieutenant*," Captain Haldeman said. "This is an elite unit investigating *real* crimes with *real* victims. Our quarry is dangerous and wily, and does genuine damage to our economy. We don't have time to solve your cases for you as well."

Jason looked out at the bullpen. One detective was watching a cat video on his computer, and one was playing a video game. Most others looked to be involved in idle conversation, feet kicked up on desks or lounging in the kitchenette.

Jason felt the tension growing between his shoulder blades. "Clearly, sir. Did I offend you somehow? I'm not sure where this hostility is coming from."

"Boy, you, personally, do not offend me," Haldeman said as he leaned back in his leather chair. "You carrying that badge around, that offends me. You being called 'lieutenant', that offends me. You being in charge of this sham of a task force, taking valuable budget money away from other units that could be putting it to much better use, that offends me. But no, *lieutenant*, you specifically do not offend me." He glanced between Les and Jason. "Any other questions for me?"

Jason felt his face heating with his rising blood pressure and ire. "Many, sir. But for now, can you just point me to someone who can talk about *kardeşlik*?"

Captain Haldeman blinked a few times before responding. "Are you serious?"

"Yes, sir." Jason picked up his phone. "This tattoo is a hallmark of that organization. Now I'm sure I don't need to tell you about how some criminal organizations use tattoos as a means of identification, such as the *bratva* or yakuza. And I know a man of your experience knows how something as little as a tattoo can identify a specific individual within that organization. And I'm certain that someone of your qualifications knows exactly how important it is to follow every lead in an investigation as complex as this. So yes, sir, is there someone I can speak to about *kardeşlik*?"

Captain Haldeman's face flickered to a deep frown before it turned into a wide smile that showed perfect, overly white teeth, a smile that never touched his eyes. "I don't appreciate your tone, lieutenant," he said. "But you're right, I do have many years of experience, so let me share some of that with you. I'm going to clue you in on something. The problem with your lead is that you'll have an easier time tracking down Santa Claus, or the Easter Bunny. The yakuza is real, the *bratva* is real. *Kardeşlik* is a story that backward hicks and urban trash tell their children to scare them into eating their vegetables and going to sleep on time. There's no such thing. So no, Lieutenant Thane, there is no one you can speak to about *kardeşlik*."

Captain Haldeman's smile didn't falter, but he said nothing else.

"Thank you for your time, sir," Jason said, spun on his heel, and left the office, Les behind him. He ignored all of the officers that stared at him as he exited. When the double doors of the Organized Crime Unit shut behind him and his partner, he finally let out the breath he had been holding.

"That went about as well as expected," Les said.

"That was humiliating," Jason replied. "So glad you stepped in back there, by the way."

"What did you want me to say?" Les said.

"Anything would have been a good start."

"To what end?" Les asked. "What was anything I could have said going to do to change Haldeman's opinions about you specifically or Gappers in general?"

"I did warn you," Les continued. "A unit of nothing but *gilapollas* glass heads." Jason grimaced. "What? I did warn you. This is why you keep your head down and just do the job."

Jason sighed. "That's what I thought I was doing."

"Seems like you're more interested in changing the status quo, the way you tend to go after higher-ranking officers," Les said. "Just saying."

"I wasn't doing that," Jason protested.

"You had a tone," Les said.

"I don't have a tone."

"I don't know if you hear it, but it's there, and it's pretty obvious." Les paused. "You wear your contempt for *bogari* on your sleeve, same as they do for you. Only they're in a position to do something about it. You're not."

They walked in silence to the elevator bank. "Do they hate me that much?"

Les shrugged. "Yes. Not you, specifically, but Gappers in general, especially any uppity ones that don't know their role, in their opinion."

Jason's shoulders slumped, and the tension between his shoulder blades grew into a full-fledged knot. "I just want to do the job."

"You and me both," Les said.

The elevator doors opened, and an officer in a uniform that marked them as an aide was standing in the car. "Lieutenant Thane? Chief Swan would like to see you on the fifth floor, please."

"Are you fucking kidding me?" Alice Swan said as the door closed behind Jason. Her tone was so calm and controlled that it sent a shiver down his spine.

"Ma'am, I think-"

Swan stood from her desk and paced behind it. "How in the name of all that is holy did you get a cop *killed?*"

The comment stung, not just because of its inaccuracy, but because Jason realized that she absolutely would politicize a police officer's death. "That's not-"

"And *then* you reassign a dozen officers to a missing person case that *may* at its best be kind of, sort of, *maybe* adjacent to a major drug trafficking ring and multiple homicide investigation." She stopped pacing and stared at Jason.

The silence between them stretched longer, and Jason began to fidget uncomfortably.

"Well?" Swan demanded.

"Oh, it's my turn to talk now?" Jason mentally kicked himself, and Swan's jaw clenched as she lowered her head in a challenging gaze. *Maybe I do have a tone.*

"You are picking a very bad time for sarcasm," Swan said, her voice sub-zero.

Jason held his hands up in *peace.* "I'm sorry, I shouldn't have said it, I take it back." He took a deep breath and let it out. "Yes, I did reassign some officers to perform a dragnet and recanvas of the area, and yes, it was in response to evidence we found in the stash house that proved Markus Kline had been in there."

"Who?"

Jason cleared his throat. "Markus Kline, the missing child. We found Markus' pin in the same apartment as Officer Novak's body, and morbidity places time of death around the same time we were sweeping the building the day of the raid."

Swan crossed her arms. "You have a positive ID on the pin? Already?"

"No, we're still waiting-"

"So, you have no proof that this pin belonged to this Gapper spawn and not to any number of other snot-nosed brats. Those pins are everywhere, every kid in the program has one, and it's one of the largest community athletic programs in The East Gaps."

Jason shook his head and censored most of the vocabulary that his brain was queuing up. "Yes, it's circumstantial but still material."

"*Not. To. Your. Case.*" Swan punctuated each word by bringing her finger down on her desk with each syllable.

She locked her eyes on Jason. "First, all that time that the officers spent asking about the street rat was time they could have spent asking about the matters relevant to *your* investigation, or about a cop killer. The time spent pounding the pavement looking for the kid could have been spent looking for evidence relevant to *your* investigation. So yes, this was a waste of time and resources. Second, if you haven't picked up on this yet, *missing Gapper brats isn't part of your investigation.* They go missing all the time, and we have a department for that. Missing persons is on it, let them handle it."

Jason heard a little voice screaming at him to shut up, to stop talking, and to walk away. "With all due respect, ma'am," he said as his demons shouted down his better angels, "Missing Persons will write this kid off. They're overworked and underfunded as it is, and we don't have any bird footage to help. This kid will just be another dusty file over there."

Swan rubbed her temples with one hand while leaning on her desk with the other. "Lieutenant Thane," she said, her voice calm and measured, "I want to be crystal clear on this, so there is no confusion or miscommunication between us. Hand whatever new 'evidence' you have pertaining to Markus Kline off to Missing Persons. Cease diverting any resources from your task force to it. Between a drug investigation, a dead cop, and two homicides, you won't have enough time to pursue any other case work."

Jason replayed her words in his head. "Wait, *two* homicides?"

Swan's lips twisted into a cruel smile. "Oh, you didn't get the file? The bakery murder is yours as well. Homicide is handing it off." She pushed a button on her desk phone. A moment later, Derrick Belford entered the office. "Derrick, did you forward the new reports to Lieutenant Thane?"

Rassgat[4] *put in his transfer already? That didn't take long.* Jason felt mixed emotions: elation that this particular headache was off his team and anxiety from not knowing when the other shoe would drop.

Les warned you.

Belford smiled his empty smile. "Of course, ma'am. First thing this morning, just like you asked."

Jason swore that Belford's default tone carried a signal that triggered some kind of evolutionary imperative in others to punch him squarely in his stupid face. Still, he forced himself to rise above his baser instincts. "No file was delivered to me or the task force, either physically or via other means."

"Lieutenant Belford, will you please get Lieutenant Thane a copy of the file so that he can do his job," Swan asked sweetly enough to rot teeth. "We wouldn't want to see his efforts hampered."

---

[4] "*asshole*"

And a promotion?

"Of course, ma'am," Belford replied in the same tone. "He has a hard enough job as it is, I'll do whatever I can to make it easier for him." He left and returned a moment later with a manilla folder in hand, one that Jason had no doubt was sitting on Belford's desk and had never, in fact, been sent anywhere.

Jason narrowed his eyes at his commanding officer as he took the file. "Just so we're on the same page: we've got the splice investigation I've been running for 18 months, *two* homicides, and you also want us investigating Novak's murder. And I'm assuming this is with no additional resources."

Swan scoffed. "You have nerve. Your task force has been running for entirely too long. Any officer from the Center City districts would have had this wrapped up ages ago." Derrick snickered. "Your deadline remains in place. By the time I conduct my press conference, I expect results. That means arrests. That means charges brought by the DA. That means a measurable, positive impact on COMSTAT. Is that clear?"

"Yes, ma'am," Jason said through barely clenched teeth.

"Dismissed." Swan took a seat behind her desk and started tapping on her monitor, pulling up reports.

Jason quietly closed the door behind him and nudged his sleeping partner's foot with his own. Les' head snapped up and looked around, and he inhaled sharply at the sudden interruption to his nap.

"I have no idea how you slept through that," Jason said.

Les shrugged as he stood and stretched. "Not the first ass chewing I've been a party to," he said, and the two detectives made their way towards the exit of Philly PD's headquarters. "This is just Swan rattling her saber to keep her bosses happy. You know, flexing a bit so she has something to talk about the next time she and the commissioner sit down. But I did warn you."

Jason shook his head. "I never understood that. Even if I was wrong, which I wasn't, it wasn't deserving of whatever that was."

"Hmm," Les said, his expression and tone neutral.

Jason side-eyed his partner. "You think she's right. You think she was right to chew me out like that."

Les sighed. "Yeah. A little."

Jason felt his ears start to burn. "You're kidding."

"Look, maybe she's not right, but she's not wrong," Les said, gesturing. "It isn't our case, and we *did* get lucky."

"Yeah, well, we're so lucky that she dropped another homicide on us." Jason passed the folder to Les.

The detectives pulled their cyclers into place, settled their goggles on their faces, and stepped through the vestibule into the heat of Center City. Everything was awash in a bluish-green light from the protective sun squares soaring overhead, all of them almost parallel to the ground as they angled on their gimbals to block the midday sun.

Jason and Les dodged in between the scores of people that filled the sidewalk, some in full UV gear, others in very little protection in response to the blistering autumn heat, or wearing more subtle versions he'd seen in the windows of several boutiques whenever he made the trek to HQ. Most wore the clear cyclers that covered their entire face without obscuring it that were apparently all the rage if Jason were to judge by his social feeds, though some still wore more "traditional" ones; whether a matter of choice, principle, or necessity, Jason didn't know.

"You're siding with her," Jason said to his partner, his voice distorted through the cycler's speaker.

"No," Les replied, "I'm watching your back. Trying to tell you that you're going all in when you're already stretched thin. You know she's gunning for you, yet you can't figure out that you need to pick your battles."

It always shocked Jason to see people outside without full gear, but here in Center City, under the protection of dozens of sun squares, ironically, it was one of the safest times of day to walk outside unprotected. He knew that in a few hours, despite the shields high above him tilting always to be optimally angled to block the most direct sunlight, the sun would dip below their effective angle, and the streets would empty until after dusk. It was a stark juxtaposition to The Gaps, where the night was the only time it was ever safe to go outside without protective clothing, and even the professionally installed shields on the eaves of some of the buildings offered only the barest respite.

Jason shook his head and signed *frustrated*. "You're the one who sent the kid's mom to me. You, of all people, knew I would want to help her. That's *why* you sent her."

Les returned *frustrated*. "I was hoping you could grease the wheels, maybe do a little digging into the case just to get things moving, not that you would divert the manpower of a massive narcotics operation."

Jason kept his eyes forward and jammed his hands in his pockets, wishing the patroller was closer so he could get some relief from the sweat dripping down the middle of his back. His coat's coolers were working overtime and still not keeping up with the oppressive heat. "You're saying I screwed up."

"I'm saying she has a point. And if we can't tell each other when we've made a mistake, then I don't know what kind of partnership we have."

They walked in silence for several blocks, occasionally having to sidestep a wayward pedestrian who wasn't paying attention, either too absorbed in their phone to watch where they were going or too busy conversing with whomever they were walking next to. None offered an apology if they bumped into Jason. Several felt the need to shoot him a dirty look clearly visible through their high-end cyclers before they returned to their phone or walking companion.

"Any movement on ID'ing our friend from the bakery?" Jason asked, breaking the silence.

Les signed *no*. He paged through the homicide file as he walked. "They didn't do us any favors with the level of detail here, or lack thereof. But looking at these photos...I really hope there aren't two people out there doing this."

"Any leads?" Jason asked. "How much did Homicide get done before Swan yanked the case?"

"Not much," Les said and flipped a page.

Jason grimaced under his mask. "So, we're back to having nothing."

"Mm... maybe not," Les said. "Might be time to go see your rabbi." There was hesitation in the suggestion. "He spent quite a bit of time working with the Organized Crime unit, not to mention stints with

Homicide and Robbery…and based on where he is…well, he probably knows more about the *kardeşlik* than anyone else, if they're even involved."

"I don't want to drag him into this," Jason said, but he felt the seed of doubt in his words as he spoke them. He mulled over his options, weighing whether he should make that call. "Think he'll mind?"

"Kid, I know I told you when we first partnered up that you would need to stand on your own two feet rather than live in someone else's shadow, for better or worse. But everyone needs help sometimes, and there's no shame in hitting up some of the old heads to see what they've got to say about things." Les nodded, seemingly to himself. "And honestly…I think he'd appreciate it."

"Yeah," Jason said, knowing he would make the call but still fielding mental doubts about his choice.

The mashed potatoes on Jason's plate had coagulated into something akin to wallpaper paste, but the texture was the last thing on his mind. He felt a knot in his stomach, and he couldn't pinpoint the cause.

Captain Haldeman's dismissal of Jason didn't sit well with him.

Can't do anything about him, though. It is what it is.

Swan's apparent vendetta against him had ramped up.

She's coming for my job, and I have no idea what to do about it.

The murders…

Don't think about that. Not here. Not now.

"What's up?" Amira asked from across the small table. "You're not eating."

Jason looked up at his wife; she had her father's eyes and cheekbones, whereas her twin brother had taken more after their mother. Jason wondered if that would have held true if he were still alive. "Nothing. Work stuff."

Amira kept her eyes on him, continuing to eat, and looked like she was satisfied for the moment with his answer.

You know what's really eating at you. You don't want to ask her.

"I think I need to visit your dad," he blurted out.

Amira's fork paused halfway to her mouth before she placed it back on the plate. "Why?" Jason could hear the concern and restraint in her voice.

"Case I'm working," Jason replied. "I'm getting stonewalled by the department on the only lead I have for these murders…" *Don't think about them.* "…and Les seems to think your dad may be able to help."

Amira placed her hands in her lap. "You want to talk to him about work."

Jason could tell he was treading on thin ice. "I don't know what else to do or who else to talk to, and after the reaming that Swan laid on me, I just…I need to talk to someone that would understand."

Amira didn't say anything and studied the food on her plate.

"If you don't want me to, just say so," Jason said. "Look, what happened to your dad…he didn't let go when Alexei disappeared, and it got him booted off the job and then…well, you know. I saw what that did to you. I can't do that to you, I can't put you through that again."

Amira cocked an eyebrow. "Is that the direction you're heading?"

Jason started to answer, but the words evaporated in his throat. "I don't know," he finally answered. "I don't think so…but if I'm being honest, I don't know. I feel this…urge…need…something, I can't find the word for it, but something that tells me that I need to solve this, that this needs to happen."

"These murders?" Amira asked.

Jason felt the knot in his stomach twist. "That…and this missing kid."

Amira's eyes snapped to his. "What missing kid?"

Jason took a deep breath and let it out. "Kid went missing from the building we raided the other day. The mom was beside herself and wasn't getting help from Missing Persons…"

"Sounds familiar," Amira said in clipped words.

"Yeah, right? So, I thought I would poke around a bit, see what I could do. But it turns out that the kid might have been at the murder scene…not a victim, just there at some point…and I think that he's somehow connected, or at least possibly a witness…but Swan doesn't want me looking into it, Missing Person's isn't doing anything…"

Amira was silent for a moment. Her lips pressed together, and her eyes weren't focused on anything, a habit Jason knew meant she was thinking. "You can't bring him back."

"What? Who?"

You know who.

"Alexei." Amira looked up at him again. Her tone softened. "He's gone, Jason. Has been for a long time."

"I know."

"There was nothing you could have done to change anything that happened."

Do I believe that?

"I think I can help this kid," Jason said instead. "And right now, your dad is the best option I have to figure this whole thing out. The only option, really." He paused to gather the words that would articulate his racing thoughts. "But it's not more important than you. If you don't want me to visit him, I won't. If you want me to walk away from this case, I'll do it in a heartbeat. I won't put you through hell to satisfy my ego. My happiness shouldn't come at the expense of yours."

Amira rose from her seat, walked around the table, and squatted next to Jason as she pulled his hands into hers. "You're right, it sucked. And I would never want to go through that again." She locked her eyes on his. "But you are stronger than he was. I've seen you get obsessed with a case and never become so detached that you drove away everyone and everything you loved. You've always been able to turn that dedication into something more, and you'll do that again. When dad was hiding in that bottle, do you know who I leaned on, who was always there for me?"

Jason felt himself blush. "Me?"

"Yeah, you." Amira ran her nails through his hair. "And you know what else? I would never have forgiven myself if I had made him stop obsessing over Alexei. No one believed us when Alexei disappeared. Everyone said he had run away or was with Mom or something. But we knew that wasn't right. We knew

Alexei would never have gone to live with Mom, not after how she treated us, how she left us. He did what he thought he had to do to find Alexei, but he wasn't in a good place to do it the right way, and it took over his life."

"That's what I don't want to do to you. I can easily see myself falling down that hole...the whole thing is just dredging up so many memories. And I could lose us everything we've worked for."

She squeezed Jason's hands. "I know you. You won't be able to look yourself in the mirror if you just walk away and play it safe."

Jason looked down at his lap. "I know. But if I use task force resources again..." he shook his head. "It just feels like there's too much at stake. If I make a mistake here..."

"So don't use task force resources." A smile snuck onto her face. "You remind me so much of Alexei." She tapped his chest. "You're thinking with this." She tapped his head. "You need to think with this."

Jason smiled at his wife. "It is that obvious of a solution, isn't it?"

Amira smiled back. "It's a good thing you're pretty. Go ahead and visit Dad."

CHAPTER 9

The drive to Howey State Prison was free of traffic and passed quickly. Jason checked in and surrendered his gun and phone to the guard station, and was led through the intentionally confusing maze of corridors and barred doors to a secure conference room. There was a single expanded steel table with benches on each side, all bolted to the ground. There were no windows, and a fluorescent light buzzed overhead. The room smelled of bleach and dust.

Jason took a seat, folded his hands on the table, and waited.

Fifteen minutes passed before he heard the clang of a secure door opening down the hall and a mix of booted feet marching and slippered feet shuffling down the sterile hallway, and Jason stood and straightened his posture. A few moments later, an orange jumpsuited figure was let into the room, hands and feet manacled and connected by a long chain running through a ring affixed to a wide leather belt.

The man was slightly hunched, whether from the restraints or the weight of his sentence, Jason couldn't tell, and he had a week's worth of growth on his face, only serving to accentuate his hopeless eyes.

The guard glanced at Jason, and then the detective's shield hanging from Jason's belt, and with a scoff began unlocking the prisoner's shackles. Without a word, he finished his task and left the room, the door swinging closed and locking with a heavy slam.

Jason took in the sight of his father-in-law, Jordan Stone. His unkempt hair almost hid his haunted eyes. Then Jason took two steps towards him and embraced him in a tight hug that the older man returned.

"Sorry it's been so long," Jason said as they pulled apart and took a seat on opposite sides of the table.

Jordan waved the comment off. "No, I get it," he said. Jason noted the texture in his voice, more pronounced since the last time they had spoken. "I remember how time-consuming running a task force could be."

"Still," Jason said. "It's not right. I need to get up here to see you more. You doing OK?"

Jordan coughed a bitter laugh. "They're forcing some new meds down my throat. But I'm guessing that's not why you came up here today, just to say 'hi', right?"

Jason felt his face flush. "Yeah, I could use your help. We hit a dead end, and I don't know where to go next."

Jordan shrank back into himself. "Oh, I don't know how much help I can be."

Jason's heart ached at Jordan's reaction to police work, the once-proud man who always had a corny joke whenever Jason came over to play with Alexei, who looked like the detectives on the shows on the media streams.

"I'm not sure where else to go," Jason said. "OCU laughed me out of the room, Swan isn't giving me any help or resources…"

Jordan's expression grew dark. "Swan's an opportunistic *rassgat* who wouldn't be able to find a shred of decency with a map and a flashlight." He placed his interlaced fingers on the table and leaned forward, and there was a brightness in his eyes that Jason hadn't seen in years. "Fill me in. Where are you stuck?"

Jason pulled out the photo of the body part with the tattoo. "This is our only lead at the moment."

"*Kardeşlik*," Jordan said.

"Yeah, that's what Les said. He also said that he didn't think they were still operating."

Jordan grunted in disagreement. "They're very good at disappearing when they need to. Very quiet, very professional. And you don't get a tattoo like that," he pointed to the picture, "unless you're in. Most tattoo artists won't go anywhere near that stuff, too afraid of reprisals."

"Reprisals like what?" Jason asked.

"What you would expect," Jordan said. "Someone goes missing, business gets torched, stuff like that."

"How about mass dismemberment?"

Jordan signed *question*.

"We've had a few murder scenes that were… messy," Jason finally said.

"Like how messy?" Jordan asked.

Jason swallowed the bile that inched its way up his throat. "It looks like someone threw a running chainsaw at a crowd of people."

Jordan was silent for a long moment, seemingly studying Jason. Then he shook his head. "That doesn't sound like them. They don't like getting flashy like the Russians or the mafia…they try to stay under the radar."

"This definitely is on the radar," Jason said and took his phone back. "I have to imagine that the *kardeşlik* have to know about this."

Jordan nodded. "I would say so."

"Should we be worried about them retaliating?"

Jordan got a distant look in his eyes, like when he played chess when Jason was younger and was envisioning the next moves. "Maybe," he finally said. "They typically don't tolerate violence against their members…only way the whole thing works. You don't fight just one, you fight all of them, you know? But if these scenes are as brutal as you're describing them…" He shook his head. "I don't know. It sounds like someone is sending a message. If any of the *kardeşlik* clans in the area got it, they might steer clear. Or they may just bide their time."

Jason felt a small amount of relief. "So, no impending gang war, you think."

"They were never a 'shoot it out in the streets' kind of organization. They thrived on being an urban legend, always working from the shadows. It's how they've survived better than just about every other organized crime syndicate. They all flaunted power, and it got the attention of law enforcement. Attention is anathema to criminal enterprises. These guys know that, and that's why no one is looking for them."

"I've got a *kardeşlik* corpse and no one to talk to about it." Jason sighed. "Awesome."

"Don't focus on the organization," Jordan said. "You'll drive yourself nuts chasing that ghost. Focus on the activity. That's the only trace they'll leave. You'll never build a RICO case against them, but you can at least make it hard for them to do business, limit the impact."

Jason frowned. "Is that the best I can hope for? Crime abatement?"

Jordan nodded. "Yeah. There's only so much you can do. The system's rigged, you know that. We can only do what's in our power to do."

Jason chuckled. "When did you get so Zen?"

Jordan reached into his pocket and pulled out an object that looked like a poker chip. "Twelve step."

I guess that is all I can do.

"What was this guy into?" Jordan asked.

"We found the body at a splice lab," Jason said. "And he was seen on drone footage running from a stash house right when the murders were happening, so at the very least, he was deep into running splice, maybe even manufacturing it."

Jordan grunted in agreement. "Sounds like them. They were never street-level with that stuff, too much exposure. If this guy was on site, he's low rank, a *malgranda estro*. So not someone with much influence outside of their *unuo*."

Jason's head spun. "OK, you just said a lot of words I don't understand."

Jordan chucked. "You have *klano*," he said, holding his left hand at eye level. He held his right hand right beneath it. "*Tribo*," and then moved his left hand under the right. "*Unuo*. Clan, tribe, unit. Each unit is run by a *malgrando estro*, a *little boss*. Each tribe has a boss, *estro*, and they all answer to the *granda estro*, the big boss. The big bosses of the clans are all a part of the *tartışma*, the Council."

Jason shook his head. "If they're this organized, how come OCU doesn't have anything on them?"

Jordan coughed a laugh. "Most of those guys are there because someone in their family made a healthy donation to the police benevolent association or a politician. They wouldn't be able to find their ass with two hands and a map."

Jason laughed. "Les said the same thing."

"Yeah, well, he's good police," Jordan said. "And the *kardeşlik* is very good at hiding their secrets. Like I keep saying, they keep a very low profile, and their members are very, very loyal."

"OK, another question then…if the *kardeşlik* is so secretive, how do you know so much about them?"

"I bothered to look. I did research. I talked to people." Jordan shrugged. "I did the work. Got an associate of one of the *unuo* to flip. But the leadership keeps everything compartmentalized, so I never got much further into the inner workings outside of the basic structure."

"Well, my one lead there is dead, so I don't think I'm going to get much more."

"Maybe not," Jordan mused, stroking his beard. "I actually worked a case years ago, right before Les and I partnered up. We get a call for a break-in at this company, a place that's an office attached to a warehouse…Greenway Protectives, I think…and the place looks trashed…but petty cash is untouched, nothing in the warehouse itself was taken. It didn't take us long to get the employees to start flipping on their bosses. Turns out the company was under indictment for human trafficking, shipping people out to staff sweatshops, and they were shredding documents and trying to cover it up."

"You get them?" Jason asked.

"Dead to rights," Jordan replied, and for a moment, Jason saw the man he knew in his youth, before despair, obsession, alcohol, and prison hollowed him out. "Anyway," he said, quieter and with less verve in his voice, "that whole operation was under the direction of one of the local *unuo*. And when it started to unravel, the *kardeşlik* cut ties with everything and everyone there. The few guys we nailed that we suspected were *kardeşlik* clammed up and took their sentences. And that was it. Anyone else faded back into the shadows."

"So maybe," Jason said, talking out his thought process, "whatever this guy with the tattoo was into, it got on the wrong person's bad side. They put a half dozen people through a wood chipper to send a message. The local *kardeşlik* leadership gets the message, and cuts bait. Now there's a bunch of people tied to this that don't have the backing of the *kardeşlik* anymore." Jason drummed his fingers on the table. "They might be willing to talk."

"That's how I'd go at it," Jordan said.

"Any ideas where to start?" Jason asked. "Like I said, I ran it past OC, and they all but laughed me out of the room. Said I was chasing boogeymen."

"It's splice," Jordan said and signed *I don't know.* "It's a pretty wide net to throw. Do you have any other ins, anything else to tie to them that would narrow things down?"

Jason wasn't sure he wanted to bring the next part up, but the words came spilling out of his mouth before he could stop himself. "So, there's this other thing…a missing kid."

Jordan froze, still as a gravestone.

"Missing persons is doing jack shit about it. The mother came to see me and asked me to look into it…and I think the missing kid may be tied to the stash house we raided, or the murders or…" Jason signed *I don't know.*

"Is the kid alive or dead?" Jordan asked, no emotion in his voice.

I don't know.

"But you're sure the kid was there?"

"One hundred percent," Jason said, then qualified his statement. "In my gut, I know it."

"Then you look for him." It was a simple statement of fact.

Jason sighed. "I've been warned off the missing person case in unambiguous and explicit terms." He laced his fingers behind his head and looked up at the ceiling. "I don't know if I can follow this. There's a lot at stake, and not just for me…"

"You gotta find the kid, Jason. That's your in. Follow it." The desperation in Jordan's voice was evident. "An investigation leads where it leads. Places you don't like. Directions that piss off the high and mighty. To consequences that you never anticipated." He paused. "But you always follow where it leads. It's the only way justice gets done…if there is such a thing, anyway."

Jordan finished the statement sounding defeated. He shuffled over to the door and banged on it for the guard.

"Do you regret it?" Jason asked. "Following your investigation where it led? Even if you knew how it would end?"

Jordan looked over his shoulder at his son-in-law. "When it comes to that, it's the only thing I'm sure of anymore. I know I did the right thing. Plenty more keeps me up at night, but not that." A guard opened the door and started affixing the shackles to Jordan's wrists.

"I'll ask around on my end, see if I can find anything out for you. But you do what needs to be done, Jason. For Alexei."

CHAPTER 10

Jason was glad for the use of a car with actual working air conditioning. It was an unseasonably hot autumn afternoon; had the leaves on the trees that still grew under the sun squares in Center City not shown the signs of the changing season with their brilliant display of colors, he would have sworn it was mid-August.

That the car was a 1967 Mustang repossessed from a busted drug dealer didn't hurt.

The car rumbled down the street, the converted 320 horsepower V8 solar engine begging to be let loose, but Jason maintained restraint and preserved the battery. Tearing through the narrow streets with that beast might be fun but more reckless than he cared to be. But the thought of seeing what the car could do brought a smile to his face.

Slowing down also let him better observe what was happening around him as he drove. Little details that could escape attention were easier to spot, like the collection of cigarette butts piling up where a stoop met the front wall of a house or the friendly wave a local shopkeeper offered up the next block over. One was evidence of a potential new corner a crew was working, and the other was evidence that the neighborhood wasn't overrun yet. He made a mental note to add those spots to the giant map of their operations back at the command center.

He eased the car around a corner, barely touching the gas, and noticed a kid, not quite yet a teenager but no longer carrying the baby fat of childhood, stapling a dayglow yellow flier to a telephone pole and running to the next one, repeating the action. It was a regular occurrence, but the kid's movements had an air of determination and urgency.

His curiosity piqued, Jason pulled over into a free spot and watched, partially to see what the kid was going to do and partially in awe of the kid's hustle. Within a minute, the kid had hit a half dozen more poles and attached his flier.

Then he noticed them: dozens of other children, youngsters to teenagers, doing the same thing. Jason put the car in gear and slowly pulled back onto the road, cruising the same route as the first kid and taking in the path of neon yellow that was slowly spreading from block to block. Eventually, he caught up with the kid and leaned over to roll down the passenger window. "Hey," he called through the cycler. "Hang on a sec."

The kid froze, and his head snapped towards Jason. Jason couldn't see his eyes or face behind the cycler that might have been a hand-me-down, judging by the outdated design, and goggles that were little more than thick sunglasses, but the kid's posture looked like a startled deer deciding whether to freeze or run. Jason was in plainclothes, as usual, but his own headgear was decidedly police issue, and given how things usually went between police and the locals, he was used to this reaction.

Jason made the sign for *friend* and said, "You're not in trouble, just have a question for you. About the flyers. Can I see one?"

The kid looked up and down the block, and his feet fidgeted like he wasn't sure which way to start moving.

Jason smiled under the mask, even though it couldn't be seen, knowing it would help. He made the *smile* sign. "Seriously, you're not in trouble. I'm Jason. What's your name?"

There was a beat where Jason was almost sure the kid would run, but then he took a hesitant step forward. "Omar," a distorted voice finally said. It sounded like he was trying to make it sound lower than it was.

"Nice to meet you, Omar. Looks like you have a lot of folks out posting these today. You all working together?"

Omar nodded and took another hesitant step forward. "Yeah, we're putting up flyers trying to find my friend."

Jason had a thought. "Are you friends with Markus Kline?"

Omar took two more steps with much more confidence than before at the sound of Markus' name. "Yeah, how'd you know?"

"I spoke with his mom last night. She asked me to help. Can't imagine that many kids go missing in the same neighborhood, right?"

Omar made a sign that meant something like dismissal, and his body language stiffened. "Kids go missing all the time, and no one cares. And the cops we told about Markus just ignored us." He held up the flyers. "So I made these."

"It's a good idea," Jason said. "And who rallied the troops here?" Omar shrugged. "You did?" Jason made the sign for *impressive*.

"Just friends. And some of their brothers and sisters. Some people from school."

Jason nodded to the stack of flyers. "Need one more?"

Omar clutched the flyers to his chest. Jason put the Mustang in park, shut off the ignition, and got out. "I swear, I'm not going to take them from you."

"A cop told us that we didn't have permits, and he called them...uh..." Omar made the sign for *thinking*. "Bandit signs. Said he would tear them down."

Jason extended an open hand. "Can I see one?"

Omar slowly peeled one off and handed it to Jason. It was a picture of Markus, similar to the one Jessie Kline had shared with Jason the previous night. It had all the relevant information needed to identify him and a number to call. And a reward of $100 for any information that led to Markus being found. Between that and the cost of the paper and printing, Omar must have been out at least $200.

"Who's paying for all of this?" Jason asked.

"We are," Omar said, and he stood straighter, shoulders back. "I mean, me and my friends. We just put all the money we had together, and this is all we could get."

Jason folded the flyer and put it in his pocket. "Well, I don't see anything wrong with this flyer. So, if anyone tells you to stop putting them up or that you aren't allowed, you tell them Lieutenant Thane said that you're allowed to post them anywhere as long as you aren't damaging anyone's personal property." He pulled out a business card. "And if anyone argues with you about it, or you see someone tearing them down, call me, and I'll straighten it out. OK?"

Omar made the sign for *surprise*. "Why...I mean, thanks, thank you, but...why..."

Jason took a seat on a stoop. "Markus must be a really good friend if you're doing all this for him."

Omar nodded. "He's my best friend."

"Well, my best friend went missing when I was a kid. And when we tried to tell people he didn't run away, no one listened to us, either."

Omar sat next to Jason. "What happened to him?"

Jason shrugged. "I don't know. We were about the same age as you. We were playing outside one day, and we were racing to the bodega a few blocks away. He was always faster than me, and no matter how hard I tried, I just couldn't keep up. But I never wanted him to wait for me, you know, to slow down for me, so that I would always try to run faster, so he just kept going. And by the time I got to the store, I figured he would already be inside but...he wasn't."

Omar shuffled his feet on the ground. "Did...did you ever find him?"

Jason felt a lump in his throat and swallowed it down. After a long pause, he said, "No. No, we didn't."

Omar's shoulders fell, and Jason felt a stab of guilt in his chest. "But here's the thing...you have something that I didn't when my friend went missing."

"What's that?" Omar said, dejection clear in his voice.

"You. And, well, me."

"Right." Omar wasn't convinced.

"Look, when my friend, his name was Alexei, when he went missing, I was sick most of the time, so I wasn't able to go out and put up flyers like this, or rally the other kids to help. Alexei had a sister, but she was too busy trying to take care of her dad, you know? But Markus has you looking for him, and that's important."

"I guess."

"And, like I said, you've got me," Jason said, nudging Omar with his elbow. "Not to brag, but I'm kind of a big deal."

"Yeah, right." Omar sounded completely deflated.

"Yeah, right," Jason replied with more enthusiasm. "Look, I can't promise anything, OK? But you see that card I gave you...see how it says 'lieutenant'? Means I can tell people what to do. So, here's what I'm going to do to help you..."

Jason dialed up Jessie Kline while he drove and put the phone on hands-free.

"Hello?"

The woman's voice was ragged.

"Ms. Kline, it's Lieutenant Thane. Jason."

"Oh, Lieutenant, did you find anything out?"

"Unfortunately, no, not yet," Jason replied. He could practically feel her energy fall through the phone. "It doesn't look like Missing Persons has done much on their end, so I'm going to start looking into this myself."

"Really?" Jessie sounded like someone who was breathing fresh air for the first time.

"Yeah, but I need to warn you," Jason continued, "I'm going to need to tear into your and Markus' lives. I'll be talking to everyone you two know, friends, family, teachers…and I will have to ask uncomfortable questions."

"What…what kinds of questions?"

Jason hated forcing the woman on an emotional roller coaster ride. "Investigations like this are about eliminating possibilities as much as they are about uncovering facts."

"You do what you have to, Lieutenant," Jessie said, her voice steel. "Whatever help you need, tell me and I'll do it. Find my baby."

"I'll do the best I can, ma'am," Jason said. "I have to run, but I'll be in touch soon."

The Mustang rumbled to a stop a block away from the speakeasy and stash house, and Les jumped in the passenger seat, two cups of coffee in his hands and a thin manila envelope tucked under his arm. When the door closed, Jason flipped on the environmental seals, and fans in the dashboard whirred to life. Once they were done cycling, Jason and Les removed their headgear, and Jason gratefully accepted one of the steaming cups.

"Anything in the report?" he asked as he accepted the file from Les.

Les coughed out a sardonic laugh. "I would use the term 'report' loosely."

Jason opened the folder and paged through the sparse pages. "Was the building on fire when they wrote this? There's barely anything here."

Les took a long sip of the steaming liquid in his cup. "Yeah," he said. He leaned forward and rested his elbows on his knees. "Twenty years later and nothing has changed."

Jason couldn't help but frown at the report in front of him.

Markus Kline, aged twelve, reported missing two days ago by his mother. Ex-husband and father living at a current girlfriend's address somewhere in the West Gaps more than thirty minutes from the boy's home, but no contact between them in at least six months, and more than a year's gap before that. No formal contact with law enforcement. Honor student at Holden Junior High School, football and lacrosse player with the Burton Youth Center.

And nothing else. No notes about any interviews, frequent hangouts, or where the officer who took the report already looked. Just the absolute barest of facts to satisfy the form requirements and not get dinged in an audit, and a single APB issued with as generic description that Jason had ever seen, one that could have been applied to any twelve-year-old kid in the Gaps.

"How is it that we have people like this on the force?" Jason asked rhetorically. He knew the answer: half the positions with Philly PD were patronage jobs arranged through money and influence.

"Looks a lot like Alexei's report, no?" Les said. "Just some missing kid that was written off before anyone looked for him." He shook his head. "And look how that turned out."

Jason pressed his lips together in a thin line. "His dad didn't do it," he said with finality.

"Yeah, I know," Les said, laying a hand on Jason's shoulder. "I know he didn't. Jordan was as good a cop as I had ever known, and he loved his kids, believe me."

Jason's shoulders sagged, and he took another sip of coffee. "Yeah, I know. Sorry. It's just...man, it's just happening again, isn't it? Or it's kept happening, and it hasn't gotten any better."

Les squeezed his partner's shoulder. "Maybe."

Jason closed the folder. "Well, maybe I can do some good before I have to start begging for help. Let's get Nguyen doing a little digging here. She's got some decent CIs in the area, right? Where is she today?"

Les flipped open his notebook and began paging through his notes.

"I still can't believe you use that instead of your phone," Jason said, shaking his head in amusement at his partner's sometimes antiquated ways.

Les didn't miss a beat. "Writing things down helps cement them into your head better than typing them into a screen," he replied with only a hint of old-timer condescension. "And I've been doing this since before you were a gleam in your daddy's eye, so just let me be, Junior." He flipped one more page. "Ah, here we go. It's lowlife payday, so she'll be sitting on the East 5th Street drop today, see if anyone's using it again."

Jason pulled the Mustang up next to Nguyen's run-down Reliant facing the opposite direction so they could speak without shouting across Les. Nguyen, as usual, had Bob Segar playing on the radio.

"Anything?" Jason asked as he put the car in park.

"Not yet," Nguyen replied. "Thought maybe someone was sniffing around earlier, though, so maybe later. Hanging back in case they're trying to test the waters, don't want to tip them off that I'm watching. Got Ryczyk on the street as a second pair of eyes."

"Where?" Jason asked, scanning the street.

Nguyen nodded to a far corner. A pile of old clothes and rags occupied a corner nestled between a stoop and a storefront. It moved slightly, and Jason could see that it was Ryczyk under the pile; or, more accurately, Ryczyk *was* the pile.

"Guess he drew the short straw," Les laughed.

"Nah," Nguyen said, "he likes it. Says it gives him a chance to commune with his spirit animal, whatever that means."

"Hey, wondered if you could do something for me today," Jason said and passed the bright yellow flyer through the window to the rookie detective. "Kinda looking into this on my own time, I wondered if you had anyone who heard anything."

Nguyen took the flyer and looked it over. "Going for extra credit?"

"Hoping you could talk to your CIs, let me know if they heard anything."

Nguyen folded the flyer and shoved it into a pocket. "Missing Persons not handling it?" Jason barked out a laugh, and Nguyen nodded. "Got it. I'm recanvassing today, so I'll ask around."

"Seeing if anyone remembers something new?"

"Yeah, figured it can't hurt. Sometimes people remember stuff or have a change of heart, you know the drill."

"Thanks for being on top of that. We're on the clock now, so we can't wait this out like usual." Jason put the car in gear.

Nguyen offered a half salute and turned her attention back to the money drop.

Les laughed as the Mustang pulled away.

"What?" Jason asked.

"You're going all in on the missing kid."

"No, I'm not," Jason said. When his partner made a sarcastic gesture, he said more emphatically, "I'm not. I'm just trying to help."

"Whatever you say, kid."

"I'm not. I'm focused on the task force. I'm just greasing the wheels a little on this other thing."

"Sure."

"I'm not going all in."

"I know."

"I'm not."

"Okay."

They rode in silence for a few minutes, and Jason could sense that his partner had more to say. "What?"

"Nothing. Just...you remind me of him. Of Jordan."

"What do you mean?" Jason asked, keeping his eyes on the road.

"Nothing, it's just...you're relentless. You have a clear idea of what's right. And you definitely have no issues stepping on toes when it comes to walking the walk."

"Look, I already said-"

"And it's not a bad thing," Les continued, holding up his hands. "It's not. We could all stand to be a little more direct, a little more honest rather than playing the same old game." Les skootched down in his seat. "It's exhausting to always have to look over your shoulder when you're trying to do the right thing on the job."

"I just don't like playing politics. It gets in the way of the work."

"Yeah, I hear you," Les said, pulling his hat down over his goggles. "Jordan was the exact same way. Hated playing politics, so he never did." He folded his arms up and settled in. "Didn't turn out so well for him, though."

Jason gripped the steering wheel tighter as he navigated a turn around a corner piled high with refuse and said nothing.

"Just don't want to see the same happen to you."

A moment later, the sky opened up in a torrent. The rain beat down on the windshield, and Jason instinctively leaned forward to see the road better between the almost ineffectual swipes of the windshield wipers.

"You know that doesn't help," Les said, bemused, tipping his hat up to give Jason a side-eyed glance.

"Maybe not," Jason replied dismissively, "but it makes me feel better."

"Well, if it makes you feel better," Les said with a shrug, "then by all means." He pulled his hat over his eyes and settled back into his standard car nap position.

Jason's stomach growled noisily, and he realized he hadn't eaten anything since the breakfast sandwich he had wolfed down on his way into work that morning. "Want to grab a bite?"

Les glanced sideways from under his hat. "No plans with the missus?"

"Nah, she has a thing with the foundation tonight, I'm on my own."

Les chuckled. "You really put your money where your mouth is, don't you? The money you got from that lawsuit could have set you up for life, never would have had to work another day. But what do you do? Give it all away."

"Rising tide floats all ships," Jason replied with a shrug. "Didn't make sense to Amira or me to live like that. So we pay it forward." Jason signaled a turn. "And it wasn't that much. Enough to get out of the Gaps, and we would have had some leftover, but it wasn't f-you money. We would have had to work either way."

"Right," Les said. "You get a settlement of an undisclosed amount from IPFC, one of the largest combat sports promotions in the world, large enough that it makes the news and causes IPFC shares to drop, and it wasn't f-you money."

Jason tightened his grip on the wheel as the car hit a puddle and hydroplaned for a moment. "Their shares dipped because the investors discovered that upper management had committed massive fraud and potentially broke several international laws. The settlement resulted from that, not the other way around." His stomach growled again. "Anyway, dinner?"

"Yeah, *podría comer*[5]," Les said, smiling under his hat. "Sweet Lucy's? It's right up the road, not too far out of the way."

"Barbeque it is," Jason said, already tasting the smoked brisket sandwich and cornbread that melted in the mouth.

---

[5] I could eat

Les settled in for his usual car nap, and Jason paid rapt attention to the road, the rain heavy enough that the lane lines were virtually invisible, the glowing signs of the businesses along the side of the road and headlights of the occasional oncoming vehicle the only indications of where he needed to be on the road.

As the signs passed, one logo grabbed his attention. He hesitated for a moment, weighing his curiosity against his rumbling stomach, and flipped on his blinker to pull into the parking lot under the sign.

"We there?" Les asked.

"Just making a quick stop," Jason said, pulling his gear on. "Be right back. Hold your breath."

The car door opened with a hiss of escaping air, and Jason quickly stepped into the torrent and shut the door behind him so the cabin could re-pressurize. He jogged across the lot, holding the lip of his hood from falling back across his shoulders, and into the vestibule of Greenway Protectives.

The lobby was much what he expected: nothing fancy, just a room with layers over layers of paint, worn industrial carpeting, a drop ceiling with fluorescent lights, ratty chairs, and a purely functional reception desk with a tired-looking woman staring into a computer monitor. Pictures of what looked to be their products in action, like sun shields of varying design and industrial outerwear, were mounted to the walls, but the pictures' corners and edges were dented and peeling.

The woman glanced up at Jason as he entered and removed his headgear. "Can I help you?" Her tone made it clear she wasn't the least bit interested in actually helping him.

Jason flashed his shield. "Hey, I had a quick question...I saw that you guys installed a sun shield over near Kensington and Sedgley, and I was wondering if I could talk to someone about that."

The woman went back to looking at her screen. "Information about clients and installations is proprietary and confidential."

Jason smiled his most charming smile. "No one's in trouble, I was just curious. It was a pretty run-down building, and it was a brand new shield...just seemed an odd match to me, but I was happy to see it there."

"Sir, all information about clients and installations..." She gestured dismissively, unable to be bothered in continuing the sentence.

Jason's smile faltered. *I feel like I used to be better at this.* "OK, well, is there a manager or supervisor I can speak with?"

"We're closing in a few minutes, and everyone is gone. You can make an appointment through the website, and someone will contact you about your interest in Greenway Protectives."

Jason's eyebrows knitted. "Couldn't...you make that appointment right now?"

"All appointments are made through the website." Jason was convinced the woman could not sound any more bored.

"Thanks, I guess," he said as he refitted his gear in place and exited into the rain.

The remains of two meals littered the table. Jason idly thumbed through the Greenway website while Les perused the menu.

"Are you seriously ordering more?" Jason asked as he brought up the corporate giving page.

"Making plans for next time," Les said. "I always like to have a plan."

Jason snorted a laugh, and he thumbed open an article link. "Well, that's interesting," he said. "Greenway participates in a grant program that subsidizes the construction of sun shields in impoverished and under-served communities."

Les grunted without looking up from the menu. "What's the angle?"

"For them? Found money. Don't have to worry about someone stiffing them on the bill." He scrolled through the article. "Looks like the grant program is through Majora Global. Sounds like something Leo would do."

Jason continued to scroll through the article that was, to his eyes, clearly written by a public relations person to look like it was a "legitimate" news article, complete with pictures and media. Workers on the job sites smiling for the camera while hanging from the supports, folks in nice UV suits pretending to stick a shovel in the ground for "groundbreaking" ceremonies, carefully posed "regular" people displaying their joy for their corporate benefactors.

Jason did a double take as he scrolled and quickly stopped the screen. "Yo," he said to Les and slid his phone across the table. "Check this out."

The picture he stopped on showed a worker inside a confined space, something that looked like it was inside a support tower, surrounded by wiring and pipes. He had his sleeves rolled up and was doing something with a scanner of some kind. He had a tattoo of a monstrous scorpion with its tail wrapping around his arm.

Les picked up the phone and looked at it closer, pinching the screen to zoom in on the picture. "No," he said. "No, what are the odds? Is that the same guy? Our vic?"

Jason expanded the photo. "No, look here." He pointed to a burn scar on the man's hand that distorted the ink. "Guy at the lab didn't have a scar on his hand. This is a different guy." Something tickled his memory. "I think I've seen this guy before."

"Where?" Les asked.

Jason began filing through his memories of the past few days.

The raid.

The bar on the first floor.

Stoned guy with a scorpion tattoo on his arm sprawled out on a couch with two women.

"Do you have your cam footage from the raid?" he asked Les.

Les fished his phone out of his pocket and pulled up the video archive. He tapped the screen a few times. "When?"

Jason closed his eyes and replayed the event in his head. "When we were interviewing witnesses after the chase. I think he was still there."

Les tapped the phone several times and placed it on the table to play. The odd point of view footage gave Jason a moment of vertigo before his brain adjusted. He scrolled through the video until he found what he was looking for and paused the playback.

Sitting on a couch. Still looking stoned beyond comprehension, still sitting with two women who seemed equally high on either side. His arms were draped over their shoulders as they contemplated the universe, and on his left hand was a monstrous scorpion tattoo marred by a burn scar.

"Him," Jason said, placing his phone beside Les. "Same guy."

"What are the odds?" Les repeated.

Jason couldn't keep the lopsided smile from his face. "Keep getting these coincidences."

CHAPTER 11

Try as he might, Jason couldn't drift off to sleep.

Amira didn't stir when he rolled out of bed. He padded down the hall to the spare bedroom they had converted into an office for the both of them and plopped down at his desk. He brought up the notes he had made about Markus Kline in his personal file and poured over them again.

He knew he was missing something, or at least that was what he was trying to convince himself of. If he weren't, then that would mean…

He refocused his attention on the notes in front of him. He needed to remain dispassionate. Emotional thinking would cloud his reasoning and make him miss something.

Crimes always had a reason behind them. Somebody always benefitted, even if just for a moment. Even crimes of passion had logical forces driving them. Find the reason, find the solution.

Whenever anyone went missing, it was for a reason. Either they ran away from or to something, or someone took them. That was the question he ultimately needed to answer. Did Markus leave of his own accord, or did someone take him?

Given his suspicion that Markus was at the stash house, Jason figured that the answer was "taken" and not "ran away", but it always made sense to cover the bases.

He brought up the DNA typing he sent in from swabbing the lacrosse pin to see if the lab had posted results yet. It was a long shot, he knew, but still...

RESULTS INCONCLUSIVE. REPROCESSING.

Jason slumped in his chair. A part of him hoped there had been enough material on the pin to give a positive ID, and an equal part knew that the odds were long against him for getting a match. The bold letters on the screen drove the reality home that the pin was a dead end for the moment. Standard procedure was to repeat the test, but Jason didn't hold out hope. It was rare that the results changed.

Who benefits?

Not Jessie. She was obviously distraught over the situation. It would be an odd strategy to raise this much attention around Markus if she were responsible. No notes from teachers about suspected abuse or sudden changes in behavior.

Dad, maybe? Jason brought up what he had dug up there. Markus Sr., in and out of the picture for the first couple of years, was seemingly completely out. No shared custody, and it didn't look like Senior had claimed Markus as a dependent. A few more clicks revealed the termination of parental rights, so even if the kid were there, dad wouldn't get any financial benefit.

So likely not dad.

Who benefits?

Jason was convinced the kid was in the stash house. Had he seen the murders and was hiding from whoever did the deed? Or did the culprit grab Markus? If they did, why take him instead of just offing him right then and there, eliminating the witness?

According to the preliminary reports on the bodies, none of them could be Markus. If Markus had seen the murders and the culprit knew that, Markus would be among the corpses. *If he ran, someone would have seen him by now.*

Or maybe not. Might be hiding out somewhere. And he would need help…

He thought back to when he ran away as a kid. His parents had been fighting again. He couldn't remember if it was over money, or him, or how much his medical bills were costing. But he did remember needing to get out of the house and away from the constant tension and yelling.

First person I told I was running away was Alexei. He helped me find that abandoned apartment to hide out in.

Memory had a funny way of warping time. He wasn't sure if he had hidden in that dirty squat for a couple of days or a week, but long enough that his parents had called the police. They only found him because they followed Alexei when he was sneaking in to bring him some food and a charger for his phone.

Might be worth talking to Omar again.

He felt his eyes droop, and decided to try to catch a few hours of sleep before his alarm went off.

His phone pulsed with an alert. A glance showed it was from Derrick Belford on behalf of Chief of Detectives Swan. A request for three, no *four* reports the chief wanted by roll call in the morning.

"Son of a bitch," he mumbled to himself. He silently got dressed to go into the office.

"I swear that Swan is trying to kill me," Jason said as Les slid a cup of steaming coffee across the desk to him. Jason gratefully brought the cup to his lips and savored the aroma before taking a sip of life-sustaining liquid caffeine. "I don't mean metaphorically. Actually trying to work me to death."

"Were you here all night?" Les asked, plopping down into his seat and spreading a newspaper in front of himself.

"She wants up-to-the-minute updates on well…everything," Jason said.

Les coughed a sarcastic laugh. "We've shut down a lab, taken at least two hundred million dollars' worth of splice off the street between buy-and-busts and seizures...what more does she want?"

"Results." Jason's eyes felt bleary, and his voice sounded gravelly to his ears. "And honestly, we don't have much on that front. No leads on who was running the lab aside from *maybe* it was a *kardeşlik unuo*, no idea who's committing the murders other than an urban myth regaled to me by an old tweaker." He took another sip and turned back to his monitor. "She's looking for any excuse to tank me on this. I figured with the seventh…is it the seventh body? I've lost track. With this latest body, I figured I'd better get ahead of it and get the paperwork in."

"The bureaucracy must be served," Les said with feigned deference and buried his face in the paper.

Jason rubbed at his eyes. "Seriously, what's next?" He looked at his partner. "I don't know the next move. We've got the vaguest of descriptions for the murder suspect that either has them wearing a police uniform or is an anthropomorphic bear, so that's awesome. Tommy Delucca is in a medically-induced coma and won't be waking up for at least a week..."

"Wait...what?" Les asked.

"One of the locals by the bakery kept saying something about the killer being a bear."

"Did he say *a* bear, or *The Bear*?"

"I don't know," Jason said. "The second, I think. Why?"

Les snorted. "The Bear is an urban legend in some less-reputable circles. Some superhuman cyborg or something like that. Whenever there's a super-violent, super-messy murder, we'll start hearing rumors that The Bear did it."

"Is this a person or a thing?" Jason asked.

"None of the above," Les said. "Ever notice that it's always, 'I know this guy who saw The Bear', but when you talk to *that* guy, they're like, 'No, it was this *other* guy who saw The Bear and told *me* about it'. Just people looking to scare the crap out of each other and deny the utter depravity in which humans can visit upon one another."

"Well, this guy says he's the one that saw The Bear," Jason said with a smile. "Maybe we should bring him in for questioning."

"You mean the old guy, dreads, lives next to the bakery?" Les said, pulling his paper up in front of his face. "Old Head Fred. Dude's nuts and he's got cataracts. He didn't see shit."

"His neighbor said the same thing. But he also said that whenever dealers wanted to make sure there wasn't a drone overhead, they'd call in fake emergencies, and that would divert the birds."

"I never trusted those things," Les grumbled. "Sending those things out for routine calls rather than a real cop? Bet those rich dicks get an actual person who shows up when they call."

"Think there's anything to it?" Jason asked, taking a sip of coffee.

Les shrugged. "What about Tattoo Man," he said from behind his paper. "Any luck there?"

Jason groaned. "*Nada.* DNA from the bakery body isn't turning anything up, which is still twisting my brain as to how that happened. And this thing with the kid…"

Les made a non-committal sound. "Still think there's a connection there?"

Jason grunted an affirmative through a sip of coffee. "Yeah. My gut tells me the kid was in there. If the DNA profile from the pin proves it was his, can't really deny that. I'm going to talk to the neighborhood kids today. They've been pounding the pavement pretty hard, maybe they've seen or heard something. Just have to do it in between literally everything else to keep Swan off my back."

"*Follarla*[6]," Les said matter-of-factly and reached for a donut from a box on the desk. "If that's where the evidence points, just follow it. You said it yourself."

"I wish," Jason said. "If I start re-assigning anyone on the task force to the Markus Kline angle, Swan will use that as the perfect excuse to dismantle the team. Eighteen months of investigation down the tube."

"So?" Les said through a mouth of cruller. "Then don't reassign anyone. Follow it yourself."

---

[6] Fuck her

"Then she takes me off the task force," Jason said. "I honestly don't care about being in charge, I just don't trust whoever she would put in to finish the investigation the way it needs to be done. They'll just wind it down as quickly as possible so she can reallocate the funds for one of her bullshit projects like park beautification or something."

Les lowered the paper. "Kid, for someone who is one of the smartest people I know, you sure can be stupid."

"Uh..." Jason didn't know how to respond.

"She didn't put you in charge of the task force because *she* wanted to," Les said. "Someone made her. You've made enough of a name for yourself that people who matter wanted you in charge, and they knew exactly what you would do: you'd run down every lead, work the case the way it was supposed to be worked, and get results. And that means stepping on the toes of people who would just as soon not be in the spotlight, people who generally do whatever they want because they have the money to protect them."

"OK," Jason said slowly, still not following Les' point.

"Kids," Les mumbled, then continued. "She *can't* just take you off the task force. She needs a *reason*. Reassigning team members for what she's deemed an 'inappropriate investigative avenue'? That's where she gets you...she can show that you're wasting *money*. But if it's just you, do it on your own time, while the rest of the team follows every other lead? Then you're just wasting *time*. More specifically, *your* time. She can't touch you for that. Good luck with her explaining that to the powers-that-be that obviously want you here."

Les picked his paper back up and returned to reading. Jason sat for a moment staring at his partner in silence, digesting the tirade he had just lobbed at him. Try as he might, he couldn't find an argument against it.

"You know, you could have just told me all of that from the get-go," Jason said with a smile. "Saved us all some time."

"Yeah, well," Les said, between annoyed and amused, "how else would you learn?"

The clouds held on to their greenish tint, threatening more rain. Jason was grateful for the respite from the storm; it made it more likely he'd be able to find Omar and his friends if they weren't sheltering from the weather.

The legion of neon yellow flyers with Markus' face posted to every possible surface looked water-logged, some mostly illegible. But they had been joined by new flyers, bright pink and laminated. The reward had gone up to $500, Jason noted.

He drove slowly down the street where he had met Omar. Occasionally he saw the corner kids out, eyeing up his car as he passed. The headgear provided them some degree of anonymity, but Jason had been working the neighborhood long enough as a beat cop and a detective that he could suss out the identities of some of them. Mookie with the red cycler that started every story with "See, what had happened was", Jojo who always wore a sports jersey over her coat, and who he had caught shoplifting when she was eleven, Ginkgo who always had the latest in fashionable goggles and was never wanting for a line of suitors.

Jason offered a small wave as he cruised by, and the ones that had been on their corners for years, the ones he knew since before they hit puberty, offered a reverse nod or wave or *peace* in return, while the other kids would give them strange looks and sign *WTF* at their compatriots.

He smiled to himself. They would learn, provided they both stayed on the corners and stayed alive long enough: they might be on opposite sides of the law, but that didn't mean they had to have an adversarial relationship every minute of every day. They would figure out that sometimes it was good to have a polite relationship with a cop, the same way that he figured out that sometimes you needed these kids to act as eyes and ears for when the crap really hit the fan.

Most of these kids weren't cold-blooded killers; they were just trying to make a buck in a world that didn't provide them many opportunities. It didn't make them right, Jason knew, and it didn't mean that some of them would be on a track to lose themselves in the game and turn into real problems. He knew that as long as there was pain in the world, there would be drug abuse, and as long as there was poverty, there would be people lining up to do whatever it took to alleviate it. Those circles would always overlap.

He rounded a corner and noticed one of the regulars, Dizzy, wasn't out with his crew. He rolled to a stop, rolled down the window, and waved over the crew leader, a teenager with a hoodie over his UV gear and hood pulled up that people called K-Dawg. It was the kid's "signature" look, and Jason always thought it made him look like one of the Jedi characters from the

Star Wars shows and movies he and Alexei had fawned over as kids. He pointed that out to K-Dawg once, but the kid didn't seem to understand the reference; still, Jason had taken to calling him "Obi-Wan", much to K-Dawg's consternation and his friends' amusement.

Jason had seen him sliding over the years further and further into the splice game, and, if he was being honest with himself, thought that the kid was rapidly approaching the point of no return if he hadn't passed it already. It always made him feel sad. Sad, and lucky. He could easily imagine where this would have been the direction he went, had it not been for Alexei and Amira, and by extension, their father.

The kid delayed walking over for a moment, engaging in the required peacocking to his friends that said it was *his* decision to walk over, *not* because the cop told him to.

"Hey Obi-Wan, where's Dizzy?" Jason asked when K-Dawg finally reached the window and leaned his elbows on the door to peer inside.

K-Dawg sucked air in through his teeth while his friends signed *smile* and *laughing* behind his back. "You should know that. Diz got that scholarship, he ain't slummin' out here with us thug-types."

Jason smiled to himself. *Maybe the Foundation is helping.* "Good for him."

K-Dawg signed *whatever.*

"Hey, looking for a kid named Omar. He's been putting up the flyers for Markus Kline. Seen him around?"

The splice dealer straightened up and yelled to his crew, and one of them said something back that Jason couldn't quite pick up. K-Dawg leaned back down into the window. "He's working at his grandma's store today. Bodega, called Fannies', few blocks up." He gestured in the direction that Jason assumed was where the store was located.

"Thanks, Obi-Wan," Jason said. "Hey, I'm coming back in an hour, I want the corner clear, OK? Pack up for the day, or I'll have to take you all in."

"Yeah," K-Dawg drawled and sauntered back to his crew.

Jason followed the direction he was pointed in and found the corner store that K-Dawg had indicated.

The interior was small but organized, Jason noticed as he pulled his headgear off. He saw all of the basic sundries that one would expect in such a store. Behind the counter he saw a kid, about twelve, working the register, ringing up a customer. Jason hadn't seen Omar's face but figured this was probably him.

"Omar?" Jason asked. "Remember me? Jason…Lieutenant Thane?"

Omar's face changed from one of suspicion to one of relief and recognition. "Yeah, hey. Any luck?"

Jason felt his heart sink. "No, sorry kid, not yet. I'm looking, but nothing yet. It's actually why I came to see you."

Omar finished ringing up the customer and accepted their payment. "I don't know where he is."

"No, I know, but here's the thing," Jason said. He waited until the customer left the store and they were alone. "I don't think Markus ran away. We agree on that, right?"

"Yeah," Omar said, an unsure look on his face.

"So that means that someone had to have taken him."

"Oh."

"Yeah. And this is where you and your friends come in. Usually, people don't just snatch kids off the street. They usually hang around for a while first to see how people react to them, where the adults are, things like that."

"Kind of like...like a hunter," Omar said.

"Like a hunter," Jason agreed. "So can you think of anyone you saw hanging around that was new, or that gave you a weird vibe, anything like that?"

Omar's eyes grew distant, like he was lost in thought. "There were some guys in our apartment the other day," he finally said. "Something about running wires, or something like that. But then when I was at Markus' apartment playing video games, one of them came over there, too. And it was weird cause, like, he kept asking us about the game we were playing, and telling us about his favorite games, but they were all, like, old." Omar blushed. "I don't know if that helps or anything."

Jason was on the fence. On the one hand, he thought it was something to at least look at...but he knew it could also be nothing. With all of the infrastructure and building improvements going on in Markus' building, it wouldn't be unheard of for contractors to come and go.

Jason could see Omar's shoulders slumping in defeat. "You know what, it does," Jason said. "It's a place to start. Can you tell me what this guy's name was, or what he looked like?"

Omar's body language picked up some with Jason's comment. "I think I heard someone call him Zeke or something like that. He was tall, like maybe about your height, and he never took his cycler or goggles off, but I think he had reddish hair. And he had a tattoo on his left arm."

Jason felt his heart skip a beat, but forced his voice to remain even. "Can you tell me what the tattoo looked like?"

"It was a scorpion-man-looking thing, like a centaur but with a scorpion instead of a horse. It was pretty cool looking. But it was messed up where it was on his hand…he was, like, burned or something, and it made the tattoo look weird."

Jason pulled up the photo from the Greenway website on his phone. "Did it look like this?" Omar nodded. *Kardeşlik.* "OK, and have you seen this man since then?"

Omar shook his head. "Does that help?"

"Yes, absolutely," Jason said. "You and your friends keep posting those flyers, and if any of you see the man with the tattoo, call me, OK?" Jason passed him another business card. His phone pulsed an alert, then another, and then another. Notifications began popping up one after the other, and then the phone started ringing with a call from Les. "I've gotta run. I'll stop by in a few days, and remember, call me if you see that guy or if you or your friends remember anything else." He affixed his headgear in place as he left the store and answered the call. "What's up?"

"Just got a hit on one of the runners from the stash house," Les said.

"We've got a name?"

"No, but a drone just made a match on the APB from facial recognition," Les replied. "I just confirmed it. It's one of our guys."

Jason opened the Mustang's door and plopped into the driver's seat. "Send me the location."

"Sending it to your phone now. I can have a tac-team there in an hour."

The Mustang's turbines whined to life. "I'm on my way there now."

"Wait for the tac-team," Les said. "Don't give her an excuse."

Jason knew whom Les meant. "Don't have time," Jason said as he pulled the car out into the street. *The sooner I close the murder, the sooner I can get these images out of my head.* "He might be in the wind if we wait too long. I'll start looking when I get there. I need you to hit up Greenway, get a name on that guy in the photo we saw."

"You got something?" the veteran asked.

"Maybe. I think all of this is connected, and I think I can prove it."

CHAPTER 12

Jason pulled the Mustang to a stop just in time for the sun to slip behind the jagged horizon of the city and for it to start drizzling.

He checked his GPS against the location data Les sent him. The building at the drone's address was a burned-out skeleton of brick and blackened windows, so dilapidated that Jason couldn't begin to guess what it had been before time and tragedy had taken it. It abutted an overpass, and in the highway's shadow, the people that no one else wanted had collected. Tents and ramshackle shelters of varying states of repair filled the expanse, protected at least a little from the sun and precipitation.

Somewhere in the mass of tired and unwashed humanity, if he was lucky, was Jason's target. Someone who might finally answer the questions that had been haunting him for the last three days, who may be able to quiet the intrusive memories of carnage and butchery.

He waded into the encampment. It was surprisingly quiet aside from the traffic passing overhead. The few people who didn't scatter as he entered the informal boundary, those either huddled in their makeshift homes or gathered around a fire, stared at him silently with varying degrees of recognition. Some, he could tell, pegged him as a cop right away. Others looked like they were seeing something from a different reality, or like they weren't seeing anything at all despite their wide-open eyes. Someone hacked like they were coughing up a lung, followed by a noisy and messy spitting sound.

It struck Jason how easily this could have been him, tossed aside as society's detritus. As he scanned what faces he could see, he absently thought of all the paths that could have led to a place like this, cast aside.

What if I had stayed sick?

Finding meaningful employment would have been near impossible…no one wanted to hire someone who would be a drain on the company's health insurance.

What if I hadn't picked up my grades and did better in school?

He could see himself easily to have turned to the less-savory activities the young, uneducated, and unemployed did when they didn't see a future after high school.

What if I had decided to use splice to keep fighting?

It wasn't hard to imagine going down a bad road, getting caught, getting addicted…

What if I didn't have Amira?

His north star.

He saw too many paths in his life that had he taken the other route he could see it ending here or somewhere like it. It made him wonder how many of the people here wondered about their path not taken, what their lives would have been like if they had made different choices, or had the opportunities that he had, options that he worked for, and that others were born with.

"Hey guys," he said as he approached a group huddled around a fire. He held up the photo of his suspect on his phone. "Seen him around?"

The group all murmured negative responses and shook their heads. Jason moved on.

He checked the screen grab from the drone again as he walked. The timing defied odds: for a brief moment, the suspect had his mask and goggles off as he was shoveling a spoonful of something into his mouth, and the drone just happened to be looking in that direction on its patrol. A few degrees to the left or right, or a few seconds faster or slower, the drone would never have gotten his face in frame, or he could have put his headgear back on. Jason would have had nothing.

Despite the luck of the picture, Jason knew it was a long shot to find the guy. He could have moved on, or if he didn't, finding someone while they were wearing headgear was nigh impossible. It would get a modicum easier once the tac-team arrived, but he knew he couldn't wait that long.

He approached an older woman who was crouched in front of a lean-to of heavy canvas and scraps of rusted sheet metal, and she scurried into her shelter before he could ask her anything.

He wished he could take his headgear off. He had never had much luck questioning people when he had to wear it. He wondered if it was because he was police or something more primal tied to not being able to see a person's eyes and facial expressions.

The grisly-but-needed childhood refrain taught in school popped into his head. *Outside is death*.

He began to approach another group when he saw a uniformed police officer slowly wading through the tents a stone's throw away.

Could use all of the help I can get.

He changed course to speak with the other cop, weaving through the haphazard neighborhood. The cop looked up and saw Jason. Jason waved and tapped two fingers on his left chest. *I'm a cop.* The officer stopped walking and waited.

"Hey," Jason said when he was close enough and flashed his badge. "Lieutenant Thane, Narcotics."

"Olafson," the officer replied with a nod.

"Did dispatch send you over?" Jason asked, pocketing his badge.

"Just on my normal patrol," Olafson said. "Everything OK?"

"Yeah, just looking for someone," Jason said. "Actually, I could use your help finding this guy if you have a few minutes."

"Sure," Olafson said. "Two eyes are better than one, right?"

Jason chuckled. "Something like that." He pulled up the photo on his phone. "Ever seen this guy before?"

Olafson looked at the picture carefully. "Doesn't look familiar. What do you need him for?"

"Suspect in a case I'm working," Jason said. "Think he might be tied to...well, some big players, at any rate. Help me look for him?"

Olafson shrugged. "Sure, but it will be hard." He motioned to his own headgear. "Hard to recognize people with these on."

"Truth," Jason said. "Want me to send the picture to your phone, just in case?"

Olafson tapped his head. "No need. Good memory for faces. If I see him, I'll come get you."

THE FALL 163

"Thanks," Jason said. "Appreciate it. I'm going to head down there a ways. You want to head up to the other side? Meet in the middle?"

Olafson nodded and started trudging in the direction Jason indicated.

Maybe there's a shot of finding this guy.

Rivulets of rainwater started forming small streams as they flowed through the camp. He followed one of them, mentally checking each person he saw against the photo.

He considered asking people wearing them to remove their masks, but it seemed wrong. To make someone breathe in even a little of the pollution just came across as cruel, even in the pursuit of…

…what? Justice? Is that what I'm doing? Or am I just plugging a hole in the damn, keeping the system running the way it always has.

The thought stuck with him. He had heard the arguments that the illegal splice trade was no different from the plethora of drugs peddled by pharmaceutical companies. People should be able to do what they want as long as it didn't interfere with anyone else.

And to a degree, Jason agreed, he realized.

If people wanted to screw up their lives on drugs, who am I to say they couldn't?

He had also seen the violence that could spring up around the splice trade, violence that drew civilians into the game in ways they never wanted. He had seen the devastation splice had wreaked on users and families alike.

Hell, I'm walking through the real-time results right now.

But was it justice he was pursuing?

What will change if I get this guy off the street? What will change?

Drug dealers would still exist. People would still manufacture splice, and other people would still mangle their genes with it, whether to get an edge at work, or in a sport, or even just to feel better for a little while.

So, nothing. Nothing I'm doing right now will matter in the long run.

Jason's thoughts drifted to Alexei.

He knew he would make a difference.

Always cheerful, always positive, always a fighter. Jason hated and loved that about him. An odd mix of jealousy and admiration fueled his relationship with Alexei. The negative parts seemed to have gotten airbrushed out after he disappeared, and completely ignored when he died. Jason wasn't sure if he should feel guilty about that or about having those feelings toward someone who had always had his back and pushed him to be better and try harder.

Alexei would have made a difference.

And he knew that it would have made a difference to Jordan and Amira if he hadn't disappeared, if he had still been around.

Like it would make a difference to Jessie if Markus were found.

That was where he should focus his attention, he decided. That's where he *could* make a difference, where what he did *would* matter.

I've got to find that kid.

The thought galvanized inside him. The one small piece of evidence he had, tenuous as it was, would need to be enough. The pin in the stash house…where the bodies were mutilated…where a dead cop was found in the ventilation system…

…wait…

The dead cop. Novak. Badge number 3427. Jason could see it in his mind's eye as clearly as if he were looking at it right in front of him.

Jason closed his eyes and envisioned Officer Olafson's uniform, the silver badge on his left breast…badge number 3427.

"Oh, gods," Jason murmured. He turned and started to run back to where he had left Olafson, or whoever he was, slipping in the mud as he did. He pulled up his phone and dialed Les. "Where's the tac-team?" he yelled as soon as his partner connected.

"Twenty minutes out, why?" Les replied.

"I need them here now…or anyone. Get anyone you can down here ASAP," he commanded. "I'm pretty sure our cop killer is here. I need boots on the ground and eyes in the sky right now."

"On it," Les said and disconnected.

Jason ran back to where he had met the fake officer and scanned the area but didn't see him. He ran in the direction Jason had sent him, hoping to catch sight of the man, but to no avail.

"Damn it," Jason muttered to himself.

Sirens began wailing in the distance. Jason figured they would be at his location in less than two minutes. The slight relief of backup did little to staunch the flow of dread and anxiety that flooded him. He had stood an arm's length away from the person who had folded a grown man into human origami.

Jason heard a panicked yell. He skidded to a stop, and his feet almost slid out from under him as the ground became more and more saturated from the rainwater overflow from the highway overhead that wasn't being captured by the reclamation system. He looked right and left for the source, and movement above him caught his eye. A man was running in the utility catwalks that hung from the bottom of the overpass, looking over his shoulder as he scrambled over the expanded steel.

Behind the man was a uniformed police officer chasing him.

"Shit, shit, shit," Jason said through gritted teeth. He spotted the nearest access ladder and sprinted to it, hampered by the random shelters scattered between him and it. He put his foot on the first rung, and it slipped off from the sludge stuck to his boot, and he fell face-first into the mud. He popped up quickly and carefully made his way up the rain-slicked ladder.

After what seemed to Jason to be an eternity of climbing, he finally spilled onto the catwalk far above the homeless encampment. He tried to gaze through the jungle of pipes and struts that clung to the bottom of the overpass in search of his quarry but couldn't see anyone.

He began jogging forward, both hands on the handrails, wary of his muddy boots on the wet metal. The walkway slanted up into the mess of utilities, then back down under them again. He could see intersections that branched to other sections or up into the works themselves, but still could not catch any glimpse of the running man or the fake cop.

The catwalk slanted down again, and at the apogee, he finally caught sight of movement. The man in the stolen uniform was turning a large valve, something Jason would have assumed took at least two people with tools to do, and water started flooding out of an open pipe embedded in the nearby support holding the highway up. He thought he heard a scream but wasn't sure, as just about every sound was drowned out by the cars passing above.

Jason ran as fast as he could without slipping, navigating ever closer to where he spotted Olafson. He hit a dead end and had to backtrack the maze of catwalks. Then he turned and found himself going back in the direction he came from and had to backtrack again.

Finally, he saw the ladder leading up to the overflowing pipe. Olafson was gone. The only evidence he had been there was the water rushing out of an orange pipe that Jason didn't think he could put his arms around. The walkway was a dead end, and Jason couldn't see anywhere he could have gone.

Jason saw patrollers pull up next to his car, lights ablaze and flashing, and cops started pouring out into the encampment. He yelled and waved to get their attention, and a few waved acknowledgments. He saw a pair run towards the ladder he had taken to get into the catwalks.

He tried to turn the valve off, but it didn't budge. He looked into the pipe to see if there was any way Olafson could have escaped through it, but Jason was sure that his own shoulders would have gotten stuck if he had tried, and he pegged Olafson to be around the same size.

Something just beneath the surface, obfuscated by the torrent of water, caught Jason's eye. Against his better judgment, he reached a hand in to see what it was.

At first, he didn't feel anything beyond the shock of cold water. Then his arm bumped against something in the churn, and he grasped at it.

And it grasped back.

Jason yelped in surprise and tried to pull his arm out, but whatever it was held fast. It took him a moment before he realized it was fingers that had grabbed onto his arm. Jason wrapped his hand around the arm in the pipe and tried to pull.

The arm didn't budge as the other fingers grasped desperately at Jason's coat.

Jason pulled again. And again.

Then other arms thrust into the water, and Jason realized two officers were next to him. He wasn't sure if he said anything or if he could even be heard between the traffic speeding overhead or the torrent of water rushing out of the pipe, but all three started pulling on the arm below the surface.

Jason realized that the fingers weren't grasping at him anymore. He redoubled his efforts, yelling with exertion as he tried again to pull whoever was stuck in the pipe out.

Finally, with a great release and upwelling of water, the body was liberated from its prison and onto the catwalk. Empty eyes stared at nothing. The face had a blueish tint. It was the same face from the stash house footage.

Jason knelt on the walkway, trying to catch his breath. He glanced out at the rooftops of the nearby buildings and was almost certain he saw a figure in a police uniform, jacket blowing in the wind, standing on a roof several blocks away.

And he wasn't sure, but he swore the figure saluted before disappearing behind the tangle of chimneys and pipes.

CHAPTER 13

Jason's headache started at the base of his skull, right where the muscles that connected the spine to the skull were. He could feel the tension there, a slow ache that was building, crawling over the top of his head and into his shoulders. Whether it was from a lack of decent sleep for four nights, or relentless stress, or from sleeping on the office couch, he wasn't sure.

He was sure that if there was something beyond "exhausted", he was feeling it.

As he stared blankly at nothing in particular, he cataloged the last few hours.

There was the man in the pipe. Scratches and bruises indicated that he had gotten stuck in the pipe; Jason figured he had crawled in as a desperate move to hide or escape whoever was chasing him. That person simply turned the water on and drowned him.

No ID on him, nothing in the system for facial recognition or DNA. The only thing that gave any clue as to his identity was the monstrous scorpion tattoo on his arm, marking him as *kardeşlik*.

It shouldn't be possible for these guys not to be in the system.

But he was dead, and his secrets went with him, as did Jason's hopes for solving the murders or finding out what happened to Markus Kline.

I can't seem to catch a break. Getting to be a trend.

The grid search started after that, which turned up nothing save for the abandoned stolen police uniform several blocks away, but no clues as to who was wearing it or where they went.

Then came the medical examiner. Then endless, sometimes insulting questions from Internal Affairs. Then a late-night visit to Dr. Misriak for a checkup in case the exposure to the wastewater from the pipe had any ill effects.

The medical examiner confirmed Jason's initial suspicions. IAB concluded that Jason, in fact, did not have anything to do with Novak's murder or his stolen gear, and that it was, in fact, a third party that committed the crimes, and happily handed the case back to him. The doc gave Jason the all-clear: no obvious complications or concerns.

Les had come by at some point, he knew, but he couldn't pinpoint the timing in his mind. The only thing Jason could remember from their conversation was that Greenway wasn't coughing up any names without a warrant. No luck on the mysterious "Zeke".

Shouldn't be surprised.

At some point, he had stumbled into the office rather than going home and waking up Amira, crashing on the threadbare couch, falling asleep as soon as he closed his eyes.

It took him a moment of blinking in the dimness of the unlit office to realize that it was early morning, judging by the pale light streaming through the windows. It took another moment to realize that his phone was buzzing. He rubbed the sleep from his eyes and checked his notifications.

FACIAL RECOGNITION MATCH ON REQUESTED SUSPECT

Jason opened the message.

The face that popped up was from a passport photo, as best Jason could tell. Cold eyes set in an emotionless face stared back at him. It was the same face as the last runner captured by the drone during the stash house raid—his last thread.

Jason was surprised that the file came with a name and criminal history: Sergei Hirokawa, one arrest for drunken disorderly six months prior.

Did he get sloppy?

He was more surprised that there was a known associate, apparently a girlfriend named Sara Dougherty, who had a place in a trendy apartment complex in Center City.

There wasn't anything else in the file, but given that the information on everyone else he had been looking for was non-existent, this read like a veritable novel. He tempered his expectations, in any case.

No sense getting excited. Nothing else has worked out so far.

Jason messaged Les to get the team together and to meet him at the office. He hauled himself off the couch and stretched, then lumbered into the kitchenette.

Good or bad…I'm going to need coffee. Lots of coffee.

While the aroma of cheap coffee brewing filled the air, Jason pulled up a search on one of the desk terminals and entered Sara Dougherty's name.

No criminal record came up. He saw a few traffic tickets, but for the most part, it looked to Jason like she kept her nose clean.

How'd she end up with this guy?

Several addresses were listed under her name in trendy neighborhoods in the Center City and University Districts.

Too many to hit at once, and if we hit one at a time, there's a good chance if he's at any of them that he'll hear about it and run.

Jason pulled up some social media platforms and searched. No pictures of Sergei, but many of her with what he presumed were her girlfriends at spas, bars, and vacation spots. She looked in her mid-twenties, pretty in the way rich girls were when they had the funds to get the gene jobs done when they were still teenagers, a weird, almost-perfect bordering uncanny valley.

Well, we know she has money. Where does it come from? His or hers?

He dug into more of her social feeds and finally found her on a professional services site among a list of a hundred other Sara Doughertys. The profile with the photo that matched had her working as an accountant at Bergman, Dougherty, and Associates.

Same last name. Too young to be a named partner...so maybe a parent or relative?

He did a map search for the accounting office and then added in the known addresses. Two were noticeably closer, within walking distance and practically equidistant from her work.

OK, but which one?

He looked up both apartment complexes. Both looked to service young professionals with "starter" apartments and amenities that would appeal to those not in the family way, like rooftop bars, shuttle services, and the like. The apartments all looked like single and two-room setups, confirming Jason's suspicion: she wasn't living with her parents.

Which means she had to apply to live at either one…and even if you're rich, they don't let just anyone rent a place like this…

Jason went to another tab on his screen and pulled her credit report. It was not as pristine as he thought it would be, but high enough to not scare away a lender…or a landlord. He finally found what he was looking for: the Verdant Shade Property Management Company, owner of the second address, had run a credit check on Sara two years prior.

Gotcha.

He sent another message to Les. REDIRECT TO NEW ADDRESS.

Jason felt his headache intensify and his stomach churn when he entered the Verdant Shade Apartments lobby and saw Lieutenant Derrick Belford standing in a dark blue pinstripe suit and loafers among the rest of the police who had gathered there. His hair was perfectly in place and held with a shellac of pomade. His smile stretched from ear to ear but never touched his eyes, revealing perfect yet overly-white teeth.

Les caught Jason as he walked across the hardwood floor towards the elevators. "Sorry, he just showed up," he whispered. "Something about oversight."

Jason ignored the comment and Belford as best he could as he strode towards the elevators. Belford fell into step beside him.

"How are you even here?" Jason asked. "You're not on the team anymore."

"We got wind of your little witch hunt, your little wild goose chase, and we thought it prudent that you had someone around to make sure you minded your manners when dealing with…well, with people who grew up having things."

"You got wind?" Jason asked, giving Belford a side-eye glance. "How?"

Belford waved his hand. "We have our ways."

"So, what's your job here?" Jason asked.

"I'm here to make sure you don't screw it up," Belford replied cheerfully.

"Didn't you forget to bring handcuffs to work?" Jason said, and Les snorted.

Belford ignored the comment. "You didn't think we would let you walk into the apartment of the member of a respected family without any oversight, did you?" There was a slight laugh in his voice.

"If Swan wants you here, I can't stop it," Jason said. "But stay out of the way. I don't need someone tripping over you. And I don't need you screwing this up on a technicality."

It was Belford's turn to snort, a derisive thing. "Oh, you misunderstand…*Chief* Swan, your boss, wants *me* to handle any questioning of Ms. Dougherty."

Jason stopped walking and finally looked Belford in the eye. "You're kidding."

"No," Belford said, the grin never leaving his face. "No, I'm not. You're not to be trusted with dealing with these kinds of people, especially when those people are large contributors to many of the political elite. The damage you could do with a misspoken word or an errant accusation could be devastating."

Jason felt his face heat. "If she's harboring a suspect, or if she's breaking the law-"

"-you will do nothing," Belford interrupted. "Chief Swan's orders."

Jason felt Les squeeze his arm, and he realized his hand had clenched into a fist, and his heart was pounding against his ribcage. Les' simple message was easy for Jason to parse: *don't*.

Jason breathed in, then breathed out, hoping that some of the tension would go with it. "Fine." He turned to address the uniformed officers who were gathering around. "The suspect is Sergei Hirokawa. His photo has been sent to your phones. The apartment belongs to Sara Dougherty. Her pic's been sent to you as well. We don't know if Hirokawa is up there or not, but we need him detained, so eyes peeled." He felt his voice choke on the next words. Jason cleared his throat. "Do not engage Ms. Dougherty. Lieutenant Belford is the only one authorized to do so. Chief Swan's orders."

Jason pointedly did not look at Belford, but he knew the man had his arrogant, lopsided smile plastered on his face.

Les stepped forward. "Team One will take the east stairwell up, Team Two, you're going up the west stairs. Team Three, you're here in the lobby, Team Four, I want you watching the rear entrances. Nguyen?"

Nguyen showed her portable terminal. "I've got eyes on the roof right now."

Jason grunted. "No chance our bird gets diverted?"

Nguyen shrugged. "I don't think so, I've got it on manual control. If call traffic spikes I'll do my best to keep us out of the queue, but no guarantees."

Jason nodded. "Good enough for me. OK, on me."

Jason's team followed him to the stairs on the far side of the lobby while the other teams split off to their assigned positions.

When Jason saw the wall placard for the twelfth floor, he could hear his team huffing and puffing behind him and realized he was three flights above them. Belford was leading the pack and breathing heavily.

Want to fight now, you soft bastard? I'm not even a little winded.

A uniformed officer was close behind, and Les brought up the rear, practically wheezing and hacking up a lung from the exertion.

Jason waited until his team caught up before pulling open the heavy fire door and proceeding down the hall. He didn't know what he expected to see, but it wasn't the relatively mundane beige walls and industrial carpeting.

He spotted Team Two as they emerged from the west stairwell. They converged silently on apartment 12C.

His nose involuntarily wrinkled, his throat closed off at the odor of rotting meat and old fruit, and his heart dropped into his stomach.

Oh no.

He turned to Les and saw that Belford's face was turning green. "That's coming from in there, right?" he asked his partner.

Les nodded, seemingly unaffected by the pungent aroma. "No doubt."

Jason turned to the burly officer leading Team Two. "Take it."

The officer, who stood half a head taller than Jason and looked like he had tree trunks for legs, squared up on the apartment door, and with one massive kick, he booted the door open, splintering the latch and lock.

Both teams poured in, guns at the ready, with shouts of, "Police!"

Jason made it three steps into the apartment before he saw the blood on the window, enough that it looked more like a work of stained glass.

Shit.

He lost all his momentum, his gun hand falling limply to his side. The shouts from the other cops stopped as they came across the scene.

Blood splattered on the ceiling and walls, and soaked into the carpet, a dark reddish-brown. A dark smear started in the living room and disappeared into one of the bedrooms.

Jason willed his feet to move, despite every thought in his mind telling him not to go in there, not to look. One step, then another, then another, he trudged to where the smear seemed to terminate.

He thought that if he were to reassemble all of the parts, there would be two bodies; one male and one female, probably.

The only thing he was confident of was that one of the bodies belonged to Sergei Hirokawa, and it was only because the head was facing the wrong way on one of the torsos, and the dead eyes were staring at Jason.

"*Madre de dios,*" one of the cops behind him muttered.

He heard Belford vomiting noisily in another room. Jason holstered his gun, spun on his heel, and walked back towards the apartment door. He passed Belford dry heaving into a trash can.

"Your scene, lieutenant," Jason said and exited into the hall.

Les quickly caught up with him. "Are you leaving?"

"Yup," Jason said. "I'm tired of having these images in my head, and if Swan has such a bug up her ass about me talking to some rich kid that she has to send a babysitter, then let him deal with it."

Les shook his head. "Why are you baiting her like this?" Les grabbed Jason's arm and stopped him. "Seriously, you know this isn't going to fly. Why are you constantly poking the bear?"

Jason looked at his partner's hand holding onto his arm, and then at Les. The veteran cop released his grip.

"Which set of rules am I supposed to play by?" Jason demanded with a hiss. "Am I supposed to investigate crimes or play politics? Because it seems like it's one or the other, and I'm sick of it."

"Just do the job," Les said.

"I don't know what the fuck that is anymore!" Jason roared.

One of the officers stepped out into the hall and looked towards them, and Les waved them off.

"If I investigate a crime, I'm constantly berated and ridiculed by my boss, and I get constant interference," Jason growled. "If I investigate and step out of this invisible little box that Swan and whoever else wants me in, but they don't tell me where the lines are, I'm threatened with demotion. If I don't investigate something that they randomly assign to me, or I do investigate something they don't want me to for some arbitrary reason, my job is threatened. So please, tell me, what is the job?"

Les pulled Jason around a corner to an elevator lobby, out of sight of the open apartment door. "The job is what it is," he said. "Those first two scenarios…yeah, they suck, but it also means you still have a job, you have a pension, you have your benefits. You get your paycheck, and you go home, that's it. Scenario three, you're out of work. And you don't think that Swan and Belford and whoever else won't try to ruin you? Keep you from getting a decent job?"

"So just keep my head down?" Jason spat. "Just bend over and take it?"

"Yeah," Les said. "Because it's the only way you live to fight another day."

Is he right?

Jason's pride kept telling him to get on the elevator and return to the office, to focus on the Markus Kline case.

I don't want these images in my head anymore. I don't want to deal with any of this crap anymore.

But Les' words rang true.

If I get fired, or if I quit, that's it. Amira and I are back in The Gaps. No health insurance, no retirement, no paycheck. She would probably have to find work and leave the Foundation, and that's her baby.

"Gods damn it," Jason muttered.

"It sucks, I know," Les said. "Believe me, I know."

Jason turned around and started walking back to the apartment. Belford pushed through some officers on his way out and walked briskly towards the elevators, passing Jason and Les without looking at either of them.

"Where are you going?" Jason called after him, but there was no response. Belford disappeared around the corner, and a moment later, he heard the *ding* of an elevator door. "Did he just leave a crime scene?"

Les shrugged. "Not my farm, not my pigs. Let's just do our job."

CHAPTER 14

The task force office was under siege. Press vans and reporters filled the parking lot.

Guess they got wind of that last one.

Jason navigated the Mustang through a gaggle of reporters that immediately started peppering him with questions when he stepped out of the vehicle. He answered all with, "No comment." By the time he reached the door, he was exhausted.

Inside wasn't much of a relief. Every phone in the office rang incessantly, and every officer assigned to the unit was juggling several phones, making notes as quickly as possible, and doing their best to contain the chaos.

As Jason removed his headgear, Les approached and muttered, "Well, crap." He nodded towards Jason's office.

"What the-" Jason started and charged into his office. Derrick Belford sat in Jason's chair, paging through case files. "Get out of my chair."

Belford *tsk*ed and wagged his finger back and forth in a scolding manner without looking up. "Respect, lieutenant, it's *Captain* Belford, and no, I don't think I will. Not until I'm done my audit."

How the hell did he get promoted again? *And after he ran away from a crime scene?*

"Audit? Are you freaking kidding me? You were there, you saw that we just had a giant shit taken on the case, I've got new leads that we need to work…we don't have time for this."

"Bring me up to speed, lieutenant," Belford said in the same calm, demeaning tone.

"Let's see, we've got a bunch of bodies that look like they've been put through a wood chipper, a connection to a splice manufacturing ring that's much larger than any of us guessed, a suspect in the wind, all other known suspects are dead, and a missing kid that's connected to all of it. That about sum it up?"

Belford put the file down and carefully closed it before taking off his glasses and looking up at Jason. "Right there, that is part of your problem…you are too easily sidetracked. You were expressly told not to pursue the missing child as an investigative avenue. Chief Swan deemed it unnecessary and irrelevant to your larger drug investigation. Am I to understand that you deliberately defied her orders?" Jason saw the corner of Belford's mouth twitch in an anticipatory smile.

"Swan said not to use any task force resources to investigate the disappearance of Markus Kline, and I didn't," Jason replied. "Any investigation was on my time, and it turns out it is connected to our case."

"More of your *gut*?" Belford asked. "I don't see any evidence here that makes that connection."

"We have multiple bodies with *kardeşlik* ink. We have a description from the missing kid's friends of someone with a similar tattoo but with scars that don't match any of the victims."

"Ah, yes, your boogeyman theory," Belford said with a chuckle and pulled out two photos from the files he was perusing. "Lieutenant, it should be obvious to anyone that these are two different tattoos."

Jason mentally groaned. "Yes, but they are both *kardeşlik* tattoos, indicating that there may be a connection between them, especially given that each was present at the murder scenes and were seen running from the stash house during the raid."

"I'm sorry, I just don't see it. I think you're drawing connections where there are none, especially with the Gapper kid. You make no mention of it in any of your reports."

"Because we don't have official confirmation yet, because the last known suspect we had a lead on *just turned up dead*," Jason said, leaving the word "moron" unspoken.

"If it's not in the reports…" Belford sighed a contemptuous sigh. "Jason, I know we've had our issues-"

Jason barked out a laugh.

Belford's expression didn't change an iota. "At any rate…I like you, Jason. I do. You're one of the good ones. A good example of what a Gapper can make of themselves if they just apply themself. You really should be commended for what you have accomplished for yourself."

Jason took a deep breath to calm himself. "I'm sensing a 'but'…"

"…but," Belford continued, "you also have limitations. It's not your fault. Some people were born with…well…benefits, like being taller or faster."

"Or richer."

"Yes, or richer. It's important that you recognize that and come to terms with that. And we've reached a point where Chief Swan and I both think you're out of your depth with the investigation and the task force. Hence the audit to make that decision."

"How exactly did you reach that conclusion?" Jason demanded. "First, I don't answer to you, I answer directly to the CoD's. Second, we've taken more splice off the streets than any other efforts *combined*. Violent crime is down in the neighborhoods we've been focused on. Civilian complaints are down. By every metric, we've done more than what was expected."

Belford folded his hands on the desk. "Except finish the investigation. And there's the little matter of a trail of dead bodies, including an officer."

Jason realized he was unconsciously cracking his knuckles. "We're working those cases and everything else that Swan's dumped on us. We need more time."

"Jason," Belford said with a sigh and heaved himself to his feet. Jason could see the athlete that Derrick used to be after years of letting himself go and couldn't help but visualize punching him squarely in the face repeatedly. "The truth is we feel that the task force has run its course, and frankly, it did so a year ago. Any other commander would have had this wrapped up in a few weeks, three months at the outside. You've been siphoning department resources for months now-"

"Siphoning?" Jason realized he was close to yelling and brought his volume back down. "I know you don't have the experience working in the field, but this is how the job is done. You chase down leads, you interview people, you walk the streets and you make sure you leave no stone unturned. Details matter, and it takes time to get them right."

Belford waived off the comment. "And now there's this…whatever this circus is," and he gestured to the outer room where detectives and officers frantically answered calls and waded through the flood of media attention.

"That? That's either you or her, and honestly, I don't care which," Jason growled. "You've both been playing these games since the task force was formed, throwing all these stupid obstacles in our way. Whether it was for fun or you are that bigoted that you would put getting a Gapper out of command ahead of the greater good, I don't know, and again, I don't care."

The self-satisfied smile that twisted Belford's face into something grotesque as he sat back down in Jason's chair told Jason all he needed to know. "I don't know what you're talking about."

Jason started formulating a plan. He was pretty sure it was a bad one, but at this point, it was better than no plan. He turned on his heel and marched out of his office. He affixed his headgear and walked outside to the reporters crowding the door. There was a moment of silence, as if the reporters were shocked by Jason's sudden appearance, and then the opening salvo of questions began.

Jason held up his hands for silence. "My name is Lieutenant Jason Thane. I'm the commanding officer of the splice task force, and we are also the ones that have been assigned the murders you've been reporting on. I wanted to clarify a few things for you and hopefully put some people's minds at ease.

"No, this is not a serial killer. The murders are directly linked to the ongoing investigation into splice trafficking and manufacture.

"What's more, we are looking for this boy," Jason said and tapped on his phone, sending Markus' picture to the nearby phones. "This is Markus Kline. He's twelve years old, and he's been missing for five days. We believe he is a material witness in our investigation, and we have reason to believe that he's in danger."

Jason sent the photo of Zeke from Greenway's website. "We are also looking for this man. We believe he is directly connected to both the murders and Markus' disappearance."

The press gaggle stayed silent, hanging on his every word.

"Questions?"

The journalists erupted.

Forty-five minutes later, Jason reentered the office. Nguyen was the first to start clapping, and soon the entire squad joined her, and some added a few whistles for good measure.

Belford, however, was not happy; Jason judged by how red his face was and the baleful glare he bored into Jason. He marched up to Jason and stopped when his face was mere inches from Jason's.

"Who do you think you are?" Belford seethed. "How dare you? You do not have the authority to-"

"I'm just playing by the same rules you are," Jason interrupted. "I have a job to do, and I'm using the tools available. You want the investigation closed, right?"

Belford stabbed Jason in the chest with a finger. "You are suspended. You are off the task force. You will be off the job when we're done."

"You're going to pull back a bloody stump if you poke me again," Jason said. "Last I checked, you don't have the authority for any of that, and if you're threatening my job, I think I would like my union rep present."

The two men stood toe-to-toe for half a minute, taking Jason back to when they did the same for the promo photos for their fight many years ago.

Belford was the first to back down. He stormed into Jason's office and gathered his things, along with several files. He started affixing his headgear and stormed towards the front door.

"Leave the files, Captain," Les said. "We need those. Or would you like to explain to the press why you're removing documents relevant to an open narcotics and murder investigation?"

Belford froze and turned to stare down Les, but the veteran had already turned back to his desk and returned to work. The ruddy captain stared daggers at Les' back for a moment, then slapped the files down on Les' desk. He turned to the rest of the squad. "Chief Swan has officially ordered that no one from the task force is to investigate the missing kid. You are ordered to conclude all active investigations by the end of the week and then report back to your precincts for reassignment. Failure to comply with these orders will result in immediate suspension, and you will be brought up on formal disciplinary charges. Are you clear?"

The room answered in defiant silence. A few of the squad were subtly making a Gapper sign that implied an inappropriate relationship between the captain and a goat, but Belford either didn't know the sign, or see it, or acknowledge it.

"You just signed your own walking papers," Belford said to Jason and slammed the door behind him.

"It'll be fine," Les finally said. "Right? I'm sure everything will be fine." Jason could tell he didn't believe his own words.

"What now?" Nguyen asked. "Want us to start a new canvas for info on Markus?"

"No," Jason said. "I don't want anyone going near that."

The squad started to protest, and Jason held up his hand. "What I did was stupid and short-sighted. We have two days to finish the investigation right, and we're not going to spend that time in a pissing contest with Swan. Focus your efforts on the murder investigation. I want viable suspects by roll call tomorrow morning."

The squad murmured their acquiescence. Jason gestured to Les towards his office. Les picked up the files and brought them with him. They took their seats, and Les closed the door.

"You're not giving up on the Markus angle," Les said. It was a statement, not a question.

"No, but I need to give the rest of them cover."

"Pretty sure they don't believe you're giving up on that angle either," Les said.

"Plausible deniability," Jason replied.

Les handed over one of the files. "What are you thinking?"

Jason pulled his notes up on his phone. "One of the neighborhood kids said he saw someone with the same tattoo working in Markus' apartment. Said he was taking an interest in the video game they were playing. Said his name was Zeke."

"Well, that's right out of the Kidnapping for Dummies handbook," Les said. "So, we've got Zeke in the room with our missing kid. We've got the missing kid in the stash house."

"Where we also have our first murder scene," Jason continued. "Second murder scene has someone with the same *kardeşlik* tattoo as Zeke, same MO as the first scene."

"Think Zeke is our perp and our kid snatcher?"

"Nope," Jason said. "I think Zeke is the snatcher, but someone else is hunting him. Someone is looking for him and is offing anyone that may have had contact with him."

Les nodded. "Yeah, that fits. But how does this tie to Markus? If he witnessed the murder and our perp knew that, he would've just killed the kid, right? We're not talking about a precise assassin here, whoever this is, it's the equivalent of throwing a running chainsaw into a fight."

"Agreed," Jason said. "The only thing I'm left with is that Markus was in the stash house at one point but wasn't there when the murders happened. Follow me on this, and tell me if I missed something."

"What are you doing, kid?"

Jason cocked his head to the side. "What do you mean?"

"I mean, *what are you doing?*"

"I'm working the case," Jason said.

"No, you're *avoiding* the case," Les said. "You're throwing yourself into the Markus Kline thing because you're avoiding the murder cases."

Jason's back stiffened. "That's not what I'm doing."

Les shook his head. "Kid, ordinarily, I would let you work this out on your own, work through whatever's living rent-free in your skull, but honestly…you're starting to scare me, and I just don't have the time to wait for you to figure it out, or the energy to break in a new partner if you don't."

"I'm fine," Jason said, returning to his notes.

"You're not," Les said. "You're starting to remind me of *him*."

"Him who?" Jason asked, but he knew the answer. "I'm nothing like Jordan was."

"Yeah, you are," Les said. "You're just too close to it to see it. And I'm telling you, this road doesn't end well."

Is he right?

Jason sighed and tossed his phone on his desk. "Look, maybe…maybe I am putting more energy into Markus' case than I should, or than I usually would…but no one else is doing anything about it."

Les rapped his knuckles on the desk. "Right there, that's what I'm saying. Markus Kline isn't your responsibility. The murders, the task force, they are."

"Yeah, and now it looks like all of it is connected, even Markus." Jason leaned back in his chair and stared at the ceiling.

I'm not avoiding anything.

He almost believed it.

"Here's the deal…I'm going to keep looking into Markus. He's connected to the stash house, which means he's connected to the murders. You can either help me, or you can leave."

Les shook his head at Jason, and he felt the silent judgment from the veteran. Then Les reluctantly nodded for Jason to continue. "Stubborn bastard. OK, shoot."

"Zeke is *kardeşlik*. Based on the last two bodies, let's assume that so were the guys in the stash house.

Let's assume, for the moment, that they were all part of the same *unuo.*"

"Makes sense," Les said.

"So, we know they were a major player in the splice trade. None of the money or drugs were taken when whoever went ham on all of them in there did the deed, so it wasn't a rival cartel or gang or anything."

"No motivation for it," Les agreed.

"Markus was the only thing that was there at one point, that wasn't when we got there. He's the X factor. It's the only thing out of the ordinary about that crime scene."

"So, what...the kid saw the operation, so whoever's higher on the ladder burns the whole operation?" Les asked. "Seems a bit extreme."

"No, I think it's the other way around," Jason replied. "I think the crew there saw Markus, and they weren't supposed to."

Les stroked his chin. "You think that this guy Zeke was involved in something separate from the rest of the crew, and, what...he accidentally crossed the streams?"

Jason nodded absently. "Yeah, it's the only thing that makes sense with what we know. If Zeke was involved with abducting Markus for whatever reason, and he stopped up there with the kid...someone finds out that the guys at the stash house have learned that Zeke is involved with a kidnapping and doesn't want the crew to know about it...that's thin, right?"

"Anorexic," Les agreed. "But I guess it could be possible. Only see one problem."

"It would mean that whoever was watching the stash house also was directing the kidnapping," Jason said, and Les nodded. "It would explain why the initial attack happened so quickly after Zeke was there. And why everyone we saw running in the drone footage has been hunted down."

"Still," Les said, "it's thin. You would need more to get any kind of support from the DA. And you still need to have a suspect for who's been offing all these guys."

Jason leaned back in his chair. The butt groove felt wrong from Belford sitting in it. "I mean...there is one suspect..."

"You don't seriously think..." Les started. "*The Bear?* You're not buying into that urban myth bullshit, are you?

"It's as good a theory as any until we know more," Jason said.

"What's the plan?"

"We don't know anything about The Bear, so the only option is Zeke. If I find him, maybe I can get some answers. He's at the center of all of this. He's also the only one left, as best I can tell."

"OK, one, what's this 'I' crap? You're not doing this by yourself," Les protested.

Jason shook his head. "Nope, I'm flying solo on this. I need you here to keep the trains running on time and to keep me in the loop. I know that Swan and Belford aren't done screwing with us, especially after my little stunt."

"Yeah, you kicked a hornet's nest," Les agreed. "I can run interference here, then, but if you need any help..."

"Yeah, I know, you're my first call," Jason said. "You said 'one'...is there a 'two'?"

"Two, how are you going to find Zeke? All you have is a name, and this guy's been a ghost so far.

Might not even be his real name. And after the media circus today, he's definitely on the run. He's too hot even for his *kardeşlik* buddies, so he's on his own."

"Got an idea for that, too," Jason said. "I think there's sufficient pressure now that Greenway will be a little more forthcoming with information."

"Probably," Les said. "You get a name, run it through the system. Then what?"

"Then I go hunting."

CHAPTER 15

The clouds finally ended their respite, and the rain returned. The streets remained clear of pedestrians; most UV gear wasn't enough to provide safety from the tainted precipitation. Jason noted once again the far cry from life just several blocks away, where the sun shields diverted and filtered the rain, protecting the more affluent citizens from the very planet that, at times, seemed hell-bent on evicting all of humanity.

To be fair, we haven't been the best tenants.

Jason sat in the Mustang, headgear on, headlights off, wipers working to keep the windshield clear. He wanted to be able to move at a moment's notice if he needed to and silently dealt with the discomfort of wearing his full gear in the stuffy car. The muted tapping of rain on the roof and windows threatened to lull him to sleep, but he shook his head and warded off the drowsiness.

He repeated the name to himself that Greenway had been more than happy to give him after his impromptu press conference. Saying it aloud made it more real to him, and kept it imprinted in his memory. "Ezekiel Falstaff."

Jason was always amazed at what could be gleaned from a name, even a fake one, as he was sure this one was. Employment records, credit reports, known addresses…so much information. Jason knew that much of the information would lead to dead ends, but it at least gave him a place to start.

Jason had started with the most promising nugget: the pickup truck Ezekiel drove to and from work, identified in the surveillance footage Greenway had also enthusiastically given him access to.

There was a knock on his passenger window. Jason unlocked the door, and K-Dawg hopped in, quickly shutting the door behind him. His hoodie was soaked through, and Jason was sure it would start falling apart within a day as the rainwater broke down the fabric. The color was already starting to bleach out where the water had saturated it.

They sat in silence for a minute, K-Dawg staring straight ahead. Everything about the kid's body language told Jason that he was nervous. None of the corner kid bravado showed, just a teenager that was scared someone would see him talking to a cop, Jason figured.

Jason jumped when his phone rang. He silenced the call without looking at it and muted all notifications.

I don't need distractions right now.

Jason broke the silence. "You ever call in a fake 911 call?"

K-Dawg sucked air through his teeth, an odd sound through his comm. "Shit, who's talking out of school?"

They actually do that? Old Head Fred was right?

"No one, Obi-Wan…just don't do it anymore, OK?"

They returned to uncomfortable silence.

"Motel up on the Boulevard. Next to a packaged good jawn," K-Dawg finally shared.

Jason made a note on his phone. "Someone saw Zeke?"

"Nah, that truck," K-Dawg replied. "If someone saw him, they'd prolly drop his ass." He mimed a gun and then *kill*. "Kid touching shithead."

"Hey," Jason said, but K-Dawg kept looking forward. "*Hey*." The teenager finally turned to look at Jason. "No bodies over this. Flat out. I need him alive, it's the only way I find Markus. If this dude's body shows up on a slab, I'm going to rain hell down on everyone, and I'm starting with you. *Everyone*. Got it?" K-Dawg nodded his assent. "Make sure people know that. Spread the word."

K-Dawg's body language shifted as his corner kid armor came back up, all swagger and attitude. He started to open the door when Jason caught his arm.

"Thank you," Jason said and signed *honest*. "You're a good kid, Obi-Wan. Don't let anyone tell you otherwise."

K-Dawg paused, and for just a moment, Jason thought the kid was going to say something, but instead, he nodded and stepped out of the Mustang. He jammed his hands in his pockets and skulked down the street.

Jason had never been on assignment to the area where K-Dawg had directed him, but he had heard stories: a den of debauchery, hell-on-earth, the gutter of the city.

The reality didn't live up to the hype in Jason's opinion as he navigated the roads into a tangle of highway junctions, rest stops, motels, and domiciles all stacked up on each other. Even at this time of night, traffic abounded as US 1 interchanged with Interstate 95 and Interstate 76, and agricultural deliveries from the grow houses that covered what used to be wide-open farmland to the north poured into the depots, ready to be loaded into waiting trucks and transported across the region.

Jason could also see how it would be effortless to get lost here, to disappear in the riot of people and commerce. If Ezekiel Falstaff was here, he had picked a good spot.

As he slowed down to allow a truck to exit the parking lot in front of him, Jason wished not for the first time that K-Dawg had been a little more specific with his information. There were dozens of motels in the district, and easily as many were next to the little shops that sold wine coolers and cold beer by the six-pack.

He pulled into the parking lot of the sixth motel and slowly cruised through. He was about to write it off and move on to the next one when he spotted a pickup tucked way in the back corner of the lot. Jason felt his heart rate pick up as he neared and checked the plate number.

It matched.

He found a vacant spot across the street from the parking lot, not wanting to draw attention, threw the car in park, and waited.

Jason drummed his fingers on the steering wheel and weighed his options. He didn't know which room Ezekiel was staying in, and he doubted he could get it from the front desk. He couldn't bring a tactical team in to seal off the area.

Minutes passed as Jason stared at the pickup truck.

I could just take a look inside.

He dismissed the idea outright, and was surprised the idea even came to him.

It would be an illegal search. None of the evidence would be able to be used.

He tried to think back to a time when he had gone outside of the rules laid out by the law, some time when he had bent the letter of the law to do something good.

No memory came to mind.

Maybe if someone else had been willing to bend the rules, they would have found Alexei sooner…before the fire…

That thought stuck with him.

The ends don't justify the means. But maybe there's some wiggle room…

He could just take a quick look in the truck. Anything he saw through the windows would be fair game. He made a decision.

He waited another minute, telling himself it was to make sure he didn't miss Ezekiel, knowing deep down it was to procrastinate.

Jason's heart beat even faster. "Now or never," he whispered to himself. He grabbed his phone, hopped out of the car with the engine still idling, and jogged across the street. He snapped a quick photo of the license plate. He pulled a sample kit from his pocket and swabbed the driver's side door handle; he knew it was a long shot that any genetic material remained after driving through the rain, but he also knew he had to try.

He cupped his hands on the driver's side window to see through the glare from the omnipresent street lights and screens blaring advertisements. There was a phone on the center console, a half-empty pack of smokes, and a book on the passenger seat, the kind that Jason used in high school to take notes during chemistry class.

After a glance around to see if anyone was watching, he stole around the passenger side, where he was blocked from sight from any of the motel rooms. He tried the handle but wasn't shocked when it didn't open. He peered in through the window.

"Don't do this," he said to himself. "This is stupid." He knew he could wait for the license plate to come back and for the DNA scan to finish running. He would have this guy's identity in a day, maybe two. Maybe enough to justify a warrant to get into the truck...

He knew that the DNA would come back negative, what with all of the crap in the rainwater. It could degrade trace DNA in minutes.

And he knew there was a chance the plate wouldn't turn up anything useful. The last eighteen months had shown him how resourceful everyone in the illicit drug trade was when it came to escaping detection and concealing their identities. And if this guy was *kardeşlik*, he probably knew all the tricks.

The case is circumstantial at best right now. No solid evidence, only a frame of video and the word of a kid.

He remembered the day Amira had been brought to his house. The day her dad was arrested. The day they found out about the fire and what had happened to Alexei and his mother. The day he first felt genuine anger, something primal deep inside that he didn't know had been there, aimed at every adult who didn't seem to want to take action when his friend had first disappeared. *"He'll turn up,"* they had said. *"These things always work themselves out."*

"Screw it," he said to himself. He reached into his jacket and pulled out the standard issue slim jim used for getting keys out of locked cars. In one smooth motion, he slid it between the window and the weather stripping, caught the mechanism, and yanked up, releasing the lock.

"Shit," he hissed. *No going back now.* He opened the door and flipped open the notebook. He snapped a picture of the first page it opened to, then turned to another and took another photo. He tried to flip to another page, but he fumbled it, and it slid to the floor. He quickly picked it up, put it back on the seat, and tried to grab the phone from the console, but he was off balance and misjudged the distance. The phone skittered away from his fingers and onto the driver's seat.

Jason collected two DNA swabs from the steering wheel and gear shift. He slid backward out of the car, and his foot slipped, sitting him down on the wet pavement outside the truck. He reached up and pushed the door shut as quietly as he could. He stole back to his car and climbed in, and waited.

The silence in the car quickly became oppressive, and Jason felt like something was missing. Then he realized he hadn't heard his phone buzz with notifications in a couple of hours. He checked it and remembered he had silenced it; he pressed the button to bring it back online.

After a moment of connecting to the network, it pulsed with a notification. Then again. Then it began pulsing in rapid succession from all of the missed notifications.

Six missed calls from Amira, plus two from Les. More missed text messages from Amira. He finally opened them.

WHERE ARE YOU?
PLEASE WRITE BACK
I NEED YOU HOME
HOW FAR AWAY ARE YOU?
COME HOME 911

Jason felt his stomach bottom out as he read the messages. Amira was not someone that panicked easily.

And you ignored her messages.

He checked his GPS. It would be 45 minutes before he would be at his house, provided that traffic didn't slow him any further.

ON MY WAY

The flashing lights in front of his house only served to raise further Jason's anxiety level beyond where it had gone on the ride over. Two patrollers were parked out front, as was Les' beat-up jeep.

Jason screeched to a stop in his spot and ran into the house. He burst into the front door. Amira was in the hall, picking up debris from the floor, and Lydia Lacroix was in the den, sweeping. Les was by Amira's side, and a uniformed officer was making notes on her phone.

The first floor was trashed. Furniture was torn to pieces like someone had taken a knife to it. A spider web of cracks marred the television screen. There were holes in the walls. Down the hall, he could see the remnants of water on the kitchen floor that had been partially mopped up. Spray paint covered just about every surface.

Jason stepped closer to his wife and saw that she had been crying. Les had a hand on her shoulder and spoke quietly to her in a calming tone. He could also see that someone had spray-painted GO HOME BLISTER BACKS and DIE GAPPER DIE on one of the walls.

"Are you OK?" he asked Amira as he tried to pull her into a hug.

She shrugged him off and went back to cleaning up. "Yeah, I'm fine, it was like this when I got home."

The anxiety that had been building in him gave way to a boiling rage deep inside him, rivaled by the immense guilt he felt for not responding to Amira's messages sooner. The way she was purposely avoiding looking at him told him all he needed to know.

I'm in deep shit.

"Any leads?" Jason asked his partner to divert his thoughts.

Les shook his head. "No forced entry, alarm wasn't tripped. Looked at the doorbell camera footage, looks like three people, but they were all wearing pretty generic-looking gear, nothing that would identify them. Sorry."

"We're going to assign two observer drones out front tonight, Lieutenant," the uniformed officer said. "We'll have a car out here as well. They probably won't come back, but just to be safe."

"I don't want to stay here tonight," Amira said to Jason, ignoring everyone else in the room.

"We'll get a hotel," Jason said.

"I already booked one," she said. "You'll have to figure out where you're staying."

Jason felt the air get sucked out of the room. "Hey, look, can we talk?"

"There's nothing to talk about," she said, then looked to Lydia. "Do you remember where I put the spray cleaner?"

Jason tried to find the words to explain what was going on in his head. "I'm sorry, I was on a stakeout, I didn't think-"

"It's fine," she said, still not looking at him. "Never mind, Lydia, I left it upstairs." She walked up to the second floor, completely ignoring Jason.

When Jason was sure she was out of earshot, he turned to Les. "You know who did this."

"Swan supporters, anti-Gapper bigoted pricks," Les said. "Yeah, after your show today, not shocked that they got their underwear in a twist, but this? This is an escalation. And we can't prove anything."

"I don't need to prove it to know it," Jason said, feeling the urge to put another hole in the wall with his fist.

"Just calm down, OK?" Les said, placing a hand on Jason's arm. "I get it, this is a huge violation. But you need to take care of Amira tonight, she's freaked out. And if you go off on a crusade for vengeance, you'll only be playing right into Swan's game."

Jason looked up the stairs. "I don't know that she wants my help right now."

Les shrugged. "I don't know what to tell you other than what I already have. Your actions have consequences. You keep flying off half-cocked, flinging yourself at a brick wall, hoping that *something different will happen this time*."

"You think that makes *this* OK," he said in a harsh whisper, gesturing to the damage.

"No, I'm not saying that," Les said, keeping his voice low and calm. "But whether you or I or anyone else thinks it's OK, it doesn't matter. It just *is*. It's the way it's always been. You need to let this go and don't go poking at it. It will only get worse."

Jason took a deep breath, but the anger didn't abate. "I don't know that I can let this go."

"You have to," Les said. "Let me handle it. If there's something to find, I'll find it, and if there's something I can do, I'll do it. But you need to steer clear of this," he said, gesturing to the room. "You're too close. Take Amira to a hotel, get a night's sleep, and we'll catch up in the morning. You can tell me how your thing went tonight, if it did at all, that is."

Jason remembered the pictures on his phone. *The illegally obtained ones.* "Yeah, it went, I think…but I need to follow up on something first thing in the morning. I'll see you at the office."

Les nodded, pocketed his notepad, and patted Jason on the shoulder. He gestured to the uniformed officer, and both exited in silence, leaving Jason alone with Lydia.

Jason grabbed a garbage bag and started putting debris into it, unsure what else to do. He was sure that Amira didn't want to see him right then. Leaving didn't seem to be an option that would result in anything other than another fight with her. So, he cleaned.

"You need to let her in," Lydia said from the other room.

"I do let her in," Jason replied.

"Not about your work," Lydia countered. "You keep that part completely closed off."

Jason started to deny it but realized Lydia wasn't wrong. "I just don't want to dump that on her," he finally said. "She doesn't need that stuff bouncing around in her skull. Hell, I don't even want it in mine."

"She's a big girl. She can handle it. Let her decide what she does and doesn't want to know." She looked up the steps. "But blocking that part of your life out entirely? That's not working. For either of you."

Jason picked up a chunk of drywall and stuffed it in the bag. "I think I really screwed up this time."

"She's not happy," Lydia agreed. "Where were you?"

"I was staking out a motel. Trying to track down this guy tied to the child abduction."

Lydia stopped cleaning. "I thought your task force was focused on splice manufacturing and distribution or something like that."

Jason chuckled. "Yeah, well, I've been kind of neglecting that part of my job entirely for the last couple of days. I've been hyper-focused on this missing kid…just my past coming back to haunt me, I guess. And I'm close to finding this guy I've been looking for, the one I'm pretty sure is the one that took him."

"And what…the splice investigation is just done?"

"No, but it might as well be," Jason said as he tied the garbage bag closed. "We found a stash house and made a huge seizure, so we were on to something, but all of the people who were there were murdered so thoroughly that we can't even ID the bodies through DNA. We can't tell where one victim ends, and the next one begins, so we're basically at square one. So that's screwed. And now…" He left the rest of his sentence unspoken as he gestured upstairs.

Lydia put down her broom and approached Jason. "Look…she just needs time. Give her space, and give her the night. She'll be OK." She put a comforting hand on Jason's shoulder. "And buy her something nice. It never hurts."

Amira came back down the steps with two bags. "I threw some stuff in a bag for you in case you want to stay somewhere else tonight," she said, and Jason noted she pointedly did not look at the destruction around her. "Lydia, can you give me a lift?"

Lydia nodded and started gathering her things.

"You sure you're OK?" Jason asked.

"No, I'm not," she said in clipped words. "Someone broke into our house and trashed it. They spray-painted horrible things on our wall. I'm not OK."

Jason noticed her hands were shaking. He reached over and took them into his. There were things he wanted to say to her, things like, "It will be OK," and, "We'll find who did this," but they all sounded to him like mindless platitudes. He opted to hold her hands in silence instead, and she didn't flinch away.

"Do you think," Amira started, then stopped. She looked like she was mentally wrestling with a question. "Do you think this had anything to do with your comments to the press?"

Jason let go of her hands and jammed them in his pockets. Guilt mixed in with his anger. "Yeah, I do," he said. "I'm sorry about that."

"It's not your fault," Amira said, and Jason almost believed her. "Maybe it's time to…you know…start looking towards the future."

Jason stilled. He didn't like the turn he thought the conversation was taking. "How so?"

"You're obviously at odds with Chief Swan, and you know she's never going to let you be promoted," Amira said. "And you've been pretty miserable the last year or so. You don't seem to like the job anymore, not the way you used to."

"It's only been miserable because of the interference that Swan constantly throws my way. If she'd just let me do my job-"

"But she won't," Amira interrupted. "You know she won't. So, wishing for that is an exercise in futility, right?"

Jason agreed but remained motionless. He knew what was coming next.

"Maybe it's time to look for something else," she said.

Jason measured his words and tone. "I'm a cop. This is what I do. I need to do *this*."

"OK," Amira said.

"You're mad."

"No, I'm fine," Amira said.

"You don't sound fine."

"I am. I'll see you tomorrow."

Lydia held the vestibule door open as Amira donned her cycler and goggles, and then both women exited into the night.

Is she right?

Jason pushed the thought away. His wife's words weighed heavy on his mind, and the pictures of the notebook weighed heavy on his conscience.

Ezekiel Fallstaff and, hopefully, Markus Kline were still out there. He hoped they could wait until morning.

CHAPTER 16

The corrections officer stared at Jason through the bulletproof glass and slowly drummed his fingers on the desk. With a heavy and annoyed sigh, he picked up the phone next to him and punched in a number. A few inaudible words were spoken. He hung up the phone, and the metal drawer in front of Jason slid open. "Gun and any other prohibited items."

Jason surrendered the items and shed his jacket into the collection bin, and the drawer slid shut with a loud scrape and a bang. The barred door next to him opened with a loud buzz, and he stepped through. Another guard was there to lead him to one of the visiting rooms.

They entered the large cell that served as a meeting room. Jason took a seat at the bolted-down bench and waited.

Several minutes later, his father-in-law was led in. The same ritual of unlocking his restraints was undertaken; the guard left, the door shut with finality, and Jordan took a seat at the table across from Jason.

"Odd seeing you this early. What's up?" he asked.

Jason felt his mouth go dry. He wanted to speak, but the words wouldn't come out.

"You OK, son?"

"I, uh..." Jason started.

No, I'm not.

"Out with it, kid," Jordan said. Not commanding, but encouraging.

My boss hates me and I keep sticking my thumb in her eye.

Everyone at work hates me because of where I was born.
My home isn't safe anymore.
Your daughter isn't speaking to me.
Oh, and then I did this...

Jason brought up the photos from the previous night and slid the phone across the table. "I may have screwed up."

Jordan looked at the phone but didn't move to touch it. "What is it?"

Jason calmed himself with a deep breath. "Stolen." It came out sounding like a question.

Jordan grunted but still made no move towards the phone. "From?"

"A suspect. Look," Jason said, trying to change gears, "I got this, and I don't know what to do with it. Anything I get from it..."

"Fruit from the poisoned tree," Jordan finished. He examined Jason's face, and a look of recognition settled in. "Jason, you aren't the first cop to get some evidence by less-than-legal means. Doesn't make it right, but it also doesn't mean you're corrupt, either, get it? What matters is how you use that information."

Jason shook his head. "I've never done anything like this before, and honestly, I don't even know if this guy has done anything wrong. It's just a thin theory."

"How thin?" Jordan asked with a cocked eyebrow.

"*Thin.*"

Jordan sighed. "Well, we're here now, can't put the toothpaste back in the tube. This for your missing kid?"

Jason nodded. "I didn't know who else to bring this to. Anyone I show it to at work, it makes them liable. I don't think anyone would go to Swan or IAB over it, but I don't want to put them in that position, and honestly," he said, "I'm embarrassed."

"Well, let's hope the ends justify the means. Let's take a look."

Jason zoomed in on one of the photos. The pages were filled from top to bottom with numbers ordered in columns. "I think these are dates," Jason said, pointing to one column. "These, too. And these here might be times. But these columns?" Jason tapped at a column of what looked like random letters and numbers. "No idea."

"What's this guy do?" Jordan asked as he spun the phone to face him and put on his reading glasses.

"Day job appears to be an installer for a sun shield company," Jason said. "But he was also at the scene where we found the stash house and the bodies, and where Markus lived and went missing. We also think he's *kardeşlik*."

Jordan silently examined the photos.

"I think you're right about the times and dates," Jordan said. "This column, I'm almost one-hundred percent sure these are coordinates."

Jason squinted at the numbers. "Doesn't look like anything I've seen."

Jordan chuckled. "Encryption via obsolescence. These are LORAN coordinates. Don't think anyone uses that system anymore, what with all of the GPS satellites. Not terribly accurate, but accurate enough."

"So, dates, times, locations…then what's this?" Jason asked, pointing to a string of numbers and letters at the top of the photo.

Jordan zoomed in on the string. "There's some repetition between the sequences, and it doesn't look random…my guess is it's a code of some sort."

"A code for what, though?" Jason wondered aloud.

Jordan shrugged. "Couldn't tell ya. You're supposed to be the detective." Jordan tapped at the string of letters and numbers again. "But experience tells me that you're onto something here. Figure out the code, you'll figure out what he's hiding. Do that, and you'll probably be able to find another way to get the evidence you need without having to use the notebook."

"What if it's just his bank deposits or something he's trying to hide?"

"If it is, then whatever, you delete the photos and pretend you never had them," Jordan said, pushing the phone back, "but I'll bet all of the money in my pockets against all of the money in your pockets that it isn't as innocent as that. This is the kind of thing bookies do to hide their business. This guy is up to something." Jordan's face sagged into a sad smile. "Old cop's intuition or something, whatever it's worth."

Jason felt the guilt of dredging up painful memories intermingle with relief that he hadn't just potentially screwed his career for nothing. "It's worth a lot to me. Thank you."

"Still didn't say where you got it," Jordan said.

"Honestly, it was a wild hunch. Saw some new solar shields going up in poorer areas, seemed out of place to me. Turns out the company this guy is working for is installing them. Saw his picture on the company website, and his ink looked the same as someone we've been looking for." Jason chuckled to himself. "Guess corporate greed might be paying out for once."

Jordan's eyebrows knitted. "What do you mean?"

"The company is Greenway Protectives, that same one you investigated for the fake burglary. They're participating in a grant program through Majora Global for the installs, so everything gets subsidized. Like I said, it's completely random that I followed this..." Jason trailed off when he saw his father-in-law's face go pale. "What?"

"Drop the case." There was panic laced in every word Jordan spoke. "Now. Walk away."

"What are you talking about?" Jason said, standing. "You told me to follow the evidence wherever, remember? You said-"

"Fuck what I said!" Jordan spat, slamming both hands on the table with a loud *bang*. A guard looked in through the window, and Jason waved him away. "Walk away from this now. Right now. Forget everything, burn that thing," he said and pointed at the phone, "and just...just stop."

Jason slowly sat back down, but Jordan was practically panting, his fingertips attempting to dig into the tabletop. "Jordan, you need to calm down. What are you freaking out about?"

"Do you want to leave Amira alone? By herself?" The words were shouted, almost bestial, spat at Jason, and Jordan was half out of his seat. "Do you?" A guard started fiddling with the lock on the door to open it.

"No, of course not, Jordan, but Jesus, what are you talking about?"

The door burst open, and three guards filed in. "Time's up," one said in a tone that brokered no argument.

Jordan fumed as he looked over his shoulder with pure hate at the guards, snapped his attention back to Jason, and stared him in the eyes. The ferocity was there, but also desperation, Jason saw, not aimed at him. "How do you think I ended up in here? Who do you think put me in this cesspool? You need to-"

Jordan was cut off when three fired tasers sent him into convulsions and dropped him to the floor.

"What the hell?" Jason demanded.

"You need to leave now, detective," one of the guards said as she holstered her taser. "You've got him worked up." She nodded to the other two guards, who lifted the semi-conscious Jordan from the floor as gently as possible while maintaining control of him. "Get him to Medical."

"Did you have to do that?" Jason felt sick seeing Jordan that way. "He was just upset."

The guard looked Jason straight in the eye. "Last time he was like this he gouged another inmate's eye out with his thumb. We can't have him on the floor like this." Her expression softened slightly, almost where Jason wasn't sure he hadn't imagined it. "He'll be all right, he just needs rest. We'll take care of him."

She gestured towards the door, and Jason slowly made his way back out to the real world.

Guess we can add breaking the man who is as close to a father as I've known to the list of things I've screwed up.

Jason jolted awake, rubbed his eyes, and checked the time on his phone; nine in the morning. He remembered getting to the office after he visited with Jordan and shutting his eyes for a moment right after setting the DNA samples to run…

He took a deep breath, wiped the drool from the corner of his mouth, and stepped out of his office. The bullpen was quiet, save for the faint ticking the building made as the structure subtly expanded in the daily heat. He figured everyone was out in the field and had opted to let him sleep. They had undoubtedly heard about the excitement at his home.

Jason plopped into his office chair, and stretched and twisted, his back making popping sounds as he did. He made a mental note that he needed an update from the team to include in his next report. He checked the coffee brewer and it was already filled with fresh grounds; from the pungent aroma, someone had filled it with the high-test stuff. He started the pot brewing and plopped down in a chair someone had brought in for their "break room". He took another deep breath, trying to clear the remnants of sleep from his mind.

While the pot brewed, he checked his phone for messages: no new alerts, no missed calls.

Jordan's reaction haunted him. He had never seen his father-in-law so out of control, so seemingly manic. It was a reaction he was used to seeing when someone was on a bad batch of splice, or was far into their withdrawal from it, from someone who had begun to lose touch with reality.

Jason held his phone for another moment, then pocketed it, retrieved a cup of freshly-brewed coffee, and took it into his office. He pulled up the DNA results he had run on the swabs from Ezekiel's truck. As he expected, the exposure to the rain last night had degraded the trace DNA enough that results were inconclusive.

The truck plates had come up as belonging to a Mildred Pierce, a 77-year-old widow living in one of the upscale townhouses across the river in New Camden. No known associates or family matched Ezekiel, so Jason was sure the plates were either stolen or scammed, a trademark move in the illegal drug trade.

"At least I know you're up to no good," he said aloud, comforting himself that he hadn't violated the rights of an innocent citizen. *Nope, just the rights of a criminal.* He didn't like the feeling that he was trying to convince himself that it was somehow different or OK.

He pulled the printouts of the notebook photos in front of him, stared at the columns of numbers and letters again, and reached for the highlighters in his desk drawer. Idly, he highlighted letters he saw repeated.

An hour later and an empty cup of coffee later, he didn't feel like he had made any progress. He glanced between the copied page and his notebook where he had scrawled down his attempts at decoding. Each time he thought he had it worked out, the decoded strings turned into nonsense, just another random jumble of letters and no words.

He sat back in his chair, rubbed his eyes with the heels of his hands, and stared blankly at the unhelpful DNA results on his screen. Then he looked closer. Under the "Inconclusive - no match" text of the test summary was the DNA breakdown, the amino acid chains with numbers following them to be used for manual analysis and confirmation. He glanced at the notebook. He quickly counted up the letters used in the code: twenty.

He counted the number of amino acid chains in the analysis: twenty.

"No way," he murmured to himself. He scribbled letters onto his notes, scratched them out, and tried again.

The coffee pot had grown cold, but Jason hadn't noticed. He scribbled and scratched more notes onto the pages next to him, stopping to tap numbers into his screen, and then returned to scribbling.

He jumped and shouted when Les knocked on the door frame. "What's up?" he asked. He realized people were in the office, but he wasn't sure when they all got there.

"What are you doing?" Les asked.

"Working. What's up?" he repeated, still staring at the screen, a pencil in his mouth as he compared the results to his notes.

"It's one in the afternoon, and you haven't left your office yet," Les said, the worry evident in his voice. "Everything OK?"

"What? Yeah, I mean, no," Jason said, "no, that's...shit. I've got something. Something big."

"What is it?"

"Not here. Too many eyes and ears." Les looked concerned, and Jason realized how paranoid that sounded. "There are a few…complications…with what I've been working on. Best not to discuss them here in the office." His stomach growled. "Let's grab lunch."

Les' mouth hung agape at the papers in front of him. "How did you…?"

"The less you know, the better," Jason said, sipping a bottle of Mexican Coca-Cola and tearing a chunk of meat off of the smoked baby back rib in his other hand. He hadn't realized how famished he was until he had pulled into the Sweet Lucy's parking lot, and the smell hit his nostrils.

"But all of these…"

"Yeah. These over here are dates, as best I can tell," Jason said, pointing to two different columns. "I can't figure out what the date means, but pretty sure that's what they are."

"I still can't believe this…each one of these…" Les scanned down the column of random letters and numbers.

"Each one of those is a DNA profile," Jason confirmed. "The letters and numbers are codes for the amino acid chains we use for DNA identification. And when I punched them into the database, each one came up with a kid that was reported missing. The second to last entry here is Markus Kline."

"Jesus Christ," Les said quietly. "I can't even…what does this mean?"

Jason put down the baby back rib he was gnawing on and licked his fingers. "I think we just stumbled into one of the largest child trafficking operations anyone has ever seen. And I can't use any of it."

Les rubbed his hand across his jaw. "You can't take it to the DA," he said. "None of this would be admissible. Case would get thrown out before it even got started."

Jason caught himself grinding his teeth. "We can't do nothing. This means that more than one kid is missing, and this asshole is a major part of it."

Les looked off, seemingly focused on nothing. "Your only option is to bring in Ezekiel," he finally said. "The evidence we had before this," Les gestured to the phone, "gives us probable cause to bring him in for questioning. We don't have to reference any of this directly," he said, indicating the phone again, Jason noticing that he was purposely not mentioning it out loud, "but if we can get him to start talking then maybe…"

"Yeah, that works," Jason said.

"We should bring the whole team up to speed on this," Les said. "This is getting very big, very fast. We need bodies to bring him in."

"No, not yet. Right now, only two people know I have these photos: you and Jordan. Pretty sure you'd be able to shake off any IAB issues...but I don't want to expose the rest of the team. They have plausible deniability, but the second I tell them, and I would have to tell them something to justify putting everyone on this guy, if it ever comes out where the lead came from, all of their careers would be at risk." Jason shook his head. "No, right now, I've got to be the only one on this."

"And me," Les said. "I'm already muddy with it, so we'll both follow this up."

"You need to stay at the office," Jason said and continued over Les' protests. "We need the trains to keep running on time, and I need you running interference with Swan, keep her off my back for a few more hours."

"I'll grab Ezekiel," Les insisted. "You head back, deal with the bureaucratic crap. That will look more normal, and you're way better at it."

"No," Jason said and held up a hand to halt Les' retort. "I'm the only one that's had any direct contact with Greenway, and I'm the only one that could be directly associated with the photos. If things break bad, I'm the only one that goes down, and it doesn't jeopardize the rest of the investigation. Better for it to look like one rogue cop than widespread corruption."

Les grumbled something unintelligible. "Yeah, that makes sense...what do you want me to tell Swan?"

"The truth," Jason said as he stood from the table. "I'm out following a lead, trying to find a CI. I never told you the name, so you have no idea where I'd be." Les nodded, and Jason wrapped his coat around his shoulders. "I'm hoping it will just be a few hours."

CHAPTER 17

Jason checked his watch: two in the morning.

The rest of the day had gone by with Jason parked across the street from the fleabag motel that rented rooms by the hour, never taking his eyes off the pickup truck in the back corner of the parking lot.

The rain had finally relented, and the sun had once again beat mercilessly down, un-filtered by clouds, slowly scouring the ground of scrub growth. He had to wear UV gear as a kid, but he also was sure he remembered a few people having grass in their front yards. Now that was a luxury only for those who could afford to live under the shields. Outside of the shields, grass was only a memory.

The district had stayed busy during the day, mostly with trucks pulling in and out of sheltered depots, but since the sun went down, the streets came alive with people.

I wonder how much time we have left.

Jason was surprised by the thought. He didn't consider himself nihilistic. He wasn't sure if grass disappearing was that big of a deal.

But it wasn't hard to see that things didn't seem to be getting better, either. It always felt like humanity kept throwing band-aids on the problems that ailed them rather than making the tough choices for real solutions.

Jason pushed the thought from his head and focused on the task at hand, and then coughed a sarcastic chuckle to himself.

Pot. Kettle. Black.

Jason waited. He itched at the cycler straps where they rubbed against the back of his neck. He desperately wanted a shower and a solid night's sleep in his own bed next to his wife, not in the back seat of his car or passed out at his desk. It had been over a week since he had made it to the gym or eaten a semblance of a home-cooked meal. He had long since shed his UV gear after the sun dipped below the horizon, and he was grateful that at least he hadn't had to spend more hours in the uncomfortable layers.

One of the motel room doors opened, and a figure emerged. Jason perked up, ready to follow, but he also tempered his expectations. None of the other guests had been Ezekiel so far. He wasn't entirely sure that Ezekiel hadn't just ditched the pickup and found different transportation.

The figure descended a flight of stairs, and made their way across the lot, and paused near the pickup. Jason felt his excitement grow. The figure looked around, then hopped into the truck and pulled out.

Gotcha.

The pickup pulled onto the main road, and Jason pulled out behind them, keeping a safe distance. The driver made several quick turns, and Jason did his best to keep the truck in sight without revealing that he was tailing them.

They drove like this for over twenty minutes. Finally, the truck pulled into the parking lot of a different no-tell motel. The driver exited the vehicle and quickly entered one of the rooms.

Jason pulled into the parking lot and parked next to the pickup. He steadied his breathing and let the adrenaline wash over him. He knew what needed to happen.

As quietly as he could, he exited the Mustang, closed the door, gun drawn, and held low behind his back. He approached the motel room door, careful not to walk in front of the curtained window lest he reveal his position to the man inside. He leaned against the door and listened; it sounded like the television was on.

Jason felt his heart rate increase. He gently touched the door knob and slowly turned it a hair; it wasn't locked.

OK, it's time.

Jason readied himself with three deep breaths. On the third breath, he burst through the door, gun raised-

-and he immediately saw white and stars.

A moment later, he registered that he had been hit in the head, and another delayed moment until he realized someone was handcuffing him to something. Then he felt someone rifling through his pockets and taking his phone.

He heard the door close and noticed that the air was decidedly cooler. *I'm inside.* He shook away the cobwebs as his brain came back online in the present. His vision shifted again when his goggles and headgear were ripped from his face. His nostrils immediately recognized the smells of bleach and mildew.

His right arm was suspended near his head, and when Jason tried to lower it, it stopped short with a metal clang. He glanced at his wrist and saw he was handcuffed to a radiator.

Before him stood a man with a scorpion-like tattoo wrapped around his left forearm. Wild ringlets of red hair framed his head, and he smelled of stale tobacco. In his right hand, he held Jason's gun aimed at the floor.

"Who are you?" he asked in a scratchy voice.

"Lieutenant Jason Thane, Philly PD," Jason said. Pain on the back of his head blossomed as the adrenaline wore off. He suspected that was where he had been clocked with a blunt object.

"Bullshit," the man said. "Who sent you?"

"Look, my badge is in my pocket," Jason said as he gingerly touched a knot at the back of his head. "I'm going to take it out and show you."

He slowly reached into his back pocket and took in the room. His headgear was on the bed, a small TV on the wall, and not much else. Jason pulled out his wallet and flipped it open to show his detective's shield.

His captor examined the badge from where he stood, disappointing Jason. He was pretty sure he could take him even with one arm literally tied.

The gun is the wild card…probably best I don't go that way.

"What kinda cop has a ride like that? What is that, a '68?" Jason noted that there wasn't panic in the man's voice and that his trigger finger rested against the gun barrel, rather than on the trigger itself. *Trigger discipline.*

"'67," Jason replied and felt a headache starting. "I work narcotics. Anti-splice task force. I've been looking for you, Ezekiel."

If the man felt any kind of way about that name, Jason couldn't see it.

"You were the one in my truck last night." Ezekiel sounded sure of his statement.

"Guilty, you got me," Jason said, tucking his wallet back into his pocket. "Like I said, I've been looking for you. And if I found you, I'm sure whoever's been leaving that trail of bodies looking for you will be able to find you, too."

Ezekiel's expression changed, and he glanced at the window. His finger crept towards the trigger. "How do I know you weren't sent here to kill me? Plenty of cops on the take."

Jason didn't take his eyes off of the gun. "I get the impression that whoever wants you gone wants you dead and gone, with extreme prejudice, right? Not someone who tries sneaking into a motel room with only 9mm."

Ezekiel started pacing in what little space there was in the spartan room. He muttered words Jason couldn't make out, sounding like he was reasoning something out to himself. "Yeah, that makes sense...yeah, you ain't him. You ain't him."

"Do you know who's after you? Or why?" These weren't the questions Jason wanted to ask, the questions about Markus, but he figured that he would need to ease into that.

"Why? No idea, but I must have royally pissed somebody off. It's the only reason why you send him."

"Who?" Jason asked. "Who's him?"

Ezekiel stopped pacing and looked at Jason like he had three heads. "The Bear."

Jason could feel an eye roll before it happened. "You're kidding me, right? The Bear? It's an urban legend."

"Yeah, well, if you think he can find me as easily as you did, then you'll get to meet him soon enough," Ezekiel said and grabbed a backpack from the other side of the bed. "He's been taking out everyone in my *unuo*. Don't think he'll care much if you're a cop or not. They're trying to erase me. And once they've sicced him on you, he never stops until he gets you."

"So, what's the plan?" Jason asked.

"Run. I'm out. Disappear."

Jason coughed a laugh. "You're trying to tell me that this monstrous assassin who never gives up is after you, and your plan is to run?" Jason laughed again. "Good luck."

"I've been doing just fine so far," Ezekiel said as he started for the door.

"You get that it's not just him chasing you, right?" Jason said. *Can't let him leave.* "Every law enforcement agency in the country will be looking for you. Your picture will be on every news feed from here to the Pacific. Think you can hide from everyone?"

Ezekiel's eyes narrowed. "Why would they be looking for me? Splice ain't that big of a deal to get that kind of attention."

"Splice? You're right, it's not," Jason said. "But child abduction and human trafficking? Those get you right in the feels. Makes for some sexy headlines and lead stories."

Jason was sure he would never want to play poker against Ezekiel with how stone-faced he was.

"You don't have shit."

Guess I'm going all in. "I've got pictures of those notes from your truck." Ezekiel's face remained locked in a look of suspicion. "Cracked the code, too. Amino acid chains for DNA identification. The same numbers are used in the police database. Clever."

Ezekiel got a predatory grin. "Illegal search and seizure, lieutenant. You can't use any of it."

"Maybe," Jason said. "But maybe a judge sees it a different way. Or maybe it doesn't matter if I can use it in court. I know what you've done. Means I can start looking into every one of those missing persons cases. Think every one of them is air-tight? No mistakes?"

Jason could see Ezekiel doing the mental calculus, and he tried to will him to stay. Every minute he stayed was another minute Jason had a chance to find out about Markus.

Ezekiel took a seat on the bed. "What if we made a deal?"

What's he playing? "What kind of deal?"

"I tell the DA that I came to you with information about human trafficking," he said. "Then it doesn't matter how you got the info, right?"

The thought of lying about evidence didn't sit right with Jason, and the idea that his career would essentially be in the hands of a child abductor made him ill, but he decided to play it out. "In exchange for what?"

"Immunity," Ezekiel said.

Jason's laugh was genuine. "Dude, I've got you on at least three dozen counts of child abduction from what I saw in that notebook alone. Don't you think some DA will find a way around how I came across the information to get that in front of a jury? This is a career-making case, on top of the fact that you've kidnapped dozens of kids. There isn't a world where you don't serve time."

"OK," Ezekiel said, and Jason saw his confidence faltering. "Protection then. Protective custody, or witness protection, something. Out here, I get torn apart by The Bear. Inside, I get killed, they can definitely get to me."

"Who's 'they'?"

"The people who hire me for the jobs."

Jason found it tantalizing. "Do you have a name?"

"No, no names-"

The temptation to even consider a deal evaporated. "Don't know what to tell you, then."

"More people are doing what I do, and I can help you get them."

Jason had to process that. "Wait…how many more?"

"I don't know, exactly…dozens, maybe?"

Jason did the math. "That's hundreds of kids every year. You're telling me you can get me to the others in this ring?"

"It's not so much a ring as it is independent contractors, but yeah, I can get you all of the information about how we operate. But you have to protect me from The Bear."

Jason decided he needed one last piece of information. "Where's Markus Kline?"

"Who?"

Jason felt his anger start to boil. "One of the last kids you took. Lived in the building where we busted the stash house on the top floor."

"Oh, him…I don't know. I just stopped in there on my way to the drop, decided to get a little buzz going before I clocked out for the day."

Jason felt the overwhelming urge to beat this man within an inch of his life with how casually and coldly he talked about child abduction. "You made the drop?" Jason hated the sound of the words in his mouth. "Markus was alive?"

"Yeah," Ezekiel replied. "Client doesn't pay for spoiled goods. So do we have a deal?"

This is a deal with the devil.

Jason was still staggered by the sheer number of kids that could potentially be involved.

"I need something more concrete than your word," Jason said. "I need something to go to the DA with. If they like what you bring to the table, and if it pans out, they might be able to work out some kind of deal. In the meantime, the best I can do is protective custody."

"I've got records," Ezekiel said. "Years' worth. Everything from when they first contacted me. Should be enough to establish a conspiracy or give you something to work with to track back to someone, right?"

"You've kept records of the highly illegal activities you've been engaged in?"

"Nah, not like that," Ezekiel said. "Nah, see, they gave me these cyclers, right, and when I'm ready to make a pickup, I'm supposed to hit this button on it. Supposed to make the kid go to sleep when they have it on. But see, I'm a little smarter than they thought," he said, tapping his finger to his temple, "and I figured out how the masks *work*. The button turns on the gas, yeah, but it *also* turns on a tracking signal. I figure that's how they know where and when to make a pickup."

"So?"

"So," Ezekiel said, pacing, "I started listening. I set my computer up to keep an ear open, and whenever one of the signals goes off," he made a popping sound, "my computer makes a note of the frequency, date, and time. Prints it out. And plenty of them happened while I was somewhere else, and I got people that can vouch for that. So, if a mask was activated, and I can prove it wasn't me…"

"…it means that someone else did," Jason finished. He squinted at Ezekiel. "Why would you go to all of this trouble?"

"It's my nuclear option," Ezekiel said. "The Bear is theirs. They should have thought of that before they sent him after me. If I'm going down, I take everyone I can with me."

Jason couldn't disagree with the logic and was grateful for Ezekiel's twisted sense of self-preservation. "It might be enough. Where is it?"

"Warehouse over on State. I'll take you." Ezekiel stepped forward and fished a keyring out of his pocket. He paused before he got within a stride of Jason's feet. "Hang on…we have a deal, right? I unlock you, give you your gun, and we're good, right?"

This is the worst idea ever. The damage this guy has done to families, to friends…

Jason's hand twitched with the muscle memory for reaching for his cuffs.

But this is my only play right now, isn't it?
Well…shit.

Jason sighed. "Yes, we're good. I'm not going to arrest you on the spot."

Ezekiel hesitated, then shook his head. "Man, I must be desperate." He inserted the key to unlock the handcuffs.

"You and me both," Jason said. He rubbed his newly freed wrist where the metal had made contact. "First thing's first." He held out his hand.

Jason thought for a moment that Ezekiel wouldn't hand the gun back. He was acutely aware of the proximity of Ezekiel's finger to the trigger. The moment stretched longer than Jason was comfortable, and finally Ezekiel passed the gun. Jason holstered it.

"OK, next on the list," Jason said and pulled out his phone. He brought up the notebook photos. "What are the dates and times? What's all of this?"

Ezekiel looked at the pictures. "This is the date when I was watching a target." He pointed to a different column. "These are times when I saw them leaving school, or leaving their home, you know, mapping out their day." He pointed at the last column. "This was when and where I figured would be the best time to harvest."

Jason cringed inwardly at how callous and detached Ezekiel was when describing the abduction and delivery of children like they were no more than a sack of flour. The urge to arrest him and accept the consequences grew in him, but he was quelled when he thought of Markus. Given how he just referred to "harvesting product", Jason figured Ezekiel was not someone who would feel the least bit compelled to help the kid to save himself.

I know I'm going to regret this.

"Take me to your nuke," Jason said.

CHAPTER 18

Ezekiel's truck weaved through the streets with Jason following close behind, slowly working their way west through the city. They occasionally skirted the edges of Center City and some other ritzier neighborhoods that fell under the shadows of the solar shields. Still, as best as Jason could tell, they never strayed far from The Gaps.

After over an hour, they pulled into an industrial park near the river. The chain link fence that surrounded it was leaning in spots, sometimes so far that the top of the fence nearly touched the ground, and it gave him a clear view of the sparse lot. No lights shone overhead or from within any of the buildings. Jason had the impression that the property was abandoned, but the open space would make it easy to spot someone approaching.

Ezekiel navigated his truck through a minefield of old pallets and potholes that would bend a rim, and pulled up to a dilapidated warehouse. The thick-shielded windows that filtered UV and kept the pollution out looked like they were all still intact, but the roof sagged in the middle.

"You certainly have an eye for real estate," Jason said as they exited their respective vehicles.

"It's off the grid, I can see someone approaching for 300 meters in any direction, and no one comes around here," Ezekiel said. "What more could I ask for?"

He led Jason through a lone door on the side of the building, pointing out a trip wire strung across the threshold that they both avoided. "Nothing lethal, just something to let me know if someone comes in."

Jason found himself standing on a catwalk that looked down on a warehouse floor littered with shelving units and detritus. It wrapped around the interior and crisscrossed at regular intervals. "What was this place?"

"Some kind of fulfillment center, I think," Ezekiel said as he led Jason further into the structure. "Place was mothballed after the retail collapse twenty years ago when all those online sellers went belly-up. Sat here forever, just slowly collapsing and collecting dust."

They traversed the catwalks over the floor, and Ezekiel pointed out other tripwires along the way. A shed-like structure revealed itself in the murk, perched in the corner of the warehouse where the catwalks met. Jason guessed it must have served as an office where a supervisor could easily look down on all of the workers on the floor below. The windows looked like they had been smashed out years before and were covered with boards.

"Welcome to my office," Ezekiel said, pushing open a door and flipping on a light.

Unlike the rest of the warehouse, the old office was free of dust and grime. It was sparsely appointed with a cot, a coffee maker on a table, a filing cabinet, and a desk with what looked like an old computer. Next to it was an ancient printer that still used paper.

"Cozy," Jason said. "So far, this only indicts you. You haven't told me anything that gets you off the hook."

"You haven't seen the best part," Ezekiel said. He walked over to the desk and pulled a binder out of a drawer that was thick with papers bound inside. "This is the nuke file. It has every ping, the frequency it was on, the date and time it went active, and when it shut off."

Jason approached and held out his hand. Ezekiel retracted the binder towards his body, but then reluctantly handed it over. Jason paged through it, studying a few of the pages filled with raw data and no labels.

Ezekiel walked over to a large cardboard box and pulled a cycler out. "Kid gets one of these. It's got a little anesthetic in the recycler, knocks them out and keeps them that way. When it's time, I activate the tracker, grab the kid."

"Then what?" Jason asked, every atom of his being wanting nothing more than to inflict violence on the man across from him.

"I'd put 'em in a shipping crate on any roof pad I could find…you know, the empty ones that anyone can drop stuff into. Within twenty-four hours the money was in my account." Ezekiel snatched the binder back. "There's a lot of data points in here. All for the low, low price of *keeping me alive*."

Jason couldn't deny that Ezekiel had been very thorough. However, he supposed that when one was dealing in child abduction and human trafficking, being able to screw over anyone who was tempted by betrayal was prudent.

All of it left a bad taste in Jason's mouth. "You never felt bad about this? Never wondered who you were working for, what they did with the kids?"

Ezekiel shrugged. "If it wasn't me, it would be someone else. Just trying to make a buck. That's the thing about people...we have more."

The absolute lack of humanity or remorse in his answer shot Jason's blood pressure up. He balled his fists and started to step towards Ezekiel, fully intent on pummeling him until he got to his candy center. Ezekiel must have realized Jason's goal and took a step back.

The sound of empty cans falling on cement stopped Jason's advance. "What was that?"

"Tripwire," Ezekiel said. He ran to the light switch and plunged the room into darkness, and then stuck his head out the door. "I don't see anyone-"

More cans fell, closer and to the right.

Jason approached the door, pulled his goggles down, and peered into the cavernous warehouse. The gear adjusted for the low light, and on the other side of the warehouse, he could see a figure approaching, little more than a silhouette.

"It's too late," Ezekiel whispered and slid down to the office floor. "The Bear is here, isn't he?"

Jason signed *quiet,* and Ezekiel did as he was told. Jason listened.

More cans fell. Then...nothing. Jason couldn't even hear footsteps.

"Can you grab the files?" Jason whispered.

Ezekiel nodded. "You want to try to outrun him?"

"I can buy us some time," Jason whispered. "Against my better judgment, I'm trusting you. Take that binder, and take it to this address." Jason handed him a business card. "Ask for Detective Les Caporelli. He's my partner. I'll meet you there in an hour."

Jason stood to meet The Bear, but Ezekiel grabbed his leg. "Are you nuts? You can't take that thing on!"

"I've got this," Jason said. "When I say run, you book it to your truck as fast as you can. Got it?"

Ezekiel nodded, and through the goggles, Jason could see, for the first time, genuine fear on his face.

More cans fell, much closer.

Jason silently counted with his fingers, and on three, both he and Ezekiel bolted out of the door in opposite directions, Ezekiel toward the exit and Jason toward the fallen cans.

Three steps later, Jason saw a flash of white and tasted copper in his mouth. His vision cleared, and he was lying on his back. He felt like he had run chest-first into a steel girder. His goggles' enhanced vision was gone, and he realized they had been knocked off his face.

The silhouetted figure was standing over him, arm outstretched in a clothesline. They were wearing a cycler that looked like it was made of a patchwork of parts and had two hoses running around the sides and behind their neck. It rattled as it breathed. The UV gear looked equally patchwork and was covered in a tattered, mud-colored jacket. The goggles they wore created the illusion of two dead eyes staring at him.

The Bear.

"What the f-" Jason started, but The Bear cut him off by jumping on top of him, raining blow after blow down on him. Jason felt the muscle memory of years of fighting kick in and avoided the punches he could, blocking what he couldn't.

One glancing blow caught his forearm, and a sharp pain followed. Jason wasn't sure that the bone wasn't broken, but he kept defending the onslaught. He felt the straps on his cycler slip, and at some point, the equipment fell off and clattered to the warehouse floor.

He finally saw an opening, kicked up his legs, and tried to wrap up his attacker's limb in an armbar submission, a move he had practiced endlessly and had won him more than one fight, both in the ring and out.

Instead of the usual yelp of pain, or the telltale popping noise as the joint began to bend in the wrong direction, Jason felt himself hoisted from the ground and slammed back down like a club. Jason felt his head bounce off the steel walkway. His vision went white again, and his ears rang.

He instinctively let go of his grapple and scooted away, trying to keep a defensive arm in front of him. His vision cleared, and he saw The Bear slowly stalking towards him, a predator moving in for the kill.

Jason rose to his feet and kicked at The Bear's leg. His form was perfect; the blow landed right at his opponent's knee...and nothing.

The Bear was not deterred from his forward movement. Jason threw punches, but none seemed to find their mark, his target ducking and weaving faster than he could imagine or keep up with.

In an impossibly fast motion, the figure unleashed a return torrent of punches, connecting and dazing Jason, and he could feel the blackness creeping in at the edge of his vision. He tried to back away and give himself a reprieve from the barrage, but the figure stayed with him, hitting him harder than he had ever remembered being hit...

...*Wait*...

Jason didn't know what round it was.

Is it the first or the second?

Hang on...what...

The canvas rushed towards Jason's face.

How did Belford hit me that hard?

...No...Why am I...

Jason wasn't sure if he heard or felt the ligaments in his knee snapping.

That's not what I'm...

The bell rang, but he didn't move...couldn't move...

...This isn't right.

Jason finally cleared the cobwebs and lurched back into consciousness. It felt like surfacing from being held underwater for too long. He figured he was only out for a few seconds, a sensation he had felt before, but as a reflex, he kicked out uselessly against the air, hoping to hit something. His other leg was raised and he on his back, being drug across the steel walkway.

The Bear dragged him towards the windows, and Jason could see the faint hints of light at the horizon: the sun was rising. The Bear turned his head slightly as they walked and regarded him through cold, emotionless goggles.

"Time to go outside," an electronically mangled voice said, completely flat and devoid of malice. It was simply a statement of fact.

Jason didn't feel his UV gear against his skin. His eyes felt naked against the air, and he breathed without restriction...

I don't have any gear.

And outside is death.

Jason kicked furiously. He grabbed onto the handrail posts, but the force of his enemy pulling him along easily broke his grip. He tried striking at their knees, but the blows might as well have been a soft breeze for all the reaction it elicited.

Then, in one lazy motion, The Bear hurled Jason by the leg through the window.

CHAPTER 19

Jason barely felt the glass shatter when his body struck it. It was more a *memory* of it happening.

There was a moment of weightlessness, of wind hurtling past him.

He barely registered hitting the ground a story below, or that the wind had been completely knocked out of him.

He lay on the ground, struggling to move, but his body wouldn't obey.

What he did register was *pain*.

The sun was peeking over the rippling horizon, and he could already feel the air rapidly heating around him in the unfiltered UV-laden sunlight.

Outside is death.

Jason tried to turn away and crawl towards any shade he could find, but his lungs screamed for oxygen, and his body felt sluggish and unwilling to respond to his brain's commands.

Outside is death.

This is it?

He gasped two shallow, unfulfilling breaths.

Does Amira know how much I love her?

I'll never get to tell her again.

Breath still wouldn't come to him. He grasped at the dust and tried to drag himself closer to the warehouse, closer to shade.

Will Alexei be proud of me?

He pulled himself another few inches across the rapidly-heating ground.

Did I do enough with my life?

Will I have mattered?

Will any of it have mattered?

After everything I've been through…I beat Horkims Syndrome…I lost Alexei…

Digging my way out of the gaps by my fingernails just to be knocked back down by that maldito *Belford, by the* maldito bougari…

They don't give a shit about people like me, like Markus or Alexei.

I'll be forgotten just like them.

It's not FUCKING FAIR.

All I wanted to do was save him, to bring that poor boy home to his suffering mother.

To bring some peace to a broken world.

But I should have known better. I should have known I couldn't do it.

I'm not lucky to have money or brains like Leo.

And did I even really want all of that? Or am I just telling myself that to feel better about myself?

I'm not special.

Jason's lungs finally responded, and he gasped down an enormous breath. He braced himself for the burning that accompanied breathing unfiltered air.

The burning never came.

With the infusion of oxygen, his body finally started to respond, and he sat up.

Then panic flooded into him, a gnashing torrent of fear and adrenaline, and he scrambled away towards the warehouse, his feet scratching and slipping in the dry dust around him, searching for any shade, any respite from the sun.

He found a small sheltered cove and huddled inside, hyperventilating, waiting.

Outside is death.

His skin wasn't burning.

Jason had seen people with less than a minute's direct exposure to the sun show the bright red skin of sunburn, and even the start of small blisters.

He checked all his exposed skin. There were no blisters. There was no sunburn.

But...outside is death...

He gingerly extended a hand from his little shaded spot. He reflexively withdrew it from the anticipated pain. He forced himself to push his hand past the threshold and into the sunlight.

Nothing happened.

He finally got his legs to coordinate with each other. Jason rose to his feet, shielded his eyes from the rising sun with an outstretched hand, and stepped out of the shadow. He turned and looked up at the shattered glass a story above him. There was nothing but a dark hole there, no figure in sight.

He closed his eyes, forced his breathing to slow down, and slowly felt the panic melt away.

He was outside.

And he was OK.

"What the hell?" he asked an empty sky.

CHAPTER 20

The fight kept replaying in his mind, always starting with that first, inhumanly strong punch, always ending with him standing exposed to a rising sun.

One question was easier to answer; the other eluded him.

Evidence. I need evidence.

Jason could already see the scene play out in his mind if he collected the evidence immediately on his own. Swan would lob accusations at him about fabricating or planting evidence, about creating a crime when there was none, anything to fit her narrative that painted him as an out-of-control cop unqualified for his position, desperately clinging on to any hope of maintaining his station.

By the book, then.

It took Jason an hour to find his missing goggles and cycler among the maze of shelves and refuse in the warehouse. He pointedly did not look at the broken window, now allowing the outside air to flow unrestricted inside during his search. He didn't go anywhere near the office. He retrieved his UV gear from the car and donned it, and tried to ignore the fact he was doing so outside.

Jason fired off a message to Les to bring the team in. Then he sat in his car and waited.

More witnesses meant it would be harder for Swan to impeach his credibility. It twisted his stomach that he needed witnesses, that his word wasn't enough anymore.

But everything is different now.

He didn't realize he had dialed a number until the phone rang.

"Jason?" Leo's voice came through. "What time is it there? Are you OK?"

No, I'm not.

"It's early…sorry, I'll call back later."

"No, it's fine, it's still the evening here…what's wrong?"

"I…" Jason started but couldn't bring himself to finish the sentence. "It's a case I'm working…I was hoping you could help."

"Sure, anything, though I don't know how much use I'll be. Shoot."

Jason ran his hand through his hair. "So, uh…remember how I had to chase that suspect outside, and they didn't have any gear on? Seemed like they didn't have any side effects until the splice wore off?"

"Yeah."

"Is there…" Jason felt the words get stuck. "Hypothetically, is that possible without splice?"

"Theoretically speaking?" Leo paused for a moment. Jason readied himself for Leo to laugh him off the call, or flat out tell him it was an impossibility. "Theoretically…yes, I suppose it is possible."

Jason's head started spinning, and he was glad he was already sitting down. He was sure if he had been standing, he would have fallen over.

"How?" was the only word he could get out.

"The human body has a wonderful ability to adapt to new situations and stimuli," Leo said. "So theoretically, yes, it could be possible for someone to develop the ability to withstand being outside…or perhaps it could be an innate ability, not something new, a mutation, like how some people can roll around in poison ivy and not develop a rash."

Jason felt his heart pounding in his ears, and a headache started to settle in behind his left eye. "But Leo…I was taught since I was a kid that going outside unprotected was death. We had to do worksheets on that in kindergarten. The sun would burn us to a crisp, and the air would eat away our lungs. You're saying that it may not be true?"

"No, no, not at all," Leo said. "It's…how can I explain this? Have you ever heard of Wim Hof?"

The name didn't ring a bell for Jason. "No, can't say that I have."

"Hof was an interesting subject. He set several records for exposure to sub-freezing temperatures without suffering the ill effects. It wasn't that he had a special gland or something odd about his physiology. Between repeated exposure to those temperatures and his willpower, he simply didn't get cold."

"So UV burns and lung cancer are just in our heads?"

"Oh, good lord, no," Leo said with a chuckle. "There are plenty of people who failed to replicate Hof's success and a few who actually died in their attempts. No, I'm saying that the human body is a complex machine that we still know little about. But within what we don't know lies great potential, the potential to learn how to heal ourselves of disease, to fight cancer, and yes, even go outside."

What happened to me?

"Do you believe that?"

Leo's voice took on a serious tone. "With all of my being. I've built my company and my career on that notion." There was a pause. "Does that help you at all? With your case, I mean."

"I'm not sure," Jason replied honestly.

"Well, if you have come across another person who can be outside unprotected and without the consequences that affect everyone else…all I can say is that person is extraordinary."

Jason didn't know how to respond and replied simply, "Huh."

"Jason, I hate to cut the conversation short, but I have a flight in a few hours. Talk soon?"

Jason agreed and terminated the call. He pocketed his phone and waited. One refrain repeated in his mind: *what does this mean?*

It took another hour for backup to arrive. It was a crime scene first, and that needed to take precedence over his own personal mysteries. Mysteries he wasn't ready to share with anyone yet.

As his team and the evidence techs worked over the scene, Jason leaned against his car and desperately wanted a cup of coffee, but he didn't want to sit in his car, and he couldn't remove his cycler. Something in his head said, *yes, you can,* but he pushed it away.

Outside meant death.

"You sure you're OK?" Les asked, and Jason jumped. He hadn't realized the veteran cop had approached.

"Yeah, I'm good," Jason said. "Just tired. What do you have on the building?"

Les paged through his notebook. "Real estate records have the last sale being to Freehold Enterprises from, drumroll please, Greenway Protectives. Looks like the title changed hands five years ago. Can't find anything on Freehold at the moment. Probably a shell corporation. We'll need to dig deeper on that."

Jason pushed himself off the car and walked toward the warehouse. "Any sign of either suspect?"

Les signed *frustrated,* and shook his head. "No, nothing. The whole lot is basically nothing but loose dust and an open field. A light breeze could cover any tracks around here. So, from the perspective of someone who doesn't want to leave much sign of their passing behind, this was a good choice."

Jason huffed a sarcastic laugh. "I don't know why I'm shocked Ezekiel didn't go to the office and find you."

"You thought he would?"

Jason shrugged. "I had hoped. Maybe The Bear got him."

They walked a few moments in silence before Les continued. "He told you everything?"

Jason signed *yes.* "Most of it. Enough to get us started. Didn't want to search the office without the rest of the team and Crime Scene here. Keep everything above board. Figured it keeps anything I did earlier from contaminating the scene."

"And the second guy?"

Jason could hear the uncertain way Les asked the question.

The fight replayed in Jason's head again. "Les, I have been in plenty of fights, and there is only one other time when I've been hit as hard as that."

"The Belford fight."

"The Belford fight," Jason agreed. "Even splicers don't hit that hard. Belford was on some kind of designer version of it when we fought, one that dramatically improves performance but also burns out of your system faster the more effort you expend. If he hadn't mistimed his last dose, I don't think I would have known that was what he did."

"And this was the same thing, you think?" Les asked, and even through the distortion of the cycler, Jason could hear the worry.

"Yeah," he replied. "Only even more so. Les, I had a full-on armbar locked on this guy, I mean *locked*, textbook, and it didn't even phase him." Jason almost continued and told his partner about the window, but he couldn't bring himself to say that part of the story.

"That's...concerning," Les said.

"Yeah," Jason agreed.

"But you think he's the one responsible for dropping those bodies?"

"He had the brute strength to do it," Jason reasoned.

They stepped into the warehouse interior. CSIs had brought in work lights to illuminate their workspace, and jumpsuited figures collected evidence while drones buzzed around the upper reaches doing the same. Nguyen waved from the catwalk when she saw Jason and Les enter. "Hey Loo, can you come up here?"

Jason ascended the stairs to the catwalk. Nguyen stood by the office door.

"What's up?" Jason asked. "Find anything?"

"That's just it, boss," Nguyen said. "There's nothing to find."

The sentence didn't compute in Jason's brain. He stepped into the office...

...and it was empty. The cot was gone, as was the coffee maker, the computer, and the printer. The only evidence that someone had been there was the lack of dust.

Jason felt his jaw go slack under his cycler. "You've got to be kidding me."

"Like I said, there's nothing here for us to find," Nguyen said. "We can swab for DNA, but I don't know what else you'd like us to do here…"

"Come on," Les said. "Let's get back to the office. I'll drive."

"I've got my car," Jason said, and he heard his own voice's complete lack of energy.

"You're exhausted, and you look like warmed-over shit," Les said, patting him on the shoulder. "Nguyen will drive the Mustang back. Maybe you can catch some sleep on the way back."

They didn't discuss the scene on the way back, and Jason didn't get any sleep. He kept playing the scenario over and over in his head.

He had been outside without gear. The sun didn't burn his skin instantly when it touched him, and his lungs didn't fill with fire when he breathed.

Maybe I imagined it?

He remembered hearing stories from alcoholics in recovery that they would have dreams about drinking that were so vivid that they were convinced that they had fallen off the wagon and gotten blackout drunk.

Is that what happened? Outside is death. Isn't it?

The beating, he knew that was real. The bruises and aches were more than enough empirical evidence that it had happened.

The strength and resilience The Bear had shown were real, he was sure. He had experienced it firsthand before. It existed within the realm of what he knew was possible.

Outside is death.

He remembered how it felt when that bully had torn Jason's UV gear, how his skin felt hot and tight almost immediately as it turned a deep red, and how the blisters started forming moments after. How it felt like he was inhaling hot, broken glass with every breath when his rebreather was knocked off his face.

Outside is death.

…but I didn't die.

He took a deep breath, but aside from aching ribs, there was no pain. He made a show of fishing his phone and wallet out of his pockets to hide him rechecking his skin, but there was no pain, no evidence of a sunburn.

Maybe I was always in a shaded spot…maybe it was a pocket of fresh air.

He didn't believe what he was coming up with, but he kept running through possible explanations for his survival in the face of everything he knew to be true.

This is how people lose their minds, trying to explain something impossible.

He tried to distract himself by shifting his focus to solving the problem of one MIA human trafficker. He gamed out what happened, trying to see what he missed, and where he went wrong with Ezekiel.

From the beginning, really.

Jason started a mental exercise he had taught himself when solving complex, abstract problems: start with the absolute basics, build on that.

250 CONNOR STEVENS & BRIAN WIGGINS

Ezekiel is either alive and on the run or dead. There are only two options.

The man was possibly dead, which would explain why he never showed up at the office.

There was no body at the scene, his pickup was gone, and Jason suspected he was squirrelier than that, though, which meant Ezekiel was in the wind.

Bastard.

Jason reasoned that if he had seen someone thrown through a reinforced window without any headgear or protectives on, he would probably think that person was taking a dirt nap, so Ezekiel probably thought he watched the only chance at a deal going literally out of a window.

The irony to Jason was that his chances of proving this case were defenestrated when Ezekiel bolted. He had zero evidence to prove any of the man's claims, or that they had even had a discussion.

I should have known. Never should have made the deal.

He tried to readjust how he was sitting to alleviate some of the stiffness and soreness in his ribs and neck, but to no avail. He knew that nothing but a hot shower, ice, and time would offer relief from the pounding he took.

All Jason knew for a fact was that he was up a creek.

His intuition was reinforced as a hollow feeling in his chest when he saw the black cars parked outside the office as he and Les pulled in.

"That didn't take long," Les said.

Jason huffed and stepped out of the vehicle. One foot followed the other on autopilot into the office.

The bullpen had more people than Jason was used to seeing there, but he wasn't surprised by their presence. He maintained his steady gait. Derrick Belford sat at one of the desks with his designer shoes kicked up on the top. Several other adjutants and lackeys took up space around the room. All of them carried similar expressions of derision, and one by one all of them moved out of the way when Jason approached, unwilling to find out if he would step around them.

Standing in the middle of the office and the tempest of Jason's career was Chief of Detectives Alice Swan with a self-satisfied smile plastered on her face. He stopped three paces from her.

"Chief," Jason said quietly.

"Lieutenant," she replied in an equal volume. "Do you have anything you would like to report?"

"Would it matter if I did?"

"No."

"OK. Then I'm going back to work." Jason turned towards his office. Belford's feet hit the floor, and he stood, barring Jason's way. His face was the definition of smug. Jason thought that made it very punchable.

"Lieutenant Thane," Swan said in the same quiet, measured tone. *She's enjoying every second of this.* "Am I to understand that you continued to pursue the missing Gapper investigation, despite my explicit orders not to?"

Jason didn't turn to look at Swan. He kept his eyes firmly on Belford in front of him. "I followed evidence that indicated a link between the splice investigation, the multiple homicides, and Markus Kline."

"I've seen no such evidence in your reports," Swan said.

"It's an active investigation. Keeping you up to the minute isn't possible." Jason felt every atom of his being straining towards Belford.

"Did your actions this morning yield any evidence?"

Jason could see her endgame. "No."

"Did your investigations in the past twenty-four hours yield anything actionable regarding the splice trafficking task force?"

Belford's smugness somehow deepened, and Jason grit his teeth. "No."

"So, what you're saying is…you have *nothing.*"

Jason didn't respond. He didn't want to give her the satisfaction of an answer.

"Were your investigations over the last twenty-four hours the result of an illegal search?"

Jason felt his heart skip a beat. "What?" The word escaped his mouth before he could stop it. He finally broke eye contact with Belford and looked over his shoulder at Swan. She was holding out her phone, with his pictures of Ezekiel's notebook on the screen.

"You hacked my phone?" he growled.

"It isn't your phone," Swan said too sweetly. "It's the department's phone, and we can access it whenever we want. What I'm hearing isn't a denial."

Jason knew there was no winning this round. He kept his mouth shut.

"Lieutenant Thane," Swan said, raising her voice so the entire room could hear, keeping the sickly-sweet tone, "you are at this moment relieved of command. Please pack your things. Report to headquarters tomorrow morning for reassignment.

Captain Belford will be taking over your post. IAB will be in touch with you."

Between the sound of his heart pounding in his ears and the squad's outburst of protest, Jason almost couldn't hear the end of Swan's order.

Live to fight another day.

Jason stepped to move past Belford when the captain grabbed him by the upper arm and said in his ear, underneath the din, "Time to go home, blister back."

Jason knew that a string of thought occurred, some internal debate that played out the pros and cons and potential outcomes. Whatever it sounded like, it happened too fast for him to make sense of anything but the conclusion he reached a fraction of a second later.

This is how my career ends.

Jason found a certain amount of catharsis with that thought, like he had let go of an enormous weight he had been carrying for years.

He laid out Captain Derrick Belford with a single punch.

Jason didn't distinctly remember throwing the haymaker. Things seemed to slow down after he felt his knuckles impact Belford's jaw. Belford's head snapped to the side with the impact. Jason saw the other man's eyes roll up in their sockets, and his body went stiff. He slowly tipped over, gaining momentum, and then hit the floor face-first with a smack of skin on the tile.

His instinct was to jump on top of his opponent, start raining punches down, and keep going until the referee stopped him.

Jason couldn't remember if that's what happened, but that Nguyen was pulling him off Belford told him it probably had.

The office was in a different kind of chaos. Besuited lackeys were fawning over a reawakening Belford or trying to interpose themselves between Jason and Swan. Swan was yelling something that blended in with the cacophony. Nguyen was trying to pull Jason into his office.

Belford lurched back to consciousness and swung wildly, hitting one of the officers attending him. Jason couldn't help but smile. The captain surged to his feet and charged at Jason, but more bodies threw themselves in the way, keeping the two men from each other.

"Always knew you were a one-pump chump," Jason goaded through the noise.

He didn't know if Belford heard him, but a moment later, a shrill whistle pierced the air, and the donnybrook waned.

Jason regained his composure and saw Belford do the same, straightening his suit jacket and wiping some blood from his mouth. He kept his eye on the other man...he knew Belford wasn't above retaliation.

Swan pocketed her police whistle. She marched up to Jason, her smile crueler and more predatory than before. "Striking a superior officer...aggravated assault...and whatever else I can think of. Your gun and badge. Now. You're suspended."

He had been anticipating those words, but hearing them aloud shocked Jason. "Yeah," he finally said. He pulled his badge out and placed it on a desk. He unholstered his weapon, removed the clip and the round in the chamber, and put it next to the badge. He pointed at Swan. "You can talk to my union rep." He pointed at Belford. "And you…you go near my family again, *te voy a matar*[7]." Jason didn't yell or seethe; he just made a simple statement of fact.

Jason spun on his heel before either of the officers could react and walked out of the bullpen, affixing his gear as he went. He noticed his squad came with him.

"Go back inside," he ordered them.

"This is messed up, Loo," Nguyen complained. "I'm not working for that asshole Belford."

"It is what it is," Jason said. "Go back inside."

More members added their protests.

"Yo!" Jason bellowed.

His squad silenced.

"Look, there's nothing to be done about this right now," he said in a more measured tone. "I appreciate the loyalty. I do. But there's still a job to do. Don't let these assholes make you less than you are: some of the best cops and detectives I've worked with. Ever."

"Sounds like you're leaving us, boss," Nguyen said.

"I'm done with the task force, Swan made that clear," Jason said. "I don't know what her plans are for me after today. But for now, you all get back in there, get Belford up to speed, and keep doing the best job you know how until they tell you to do otherwise. Got it?"

---

[7] I will fucking kill you

There was a murmured round of "Yes, sir" from the gathered squad. They all shuffled back to the front door, except for Les.

"Need something?" Jason asked.

"Why are you doing this to yourself?" Les asked.

"I don't know what you're talking about."

"Yes, you do," Les said. "You're picking battles with your commanding officer you know you can't win. You just punched a captain who's also *bogari*, in case you forgot, and you're flushing your whole career down the tubes, and for what?"

"Really?" Jason snapped. "Markus. Kline."

"Jason," Les said while shaking his head, "I don't know any other way to say this, but…kids go missing all the time. We can't find them all. It's just how it is. It sucks, but there it is."

Jason stared at his former partner. "'There it is'?"

Les shrugged. "*Esso si que es*[8]."

Jason felt like a dam burst somewhere inside him. "You are the laziest asshole I have ever met."

Les stiffened. "Excuse me?"

"You always play it safe, never break the rules, comfortable right where you are," Jason said, each word dripping venom. "Never any ambition to do more, to be more, content to just work an ass groove into your chair."

"Yeah, I'm comfortable where I am, what's wrong with that?" Les retorted. "Maybe because I know that I'm good at this. Maybe because I know how things are."

---

[8] It is what it is

"Maybe you're just afraid to try."

"No, I'm afraid one of these glass-faced pricks will take my pension away because they can. I'm afraid they'll trump up some BS charge and have me tossed off the force or in jail because I looked at one of them cross-eyed. So yeah, I keep my head down, I do my job, I don't ruffle any feathers *because that's how things are*."

"I don't accept that," Jason threw back at him. "It's a shitty way to live, and no, I don't accept that."

"You're going just to give your career away because you won't play along? Because you think that you can change the system?" Les made an insulting gesture. "*Pendejo*."

Jason turned his back on Les and walked away. "*Vete a la mierda.*[9]"

"Need a ride?" the veteran detective yelled at Jason's back.

"I'll walk."

---

[9] Fuck off; literally "Go to shit"

CHAPTER 21

Jason didn't remember his walk home. He was vaguely aware of the act of walking, but when he arrived at his front door, he had no direct recollection of the route he took, what he saw along the way, or how long it took. He wasn't even sure if he was asleep for the journey. But he found himself at his house nonetheless.

He was profoundly aware of the hollow feeling in his chest as he plodded up the steps and entered the house. He pulled his headgear off when the door closed behind him, but he didn't hang it on the wall next to Amira's, instead holding it in his hand at his side. The graffiti and damage to the house barely registered.

"Hello?" Amira called from the second floor. He heard her walk down the hall, and then she appeared at the top of the steps wearing one of his college hoodies and ripped jeans. "Jason? What are you doing home? Is everything OK?"

Jason didn't respond right away. He honestly didn't know how to answer the question.

"Babe?" she asked and started descending the stairs.

"Not really." It was the most straightforward answer he could think of. *I don't know what I am anymore.*

She hurried her pace to her husband. "What happened?"

I went outside. "I got suspended."

"For what?" She was at his side, her tone somewhere between shock and anger.

For trying to change things. "I hit Belford."

Amira's mouth fell open. No words followed.

After a moment of silence, she finally asked, "Why?"

Jason shrugged. "I don't know," he answered, and he honestly felt like he believed it. The anger, the rage he had felt in that moment when Belford had provoked him wasn't there anymore. It felt like it had belonged to someone else, or that he dreamed it rather than lived it.

Amira's lips moved with an unasked question, like she couldn't find the words to articulate what was going on in her head. He could tell she was confused, worried, and angry, and the emotions were fighting for dominance.

"He goaded me," Jason said, trying to recount the factual events. "Swan had just taken me off the task force, and he probably saw I was already on my last nerve, and he took the opportunity to get me to do something." Jason chuckled ruefully. "He played me good."

"Wait," Amira said, "you…you're off the task force…what the hell happened?"

Jason tried to find an explanation, and he felt like his insides were scooped out. His chest wanted to cave in, and his knees felt like they were about to buckle under him, but he kept his composure. "I tried," he said, and was surprised how his voice quavered. "I tried to make things better, and this is what I got for it."

Amira pulled him into a hug and squeezed him tight. He couldn't bring himself to return the embrace.

"You have done good," she said into his chest. "You have made things better."

"Have I?" he asked. In his heart, he knew the answer was a resounding "no". "Things aren't any better than the day I started on the force. Nothing's gotten better for anyone in the Gaps."

"What are you talking about?" Amira said and pulled away. "You've helped a ton of people. You've gotten kids off the streets, you've helped people get back into society after they've gotten out of jail, you've made neighborhoods safer-"

"For what?" he interrupted. Every point she made felt like a punch to the gut. "All I've done is rearrange some deck chairs. The ship is still sinking."

"You don't think that you've had a positive impact on people?" Amira asked with more heat in her voice. "You don't think those people think you've made a world of difference?"

Jason shook his head. "I had this stupid idea that I would be able to make a *real* difference, change the things that *cause* the problems. I was stupid. It was moronic of me to think that somehow, I would be able to do what no one else has been able to, to go up against an establishment that will do anything to keep the game stacked in their favor."

"You're right, that is stupid," Amira said. It felt like a smack to Jason's face. "What? It's stupid to think that one person will change the world when they get knocked out once and are out of the fight."

"That's...that's not..." Jason didn't have the words to argue with her. "I'm not going to be a cop after this. I don't know what the world is anymore." *I went outside. Outside is death.*

"So, it's fighting all over again?" Amira said, crossing her arms in front of her. "You're just going to walk away because you don't like how the game is played?"

"What do you want me to do?" Jason yelled. He didn't mean for it to come out that way, and he immediately wished he could take the words back.

"I want you to fight back!" Amira yelled back. "Like we've always done! We didn't get where we are by accepting that this is the way things are, that this is all things could be. We've fought and worked our asses off for everything. We wanted to get out of the Gaps, so we were the hardest workers in the room, and we did it. You wanted to be in command so you could change police policy by even a little, so you fought and worked. I wanted to start a legitimate foundation that could move the social equality needle just a little bit, so I fought and worked."

"You think we've made a difference?" Jason said. He couldn't help but lace each word with a hint of poison, and he hated himself for doing it and aiming it at Amira. "Even a little? The rich still have everything, everyone else is left to tear each other apart for the scraps. I was stupid for even thinking we could be more than a couple of Gappers. And how long do you think it will be until one of those rich assholes comes after the Foundation, takes it all down because they don't like what you're doing?"

"I think every person who I've helped, every person *you've* helped, has made things better, yes," she said, standing her ground against his unwarranted verbal assault. "Each person we touch changes the system just a little bit. And if someone does decide to come after the Foundation because they're so small that they're threatened by everyone doing a little better, then let them fuck around and find out. *Joder y averiguar.*" She got a tired look on her face. "You just need to decide whether you will be there with me." She turned and walked with purpose towards the kitchen.

"I'm sorry," Jason finally said. "I just...don't know who I am right now."

Amira paused but didn't turn around. "I do. But that doesn't mean anything if you don't." She continued into the kitchen, and he heard scrubbing noises a moment later.

He thought about joining her in cleaning up, but he sensed she needed some space away from him. He knew that she used cleaning as a meditative thing to calm herself down and clear her mind. He would just be in the way.

He felt like he was in everyone's way. So, he decided to take a walk.

Jason let his feet carry him aimlessly as he once again retreated into the solitude of his thoughts.

He wondered what was going to become of the task force. Every scenario he imagined ended poorly and made his stomach twist. It was like when his first girlfriend broke up with him in high school, and she started dating someone else, and he couldn't stop the pangs of jealousy or the faint ember of hope that she'd see the error of her ways and come back to him. Thinking of Belford leading the task force felt the same way.

He followed a random path down blocks, around corners, and across streets. He wondered what was going to happen with Markus. He knew there was a ticking clock on the kid, if there was still a chance...and he had blown it. If he weren't suspended, he'd still be able to do something, but now…he wished he could take back that punch. The jealousy towards Belford gave way to anger aimed at Belford and himself. There was enough blame to go around.

Buildings and breezeways passed on either side and overhead, but Jason looked ahead, focused on nothing. He was worried about the fight with Amira. They had fought before, about the usual stuff couples fight over. This was the first time that a fight felt *real*, like it was about something more, something that could shake the foundation of their relationship.

Her words haunted him. *You just need to decide whether you will be there with me.* She had never said something like that to him before. She had issued an ultimatum.

He wanted to say "yes". He knew that was the right answer. But something felt like it was chaining him to a wall, choking him when he tried to reach the bright light of the door that would let him out of this dungeon he felt trapped in.

How can I be there when I don't know what I am?

He wanted to be in the fight. He didn't want to give up. But how could he stay in a battle that no one wanted him in? A war that was all but impossible to win?

The wall of change seemed insurmountable to Jason for the first time. Maybe it was the first time he was seeing it for what it was, rather than the thing he imagined it was. Perhaps he had been fooling himself for all these years that he was special, that he could tear down the wall erected over the years so carefully to protect the powers-that-be.

He found himself at a literal wall and finally took stock of where he was. The buildings were vaguely familiar. He spun slowly and saw the apartment complex across the street. It was where he and Alexei and Amira had grown up. He had walked home.

He remembered the wall. They had used the pipes and gutters that snaked their way up the side to reach the roof of the building. They would see who could climb fastest. Alexei would sometimes win, sometimes it would be Amira...Jason never won. He constantly got tired quickly and couldn't scamper up as quickly as his friends, but he always tried to go a little faster each time. His friends would hang over the roof's edge and shout encouragement down to him.

Once up there, they would run across the rooftops, over and under and through an obstacle course of pipes and utility boxes, over alleyways and across breezeways until they reached a spot they had discovered that offered an unparalleled view of Center City and all points west until the buildings disappeared in the hazy murk of the horizon.

Without giving it much thought, he reached out and grasped a pipe in his hand and tugged at it. It didn't budge. He tightened his grip, placed a boot on the wall, and pushed up. He found himself pulling himself over the lip at the top and onto the roof in just a few movements. It had always seemed like a longer climb as a kid, he thought.

He realized this was one of the last places he had seen Alexei. They had climbed to the roof like they had hundreds of times before. His Horkrim's Syndrome was at its peak, and he was exhausted from the climb. Alexei still wanted to run the roof race, and Jason remembered feeling like death warmed over.

"You're going to beat me this time," Jason remembered Alexei saying.

I'm never going to beat you.

"How do you know?"

I never do.

"Doesn't mean you never will."

It's not fair, Alexei. I'm sick, and you're not.

"So? You get faster every time. And it doesn't mean you'll always be sick."

This is stupid. Why even try? What's the point?

"Because if you don't try, you won't ever know. You've lost before you've even started."

And Alexei had taken off on their well-trodden path. Jason remembered feeling angry at his friend for not recognizing his limits and for trying to make Jason be something he wasn't. He wasn't fast, or strong, or good at school. Alexei was.

Just once, he wanted to beat Alexei, not to feel jealous of his best friend. So he pulled himself up and ran after his friend, his feet falling into place without him needing to think about it. Every foothold and handhold had been practiced so many times over the hundreds of times they had run their course, a completely made-up thing known only to them and the select friends they showed it to, that he could practically run it blindfolded.

Over. Under. Duck. Jump. Roll. Balance. Jump, then jump again. Swing from the pipe. It all came back to Jason. And as short as the climb had seemed in retrospect, the course he, Amira, and Alexei had devised seemed longer.

When they had finally reached the end of the run that day, it had been sunset. The sky to the west was an explosion of purple and red. The sun shields over Center City were at their steepest angle of the day, providing as much protection as possible during the short period of the day when direct sunlight could slip under their shadow and shine into the usually shady streets. The buildings were starting to light up, and drones flitted about the city sky, glinting as they caught the sun the right way as they weaved about.

"We're going to live there one day," Alexei had said, sitting on the edge of the roof with his legs dangling over. Jason had remained standing, worried that if he sat down, he wouldn't want to get back up again. His lungs had burned from running and breathing hard, and they had felt like he hadn't been wearing a cycler at all.

"Yeah, right," Jason had replied. "No one makes it out of the Gaps."

We did.

"We will," Alexei said. He wasn't bragging; he was just confident. "And one day, I'm going to see the sunset with my own eyes."

"What do you think you're seeing them with now?" Jason had said between labored breaths. He intended all of the sarcasm.

"No, I mean without these," Alexei had said, tapping his goggles. "I want to see what the world really looks like. I want to know what it's like to go outside without all of this gear."

"You're stupid. If you go outside without your gear, you die." He had wished he could have taken his UV gear off; there was so much sweat accumulating under it.

Outside is death.

Alexei had shrugged. "It wasn't always like this. So maybe it doesn't always have to be like this. Maybe we can make it better."

"Who's we?"

"You and me and Amira," Alexei had said. "All of us. We'll fix everything."

"How?" Jason had said, and he finally sat next to his friend. He remembered how angry he was at his friend for thinking any of that was possible. Alexei hadn't been burned; Jason had, and his friend didn't know how that felt.

"Maybe we only don't do things because we're told we can't." Alexei had signed *smile*. "So I say we can. The same way we figured out our obstacle course. One thing at a time. And together."

Jason found himself sitting in that same spot, the sun starting to kiss the horizon.

I went outside.
Outside is death.
But I didn't die.
What does that make me?

The last thing Jason could recall about that final conversation with his friend was Alexei nudging him on the arm. "We'll always be friends, right?" He hadn't needed any signs to hear the smile in his friend's voice.

It's a place to start. Maybe Alexei's words had stayed with him more than he realized.

That had been the last time they saw each other. Alexei didn't show up to school the next day. After that, Jason had been in the hospital getting his new round of treatments, so he couldn't get any updates on what was happening for several months. Then they got the news that Alexei's body had been found with his mother's in her house when it burned down. Jordan was arrested…

He felt the hollowness in his chest. It felt the same as when he was told his friend had died. He had defined himself so much by his friendship with Alexei that when that had been taken away...

No...no, that's not right. He had defined himself by comparing himself to Alexei, and Alexei had never settled for that. Alexei had always pushed him to be more, to try harder, and not to let the limits that Jason put on himself be what defined him.

You'll never know unless you try. Jason had decided to fill that hollowness by doing what Alexei had always done: he pushed himself harder. The treatments had been successful, and he could keep up with the other kids. He worked harder at school and sports and didn't accept any limits that anyone put on him.

When a teacher had told him he would never do well in AP English, Jason studied harder and pulled top marks in the class.

When a coach told him he'd never make varsity, Jason was at the track first thing before school and then again after school for practice. He set four state records.

Who am I?

He thought back through his life. Whenever someone told him he couldn't do something, he kicked into a higher gear, worked harder, and proved them wrong. Every time he got knocked down, he got back up.

This is who I am.

Jason pulled his UV gear down off his torso. He anticipated searing heat as he exposed his skin to the dying sun, but instead, he felt the gentle embrace of the light.

I have made a difference. I've helped people.

He removed his cycler and took a deep breath. It should have filled his lungs with the feeling of broken glass, but instead he was met with a thousand smells: car exhaust, and food, and garbage, and so many other things that he couldn't identify, and the breath came easy.

It's not the big problems. It's dealing with the little ones. The ones I can fix.

He pulled his goggles off and opened his eyes. The sun was a hazy ball at the horizon, and the world was a much brighter place than he had imagined. The goggles had always subdued the colors and sharpness of everything, and it was like the world suddenly snapped into focus.

He imagined the insurmountable wall in front of him again, only this time, he saw it for what it was: not a monolith, but a stack of bricks. Bricks that could be moved, shifted, removed, and smashed one at a time. And before him, in his unfiltered vision of the city, he saw thousands of people who could help. Every time he helped one of them, they started chipping at the mortar holding that wall.

Jason took in the riot of color that reflected off the swarms of drones that danced in the sky.

This is who I am, Alexei. You were right.

Jason knew: it was time to get off the mat and back into the fight. Swan and Belford had told him "No". They told him what his limit was. He had, somewhere along the way, accepted it.

That was their definition of his limit. Not his.

CHAPTER 22

Jason was tearing his gear off as he burst through his front door. Amira was scrubbing the spray paint off the wall, spun around, and yelled in surprise at his entrance.

"Where did you–"

Jason cut her question off with a deep kiss and embrace that lifted her feet off the ground.

"What was that for?" she asked when he put her down.

"You were right," Jason said. "You were right, I should never have doubted you, and I need to get to my computer." He bounded up the steps to the office.

"What happened?" she asked as she followed him up the stairs. "You're worrying me."

"I went for a walk," Jason said as he plopped into his chair and brought up his work login. "I wish I could explain it, but you were right. It's not about making the big changes, it's about changing what we can. If we can get a thousand people chiseling at the wall, the bricks will come out one at a time, and…" He trailed off when he realized he hadn't shared his mental metaphor with her and that he must be coming across as having a manic episode. "Never mind, I'll explain that part later. But right now, I'm doing what I can to make one life better…I hope."

He logged into his work virtual terminal and felt a surge of relief when he saw his access hadn't been shut off.

"I thought you were suspended," Amira said as she stepped around behind his chair. "How do you still have access?"

"Bureaucracy is slow as shit…budget cutbacks…or maybe they can't until there are formal disciplinary charges against me, who knows?" Jason said as he navigated through the reports menus.

"Could you get in trouble for this?" she asked, biting her lip.

"Not doing anything illegal," Jason said. "And you know what? I'm getting more good done by breaking the rules than following them. I played their game, and the splice investigation took over a year and a half. I gave the rules the middle finger, and boom, I uncovered the largest child trafficking ring anyone's ever seen."

"Wait, what?" Amira's shock was plain.

"Oh, yeah, I didn't tell you that, did I?" Jason said. "It was an eventful day. But I think I have a way to figure out where Markus was taken, and if I'm lucky and I *can find the stupid report-*"

He clicked through more menus and reports settings until he finally found what he was looking for. He brought up the notebook photos on his phone and typed in the parameters the report required.

"This is a missing person's report," he said and started bringing up new tabs on his screen. "And this," he said as he typed in more information, "is the location data for when my perp made his move."

"What perp…?" Amira's voice trailed off.

"It's a lot," Jason said, bringing up another screen. "But trust me on this. I know the date, time, and location of when a bunch of these kids went missing, so with that information…" He brought up an archived video feed. "Boom," he said when the video loaded. "Got it."

"What am I looking at?" Amira asked and put her glasses on as she leaned over his shoulder.

"This is drone footage from right before Ezekiel…"

Amira gave Jason a questioning look.

"Ezekiel is the bad guy, or one of the bad guys, sorry, but this is when Ezekiel activated the tracker…"

The drone footage suddenly veered away.

"Was something supposed to happen?" Amira asked. She squeezed his shoulder, and Jason could sense her worry.

"This is supposed to show when the kid was taken," he said. "Hang on, must have gotten diverted. Let me check another one."

Jason brought up the footage from a nearby drone that offered another angle of the same location. He forwarded to the time stamp of the tracker going active…and the drone footage veered away again.

"No," Jason said, "that can't be right…"

The words no sooner left Jason's mouth than his terminal blinked off.

"No, no no no…well…shit." Jason checked the time. "Maybe Nguyen is still at the office." He stood from his desk and started gathering his coat and mask.

Amira stepped in front of him and put her hands on his arms. "What are you doing?"

"I need to do this," Jason said.

Tears rimmed her eyes. "It won't bring Alexei back," she said.

He took her hands into his and kissed her fingers. "But it may bring someone's Alexei back."

"So, you find out where Markus is, and then what?" Amira said, crossing her arms. "Go in, guns blazing?"

Jason could tell his wife disapproved of that plan. "No, I'll…I don't know. But no one else is doing anything, and if there's any chance I can find that kid alive…"

Her shoulders relaxed. "No, I get it. I know you'll be as safe as you ever can be." She kissed him. "You're a good person."

"Yeah, I'm starting to get that now," Jason said. "And you know I'll always be in the fight with you, right?"

"Yeah, never doubted it. Just glad you figured it out. Now go be a big damn hero."

Jason traversed the Gaps for the third time that day. *Getting my steps in today.*

With the devastating rays of the sun safely hidden behind the horizon and beaming down somewhere else, the Philadelphia streets came alive with people and activity. The denizens gladly shed their second skin of UV gear and bared their skin to the open air, a welcome relief from the necessity of being clad in unbreathable materials during the day.

Jason saw the signs of the social and economic barriers that seemed to disappear with the sun. More *bogari* ventured out of the shadows of the sun shields into the Gaps at night, which had become a riot of color and sound.

Gapper musicians co-opted disused buildings and underground clubs sprang up, the thumping beats permeating the streets outside, flashes of strobes and a press of humanity glimpsed through the doors. On the corners, the pushcart merchants barked at passersby, enticing them to peruse their wares that ranged from energy drinks and skin supplements to music compilations and bespoke fashion.

The *bogari* walked through the streets where the border between Center City and The Gaps was blurred, all pretense of their perceived station in life seemingly shed in favor of simply enjoying the spectacle, searching for a new dealer or artist, seeking a place to unwind and simply be.

Jason wished he had noticed…no, that wasn't the right word…*appreciated* the beauty of what happened every night. He always knew this blending of worlds happened, but knew it in the way that he was aware that he was eating something without appreciating the depth of flavor and nuances of textures. This was more than simply a source of sustenance for the city; it was the lifeblood of it.

The reverie had its limits, though. Within a few blocks of moving into The Gaps, the melting pot thinned, and the sounds of music and people faded, eventually giving way to the bustle of a city trying to accomplish as much as it could as quickly as possible. The lights of bars, clubs, and merchants were replaced by the glow of corner stores and street lamps. People walked briskly, heads down, carrying groceries or supplies, or towing children behind them as they hurried to or from work, people who had to make as much use of the little time they had between the sun going down and allowing them free movement, and needing to either get to their shift or catch as much sleep as they could before reporting back to work.

Several more blocks and Jason could almost feel the shift from working class to working poor. The streets were quieter, fewer people traversing them, fewer lights illuminating them. There was music in the air, but a less joyful kind, and it floated into Jason's ears from the occasional passing car blaring a song on a poorly-installed aftermarket sound system, or from the phone of the corner kid showing off to their crew.

It was only the span of maybe a dozen blocks between Jason's home on the edge of Center City and where he stood, and he lamented, not for the first time, that the walk towards the safety of the sun shields was not one that most in The Gaps would ever make.

The mixing at the border was nice, it was life-affirming, but it was not permanent. In a few hours the merchants would start wheeling home, the clubs would play their last song, and everyone would return to where they came from.

A few Gappers might have a few more dollars in their account, both legally and elicitly gained, maybe enough to survive another week, maybe sufficient to inch a little closer to the safety of the shade.

Bogari would have a fun story to tell their work or college friends, or maybe they "discovered" a new artist or something they would leverage for clout with their social feeds. Perhaps a few would be moved enough to reach out and offer a hand up to someone or to start questioning the state of things.

Small victories. The Gapper that successfully inched forward, the *bogari* that looked back and acted, each was a drop in the bucket, a grain of sand, Jason knew. He also knew that enough sand eventually became an entire beach.

Jason traversed from one pool of light to the next cast from the street lamps overhead. His mind had wandered, but as his office...*former* office...came into view, he refocused. There was a missing kid that needed to be found.

He hoped. His brain told him that the odds were low that he'd find Markus and that even if he did, they were even lower that he'd be OK. But the spark of hope remained.

The parking lot was barren of cars, save for the Mustang. He tried to keep from thinking of it as *his* Mustang. It belonged to the department, and even if he wanted to buy it, the price would be well beyond anything he could afford. But again, the spark of hope remained.

Lights were shining in the windows. He swiped his ID at the door, but a flashing red light and a rejecting tone told him what he already knew. He pounded at the door and waited.

A full minute passed before he heard the buzz and click of the lock disengaging, and he pushed his way in. Nguyen stood by the remote entry button, the top shirt button undone, her tie hanging loosely around her neck.

"Hey, Loo. What're you doing back?" the younger detective asked. It wasn't an accusation, Jason could hear.

"Couldn't stand the coffee at home," Jason said. "Shouldn't you be gone for the day?"

Nguyen huffed. "Well, even if you hadn't knocked Belford on his ass, it was still going to be a shit show after you left. Transfer of command and all that.

Our new CO wants a full summary of the entire investigation since its inception, along with productivity reports and…" She trailed off. She gestured around at the stacks of reports around the office. "…I'm low man on the totem pole."

"I'm sorry that it went down the way it did," Jason said.

"You mean keeping on Markus' case, or punching the captain?"

"Punching Belford, I suppose," Jason said. "I shouldn't have done that. I mean, it felt good, but still…but I can't apologize for trying to find Markus. Or how I went about it."

Nguyen nodded in a tight motion. "Good. You shouldn't apologize for that. And as for punching Belford in his stupid face, well…asshole had it coming."

Jason shared a brief chuckle with his subordinate…*former* subordinate. He mentally chastised himself. It was a new world he was living in, one that he needed to wrap his head around.

"Seriously, though, I do want to get some sleep tonight, so what can I do for you?" Nguyen said, and she plopped back down in her chair.

"I have a lead on Markus…or, at least, I think I do, and I need to confirm it."

Nguyen leaned forward, all signs of exhaustion gone from her face. "Anything I can do to help."

"Might mean getting on the captain's radar in a bad way," Jason warned.

"Meh," Nguyen replied. "Let him fire me. I'll just go get a job in the private security sector and make twice as much money."

"You sure?"

"I'm in, boss," Nguyen said. "What do you need?"

"OK, so I tried looking at the footage from another abduction that this guy Ezekiel did," Jason said, pulling up a chair to the younger woman's desk. "But all of the drones were diverted. Can you pull up the footage from another incident?"

"Sure," Nguyen said and began pulling up tabs on her screen. "What's the date and location?" Jason pulled up his phone and gave Nguyen the information. "OK, got it," she said and pulled up the video feed.

As he suspected, the drone footage veered away from the location as the timestamp reached when the tracker was supposed to have gone active.

"Weird," Nguyen said. "Same thing happened with the Kline kid."

"And two others," Jason said. "So if a drone gets called away, what happens when they reach the site they were sent to."

Nguyen scratched her head. "Well, I guess it depends on the type of call. Most of the time, the drone will do a flyover and get footage. If the heuristics spot someone they need to speak to, like, say, a driver of a car if there's an accident, they'll fly in and interact with whoever it is. Why, what are you thinking?"

"What if there is no actual crime when they show up?" Jason asked.

"Like if no one's there?"

"No, if there was never a crime at all. Like if someone called in a car accident, but there wasn't actually a car accident?"

"Probably gets filed under 'no call' and they go back to their patrol route," Nguyen said.

"Do me a favor," Jason said. "This drone we just looked at…can we see if whatever call pulled it away ended up on that 'no call' list?"

Nguyen tapped a few keys. "Yeah, look at that…it was."

"Can I hear that call?"

Nguyen tapped a few more keys. A waveform appeared on her screen, and a female voice played from the monitor's speakers.

"Hello, I'd like to report an accident…I think a kid got hit by a car. The address is…"

Jason stroked his chin. "OK, this is going to be an odd request…" He grabbed a pen and a random piece of paper and started scribbling information from Ezekiel's notebook from memory. "Can you pull anything that ended up being a 'no call' on these dates, at these times, at these locations?"

Nguyen examined the list. "Yeah…shouldn't take more than a couple of minutes."

"Really?" Jason was legitimately surprised. He thought it would take a few hours.

"Boss, I don't know if you've noticed, but I'm kinda a genius."

Nguyen was good to her word. Within three minutes, she had started compiling a report of the calls Jason requested, and Jason began listening to them. Call after call, all for what he would consider low-key and even mundane things, calls that would rarely rise to getting a live person dispatched. He wasn't sure how he felt about that.

"Yo, there's a dumpster on fire, someone better put that thing out…"

"Um, I'd like to report a mugging…someone stole my purse…"

"Hello, I'd like to report an accident…I think a kid got hit by a car. The address is…"

"Wait," Jason said. "Wait, that one…I heard it before. Play the first call you found again."

Nguyen tapped on her keyboard.

"Hello, I'd like to report an accident…I think a kid got hit by a car. The address is…"

"Is…is that the same voice?" Nguyen asked. She played both at the same time. The same voice played in sync and then diverged when they read the address.

"Holy crap," Jason said. "How is that even possible?"

"It's not hard," Nguyen said. "Probably just a computer-generated voice reading through a script."

Jason looked at the list of 'no calls' that was still compiling. "Each of these dates has over forty 'no calls' each," he said, partially to himself, partially to Nguyen. "That's how they're doing it."

"Doing what, Loo?"

"They're setting up robocalls or something," Jason said, saying his thought process aloud. "They jam the system for a few minutes, clear the drones out. Abductor drops the kid in the shipping crate on the roof. Then the shipping drone picks it up, and no one's the wiser; it's just another drone in the sky." A thought occurred to him. "How hard would it be-"

"Hard," Nguyen said, finishing Jason's sentence. "I could set up something to monitor the dispatch calls for anything that's a repeat of something on the 'no call' report we already generated…but with the average call volume that comes in, by the time I identified the call, we'd probably be too late to respond. It would also take a fair amount of processing power, enough to make someone in IT notice."

"Crap," Jason said, his hope deflating. "Wait…what if we could narrow the window?"

Nguyen stared off into space, and Jason imagined she was doing complex math in her head. "Yeah, that would help…depending on how small of a window, it could take the time down from hours to…thirty minutes."

Jason closed his eyes and envisioned Ezekiel's binder. He reconstructed the pages that he had seen. The dates and times…and a frequency on each page. "What if we knew exactly when they were starting?"

"Well…yeah, then I could isolate those calls in a matter of minutes at worst," Nguyen said. "But how?"

Jason wrote the frequencies he saw on the piece of paper. "This is the frequency they ping when they take a kid. If we can catch that ping when it activates, we'll know it's time to start listening to calls."

Nguyen was already typing code into a new tab. "Already on it. I can use our current communications network to listen to those frequencies…"

Jason lost the rest of what Nguyen was saying in a garble of technobabble that he couldn't understand, but he was sure the woman knew what she was doing.

Jason was impressed with Nguyen's work.

The rookie detective had set up the monitoring for the trackers and the listener for the dispatch calls in less than an hour.

I knew she was brilliant but damn…

Then it was time to wait.

Three hours and three pots of sludge-like coffee later, Nguyen's computer beeped.

"Tracker just went active…" She started tapping on her keyboard. "Listener is active…there's one…another…yeah, it looks like it's started. I think we've got one."

Jason ran to Nguyen's side. "Cross reference the calls with where they were sent." Nguyen tapped a few keys, and a map appeared on the screen with red dots for every call. "Zoom in there," Jason ordered and pointed, and Nguyen enlarged a map section. "Right there. Where is that?"

Nguyen looked at the addresses scrolling on her screen. "Looks like 60th and Sansom. That's at least an hour on foot, maybe longer."

Jason went to Nguyen's desk and opened the top drawer. He fished around and pulled out the Mustang's keys. "Not walking."

Nguyen didn't even attempt to hide her smile. "I didn't see anything."

Jason pulled his headgear on. "Can you keep an eye on dispatch? Let me know if anything I should know about in that area pops up?"

"Will do," Nguyen said. "Good hunting."

CHAPTER 23

Four square blocks was a lot of ground to cover, especially when Jason didn't know what he was looking for, or when it would happen.

Nguyen had confirmed that the dispatch spike was still in play, which gave Jason a little relief. The window wasn't closed. There was still a chance he could catch...someone. He wasn't sure who.

Not for the first time, he wished he had gotten his drone pilot license. It would have made easy work of finding what he was looking for: fly a drone over the area and search the rooftops for a delivery pad.

If wishes were horses...

He needed to find a way up to the roofs to explore the old-fashioned way: mark one eyeball. He knew the Mustang would garner attention, especially if he spent hours circling the area. He didn't want to spook whomever he was looking for. He parked it in the first available spot. He returned to how he started his career: a cop walking a beat.

There was no better way to learn a neighborhood, to learn what to look for, than being at eye-level with the people, Jason thought. He remembered his training officer, Banks. Banks was one of the good ones. He drilled into Jason repeatedly that the job was knowing who everyone on the beat was, what they did, and when they did it. Banks had never intended it as a surveillance tactic, more from the angle of taking a genuine interest in people. The job, at its core, was people.

Jason felt like Banks was walking beside him as he felt the concrete beneath his boots. It was a new neighborhood, unfamiliar to Jason, so he started with the basics. He saw where the storefronts were, and where the apartment entrances were located. He saw which breezeways connected which buildings, and which alleys had delivery entrances.

He watched the people as they walked by; he saw who was in a hurry, who was in no rush, who seemed to be having a bad day, and who looked like they just wanted to get home.

He saw the slow decay of a neighborhood. Some potholes had been in the street so long that the edges were caving in. The sidewalks were crumbling, and he couldn't take more than a couple of steps without needing to catch himself from stumbling over where it dipped down, heaved up, or sat at an awkward angle. The buildings seemed to sag and lean, and there were so many layers of graffiti that Jason found it impossible to discern anything legible or recognizable.

The people matched the buildings: slumped shoulders and curved backs, a slow, plodding gait of a weariness that had sunk into the bones.

The distant lights of Center City offered enough illumination to outline the wreckage of an enormous solar shield jutting out of the ground at an obtuse angle that served as the backdrop for The Western Gaps, the result of a forgotten accident that left a swath of the city uninhabitable, abandoned, and off limits. If the area had a name before the accident, Jason didn't know it; he only knew it as The Falls.

Jason recalled driving through neighborhoods like this when he first got on the job, but he didn't remember the sheer level of hopelessness that seemed to permeate the very air. It seemed like the rot of The Falls continued to spread one block at a time.

Banks had told him that he would know his beat when he could set his watch to the ebb and flow of the people. Jason didn't have that kind of time, but he strived for the spirit of the teaching: to know what was happening, and when.

He checked his phone. No messages from Nguyen, so the window was still open. Yet still, he couldn't find a clear route up to the roofs. Every door he tried was locked, and no one answered when he knocked.

Don't blame them. I wouldn't answer the door at this hour.

This was the work, though Jason wished it was under better circumstances. Just a few short hours prior, he could have had five cars stationed in the area keeping watch and a drone tasked to their position. He could have created a net that, with one word from him, would snap shut and ensnare his quarry. He would have the backing of a team to ensure no one escaped and the luxury of at least a little time to interrogate suspects.

Another lap around the area, and still no route revealed itself. He varied his route. Familiarity bred laziness, and Jason didn't want to miss something because he fell into a routine.

He wiped a layer of sweat from his brow and rechecked his phone.

I've got to be running out of time.

Many street lamps were out, either smashed or simply not working. Jason was sure there was a moon somewhere in the sky, but it remained hidden behind a curtain of clouds and haze, providing no light. His goggles attempted to constantly adjust to the sporadic illumination and always seemed a step behind. He eventually gave up on them, hanging them from his belt.

He could hear sirens in the distance and figured it was a patroller responding to one of the dispatch calls. The thought of how many crimes were being ignored because of the robo-dials to divert attention from a four-square block area sent a shiver down Jason's back.

He began another circuit of the area, and his phone pulsed. He checked the message. It was from Les, not Nguyen, and it was a single word: HIDE.

The sirens were getting closer. Just below that sound, he heard a high-pitched buzzing. *Drones?* He ducked into an alley and found a spot between some dumpsters to hunker down.

WHAT'S HAPPENING? Jason messaged back.

There wasn't an immediate response. He heard a patroller speed by the alley and saw the flashers reflected on the walls as it passed, followed by a loud *bang* as it hit one of the large potholes that Jason knew was just up the road. He listened, and it sounded like the patroller continued on, but he knew that the car would need major repairs soon, especially if they kept driving at that speed and hitting holes that a family could live in.

His phone pulsed. BELFORD PRESSING CHARGES. A pause. ASSAULTING A POLICE OFFICER. Another pause. THEY TRACKED THE CAR. GET OUT OF THERE.

Each message ratcheted up Jason's heart rate a notch. He went from suspended, to misdemeanor, to felony, to grand theft auto in ten seconds.

A swarm of drones buzzed into the alley, and Jason pulled himself into a tight ball and wedged himself further between the wall and the dumpster. Three flew by in formation, cameras darting about on their gimbals underneath, and continued down the alley without any notice that they had spotted him.

OVERKILL MUCH? Jason replied.

There was no response. He waited and gamed out his options. He could make a run for the car, but they would just track him, and were likely waiting there for him. He could try to make it home, but he figured Swan and her stooges would also have eyes on that.

He needed a lawyer. He wouldn't be able to get one until the morning. He had no intention of sitting in a jail cell all night, which was where Swan and Belford wanted him to be. He wouldn't give them the satisfaction of that visual.

His phone finally pulsed, and Jason realized it was only a matter of time until they zeroed in on his location through the device. He glanced at the message. SORRY, S & B ARE HERE. WINDOW STILL OPEN.

Jason pulled the back off his phone and removed the battery and sim card. The drop window was still open.

That means there are no eyes in the sky. He looked up and down the alley. There were no fire escapes that he could access at ground level. No obvious entrances into buildings, just one-way fire exits. Utility pipes running out of the ground to the higher levels…

…finally, a path upward.

Jason took stock of the alley again. No sirens or flashing lights nearby, no buzzing of a drone swarm searching for him…

He sprinted across the alley and, without breaking stride, planted a foot on the wall and pulled himself hand over hand up the pipes until they bent into the brick wall. He craned his head around and saw a window sill just above him. He launched himself up, caught the edge with his fingertips, and slowly pulled himself up, bracing himself against the inside of the window cut out until he was pressed against the darkened glass, standing on the thin sill.

He found more points of purchase: other windows, missing bricks, more pipes that climbed up, architectural flourishes, and slowly made his way up the side of the building until he pulled himself over the lip of the top and onto the roof. He took a moment to catch his breath, stretch his fingers, and then surveyed the alley beneath him. The drone swarm entered the alley again and began another sweep. He counted three drones again and breathed a small sigh of relief.

Jason scanned the rooftops. A jungle of metal rose before him, blocking his view of anything more than a few dozen feet in any direction. He needed to get higher to see anything. He clambered over ducts and fences, and pulled himself over access ports and water tanks until he finally had an unobstructed view.

He could hear the sirens below still, and occasionally the flashing lights reflected high enough that he could see them from his perch. Radios and mask-dampened voices sounded muffled in the distance, but it was clear to him that the search was still on. Jason figured that this kind of response could only mean one thing: Swan and Belford were coming for his career. His position in the department wasn't what threatened them anymore…the fact that he was even on the force was what they feared.

He tucked away the thought to process later. His most immediate need was escape. He began plotting out routes he could take over the rooftops and breezeways that would get him far enough away from the search grid when he heard the squeak and squeal of a door opening, and he froze.

Movement caught his eye from three rooftops over. He saw a rectangle of dim light; then a silhouetted figure awkwardly pushed something out onto the roof. They stopped, kneeled out of sight, and the figure stood back up a moment later with some effort. Jason squinted, trying to see more through the relative darkness, but from his obstructed view, the details eluded him. The figure walked back to the door and went back inside without whatever load they had carried up.

The door hadn't finished closing by the time Jason's boots hit the graveled rooftop. He took off at a full sprint, paying no heed to any of the objects in his way, leaping over them and dodging around and under them without slowing.

In less than thirty seconds, he made it to the door but hesitated before opening it. The hinges had made an awful squeal that had to have been heard from the street; if he opened it now, it would surely grab someone's attention, including the figure likely working their way back down the stairwell.

He decided to instead look for whatever they had dropped. It didn't take long. A single black delivery crate sat on the roof where he had seen the figure stop. He didn't recognize the chemical names on the labels, but he did recognize the hazard and biohazard placards that were in plain sight.

He turned to continue his pursuit down the stairs when he heard a noise from within the crate. It sounded like something shifted, followed by a dull *thump*. He approached the crate again and slowly pried the lid off.

He suspected he knew what he would find, but the sight of an unconscious child still surprised him. He stared in shock for a moment.

It was a girl, barely on the edge of being a teenager, though it was challenging to be sure with her headgear on. He reached in and pulled her out as carefully as possible, taking care not to knock her cycler off accidentally. He noticed it wasn't a normal one that he was used to seeing; this one was configured differently, almost identical to the one Ezekiel had shown him.

His heart pounded in his chest as he weighed his options. Whoever had dropped the kid on the roof was likely still nearby...but the kid needed his help first. He powered on his phone, deciding that the risk was worth it. Moments later, he had sent the message to Les with his location.

He eyed the girl, and then the crate.

A plan formed. He moved the girl and tucked her away out of sight. He messaged Les again. WAIT UNTIL AFTER WINDOW IS CLOSED FOR RECOVERY. He followed it up by describing where he had moved the girl. He removed his long jacket and covered her as best he could, just in case the sun rose before help arrived.

Guess I don't need it.

A few moments passed before he got the pulse of an incoming message. WHAT ARE YOU DOING?

Jason stepped into the crate. GOING DARK. He powered off his phone, worked his way into the cramped crate, barely large enough for the child, and pulled the lid closed, sealing himself in darkness. His knees were pressed into his chest, and he had no room to move his arms.

And he waited.

If there were any sounds outside his self-imposed prison, they were muffled by the thick plastic of the container. He could only hear his cycler cycling and his heart beating in his ears.

He had no idea how much time had passed, whether it had been mere minutes or closer to an hour, when he finally heard the whine of the dual turbines of a delivery drone. It got louder until it was directly over him, then he listened to the graspers slide and click into place on the haul points on the sides of the crate. A moment later, there was an increase in the turbines' pitch and a slight lurch as he felt the container lifted into the air.

Really hope I don't exceed the weight limit of this thing.

Time was beginning to lose meaning for Jason in his near-perfect darkness. He had tried to count to himself but abandoned that quickly after he measured out ten minutes. Even if he knew how long they had traveled, the radius had grown so large to make it useless information, and he had no idea which direction he was traveling. So he waited.

Eventually, he heard the turbines change pitch again, and after a few moments, he felt the crate alight on something solid, much more gently than he anticipated. The grasper servos whirred as they disengaged, and the drone sounds faded as it flew away.

Now?

He started counting. He decided when he got to one hundred that he would exit the crate.

He got to eighty-three when there was a mechanical sound of metal sliding on metal, and then he felt himself being lowered like he was on an elevator. He concluded that was precisely where he was when he felt his ears pop from the rapid change in altitude. He gathered he was in one of the taller skyscrapers.

The elevator came to a rest, the doors opened, and there was nothing. Then something slid underneath the crate, and he was being moved again. A few turns followed, and he was brought to a rest.

His legs had moved beyond cramping, and he felt the pins and needles as he lost feeling in them. He needed to stand, to stretch, or else he worried he would be in no condition to defend himself or move quickly if necessary. He decided to risk it and slowly pushed the lid open a crack to see where he was.

Wherever he had been taken, it looked like a morgue. The room was spartan, with dark-tiled walls and utility lighting. A few shelves with what looked like surgical gowns stacked by size lined one wall, and there was a wheelchair with restraints on the arms and legs in the corner. A figure in a white cleansuit had their back to him as they tapped information into a screen next to a set of double doors.

Jason slowly rose from the crate, careful not to let the lid make any noise. He stepped out and tested his weight on his legs and felt the painful sensation of blood rushing back into them. He carefully, silently crept towards the figure, willing them not to turn around.

Ten feet away.

Five feet.

Three.

Jason's boot squeaked on the tile floor, and the figure spun around.

CHAPTER 24

Jason had only a fraction of a second to register the look of panic that dawned on the person's face before they yelled something muffled by the suit's mask. Jason palmed the faceplate of the cleansuit and slammed their head backwards into the screen, smashing the piece of equipment into uselessness. They stumbled and fell.

The cleansuited figure attempted to rise to their feet, and Jason kicked their legs out from under them, sending them to the ground in a heap. He grabbed them by the scruff of their suit and drug them over kicking towards the shelves of gowns. He grabbed one and secured their hands behind their back before flipping them onto their back and ripping the headpiece off to reveal feminine features. He clamped a hand over her mouth.

Her eyes were open wide with panic, and Jason could see the whites all the way around her irises. Her chest rose and fell quickly as she hyperventilated.

"I'm going to take my hand off your mouth," Jason said calmly. "When I do, you aren't going to scream. Understand?"

The woman nodded her head. Jason slowly removed his hand, and she remained silent, breathing rapidly and heavily.

"Take a deep breath," Jason said. Whether she tried or not, he couldn't tell, as she continued breathing in a panicked pant, though he thought maybe it slowed down a hair. He jammed his hands in his pockets and felt around for his phone. "What is this place?"

"It's…it's…it's a…a research… research center," she stammered out between breaths.

"What are you researching?"

"Congenital and…inherited…genetic defects and…defects and diseases," she answered.

"And you experiment on kidnapped kids?" Jason spat.

The woman glanced over at the crate in the middle of the floor. "We…we need specimen material…what we're doing is cutting edge-"

"You know what, shut up," Jason commanded as he felt his rage building.

He searched the woman and found a keyring with several keys and a white access card. "Where are we? Specifically?"

"If you let me go, I'm sure that we can work out-"

"Lady, does this look like a negotiation?" Jason said quietly. "If you think for one second that I will hesitate to start breaking your fingers…"

"The delivery room," she quickly responded as the color drained from her face. "Where the specimens are prepared before being held for the procedure."

"Right," Jason said, not liking any words she just used. "By 'specimens', you mean other kids, right? Where do you take them?"

"The specimens must be kept in pristine condition," the woman said. "We've learned that external contamination can dramatically affect results…"

"If you refer to kids as *specimens* one more time…" Jason's voice trailed off. "Where do those doors go?"

The woman swallowed hard. "The research center. Operating theaters. Lecture halls. Records room."

Jason felt his hand involuntarily ball into a fist. Answers were on the other side of those doors. "And the elevator you brought me down on?"

She shook her head. "It's automatic. Deliveries only come down, nothing can be sent back up. That's what I'm trying to tell you, we can't let the specimens leave-" She flinched under Jason's glare. "…it's a completely secure facility. You won't be able to get out. But if you let me talk to management…"

"Do you live here?" Jason demanded.

The woman looked confused. "What? I don't understand…"

"Do. You. Live. Here." Jason repeated.

"No, I live in Society Hill."

"Then there's an exit," Jason concluded.

He started playing scenarios in his mind. Something the woman said stuck with him, however. "What's the procedure you mentioned? What do you do with the kids?"

"I don't know," the woman replied and yelped in fear when Jason grabbed her little finger in his fist. "I honestly don't know, I just do intake, honestly! Once I process the spec-kids! Kids, once I process the kids for intake, that's it, I don't have anything else to do with the procedure!"

Jason looked at the stacks of surgical gowns. "How many?" he growled.

"What? I don't-...I mean, I processed twelve kids this shift. Twelve. So there are probably just as many procedures scheduled for today. We don't hold inventory…"

Twelve?!

"How long before they start?"

The woman looked like she was trying to recall something. "I mean, it's about five in the morning, so they'll probably start in the next fifteen minutes if they haven't already."

Jason reached into his pocket and pulled out his phone. Les' number was still on the screen, and he tapped the "unmute" button. "That enough?"

"More than enough," Les replied. "Got your location, too. I'm calling in for a response team right now, warrants will be on the way."

The woman paled. "Wait, what…what have you…"

"Stand down and sit tight, we'll be there in less than fifteen minutes," Les continued.

She had said that the procedures would start in fifteen minutes, if they hadn't already.

Standing down wasn't an option.

Jason knew he needed to get the kids out; that was the top priority. But once he got them out, would he be able to get back in? Not likely. He didn't see a scenario where he was able to escort a bunch of kids out of a highly secure facility without someone noticing.

He also knew he would need more information about what was going on to shut it down permanently. They would go out and get more kids and build a new facility; he was sure of it. There was too much money invested in this to abandon the project.

Kids first. It needed to happen.

"Negative," Jason replied. "Clock's running."

"Jason, you don't have your badge anymore," Les said. "You can't just go charging in-"

"I'm doing it," Jason said. "Arrest me when you get here if you need to." He disconnected the call.

He used more gowns to secure the woman's ankles and then jammed one in her mouth and tied it as a gag.

Jason pushed the double doors open a crack and peeked through. It was a sterile-white, hospital-like hallway. He heard voices further down the hall, out of sight around a corner, and he froze. He waited and listened. The voices grew louder, then grew more distant with each passing moment. Once he was satisfied they were moving away, he moved down the hallway as quietly as he could.

He approached the end of the hall and slowed, eventually stopping where it made a sharp left. He poked his head around the corner to get the lay of the land, and he was shocked.

The hallway became more of a mezzanine, with a waist-high glass barrier on one side. Beyond that opened into an indoor quad, looking down onto a large tree growing several floors down. He could see similar glass-lined halls affording the same view above and below his position. There were lounge areas, communal work areas, screens everywhere that flashed media streams, and more esoteric information that Jason couldn't begin to interpret. Two staircases twisted and winded their way up the interior perimeter in a great double-helix, stopping at each level's mezzanine.

The facility, though, appeared empty and dimly lit, waiting for the workday to begin, which Jason was grateful for as it made his search easier. He couldn't imagine navigating the maze of hallways and offices while trying to be stealthy.

Room after room, he kicked doors in and cleared them, and for the life of him, if he didn't know any better, he would have thought he was in a typical, if swanky, hospital. He found exam rooms that looked no different than any he had been in, offices with diplomas and awards hung on the walls next to real-wood bookshelves and real-wood desks. There were conference rooms with large screens arrayed for presenting…Jason wasn't sure what, but he was confident that's what they were for. There were labs with microscopes, centrifuges, and other equipment he had never seen before.

Every room he checked had terminals, and all of them were locked, preventing him from accessing any data, furthering his frustration.

The most significant difference between this and a real hospital, Jason lamented as he kicked open another door to another communal workspace, was that there weren't any signs indicating where anything was. Every hospital he had ever been in as a kid, and he had been in plenty up until the final treatments for his Horkrim's Syndrome, had signs everywhere to tell you where to go. This place was sterilized of that information.

He came to another set of double doors that actually had a label over them: *Auditorium.* A screen next to the door had the current date, with a message that read, "*10:00 am: Mortality and Morbidity Review of Potentiality Reallocation by Exchordic Nucleatic Ablation.*

He pushed the doors open and found a different kind of room. It looked more like a theater, with seats arranged in an arc before a stage, each row lower than the one behind it to allow an unimpeded view.

He could see this was the corner of the building, facing east. Windows ran from floor to ceiling, almost two stories high, and in the corner of the room, where all attention would be directed, was a small stage and podium and a large screen behind. Outside the windows was some kind of terrace surrounded by scaffolding.

He noticed flashing on the podium and saw an active screen. He almost turned around to resume his search but decided he would kick himself if he didn't at least check.

He approached the podium and saw that the screen was active and, to his shock, not locked. He tapped it to bring up what was last accessed, and he saw a directory labeled RESEARCH NOTES ARCHIVE: SITES ALPHA, OMICRON, UPSILON.

He opened the folder and looked for the most-recently accessed file. The date was from two days prior, and he opened it.

The screen behind him lit up with the image of an overhead shot of an operating theater. There was a table with what looked like platforms sticking out where someone's arms would be, were they to lay on it. A time code was running in the corner.

He heard voices from the recording.

"Plans for the weekend?" one said.

"I'm behind on my data analysis," the other said. "I need to get it wrapped up, or I won't get credit for the class."

"Oof," the first said, and they entered the frame. Both wore scrubs and surgical masks. One was pushing a wheelchair with an emaciated-looking kid in it. "That sucks. Anyway, ready? On three?"

The second figure kneeled and held onto the child's legs while the other placed a hand on the child's shoulder and used their free hand to manipulate something on the chair. Restraints released, ones that Jason hadn't noticed were there, and both figures grabbed firmly onto the child who started fighting them.

"No, no, no," a small voice was begging. "Please, I want my mom, please…"

The adults wrestled the squirming child onto the table face-down and began securing new restraints, the whole while the child was begging for them to stop, begging for their mom and their dad.

Jason's heart broke as he looked on.

Once secure, the adults continued their idle chatter as one moved a piece of equipment over the child, a curved rack with thin spines sticking out from the top, and the other removed the surgical gown covering the child to expose their back.

"OK, moving to ready position," one adult said and tapped some keys on a keyboard. The table adjusted position, forcing the child into a position where they were curved forward like they were slouching, and Jason could see the bumps of their vertebrae.

The other lowered the curved mechanism until it touched the child's back and locked it into position. "Extraction halo is locked."

The child was sobbing. The adults didn't seem to notice.

"Engaging delivery nodes." There was a hiss of air, like a nail gun firing, and each of the spines of the device lowered in an instant, one after the other. The child jerked with each one as much as the restraints would let them.

The scream from the child ripped Jason's heart out of his chest and shattered it into dust.

"Delivering enzyme solution into the L4/L5 Intervertebral Disc."

"OK, doing T9/T10."

"All readings are normal."

"Hm, that one didn't seem to take. Re-extracting from T1/T2."

With each step, the adults narrated the procedure, and the child's screams of pain were only broken up by uncontrollable sobbing and begging for them to stop, begging for their mom. Never once did Jason see or hear anything that indicated pity, or remorse, or that they even acknowledged that there was a *human child on the table.*

"Ready for final extraction?"

"Hang on, let me check…yeah, looks like we have everything."

The table lowered, and one of the adults approached the child. They palpated the back of the weeping child's head, and when they found whatever they were looking for, they picked up a long syringe from a table and inserted it where the skull and neck met. They started pulling back on the syringe, and the child started convulsing violently.

And then they went silent and still. Even with the restraints in place, Jason could see that the child had gone completely limp.

"Extraction complete," the adult said. "That was a good one."

"Very smooth," the other said. "This will really help someone."

The video went black, and Jason realized tears were streaming down his face.

A new video came up on the screen, and Jason frantically tried to find the control to turn it off but couldn't find anything. He started to walk up the steps, not wanting to see the procedure again, not knowing if he could.

This time, it was another operating room with a child lying face up and anesthetized from what Jason could see. Someone different from the first video, an adult in scrubs, stepped into the frame. The time stamp put the footage from a day ago.

"This is the documentation of procedure 836-A-2B. Patient was tested, and results were positive for Huntington's Disease on March 30 of this year. Procedure has begun at 14:21, please mark the time. While we know that the procedure has been successful for those without any ailments and those with chronic genetic diseases after the onset of symptoms, the 836 protocol is to test the efficacy against disorders prior to onset and activation. Ten blade."

Jason paused and turned around. He watched the procedure as the doctor calmly explained the technical aspects in terminology that Jason didn't understand. He was able to pick up one thing: that whatever was extracted from the first child was used on the second to treat a horrible and incurable disease that would ravage them later in life.

For the briefest of moments, Jason had thought about the good of the procedure, what an incredible thing it was that they had a potential treatment for such a debilitating disease. But then he remembered the cost. His heart broke all over again.

He returned to the podium and looked at the directory. The file was named in a naming convention that Jason didn't understand, a date, and was followed by the word SUCCESS. The list of files filled the screen.

He started scrolling, and scrolling, and scrolling. File, after file, after file scrolled past, fifty files, a hundred, then more, each date on the file going back weeks, then months, then years…Jason lost count as he scrolled through, unable to bring himself to open any and look at another procedure.

Most of the most recent files ended with "success", and only now and then was one followed by FAILURE. As he scrolled back in time, the failures appeared more frequently, from when the procedure was less refined, Jason surmised.

Soon the failures outnumbered the successes. More and more filled the screen until there were no successes. He found the first file marked "success" and counted back. He estimated at least 50 failures before the first one succeeded. He scrolled back to that one. It was from twenty years ago.

The date.

No.

It was the date of his procedure.

No, no, no that can't…that can't…

His finger hovered over the file. He was at war with himself and couldn't bring himself to either open the file or move his finger away.

I'm sorry.

The video began to play.

The quality wasn't as good as the one he had just seen, but it was clear that it was an operating room. Doctors and nurses moved about the surgical table.

He saw his younger self, thin, small, barely breathing on it. He remembered how hard breathing had been then, how each breath was a struggle. Walking, sitting up, and even eating had become exhausting.

But his parents had told him that this new procedure would help him, could make him better.

IVs trailed out his arm, and monitoring devices were affixed to his skin. The anesthesiologist placed a mask over Jason's young face and told him to count backward from one hundred. He only made it to ninety-six.

Another table was wheeled in with a curved device, similar to the one that Jason saw in the first video, and his stomach tied itself into a knot. The device differed in that long tubes were coming off of it, and it looked less sleek, less refined, and Jason watched as they inserted more IV needles all over his body and connected them to the device.

Then he heard a crash from off-screen and yelling. Three figures in scrubs entered the frame, trying to restrain a child about the same age as the younger Jason as they carried him in. The boy thrashed and fought, and Jason could see that the adults struggled to hold on to him.

The boy saw Jason lying on the table and started yelling. "No! Jason! Jason, wake up! No!"

A chill washed over Jason in the present. That voice…he knew that voice. The boy thrashed more, and for a moment, Jason could see his face.

It was Alexei.

Jason felt his body convulse as he watched them wrestle Alexei onto the table and strap him down.

"Don't you do it! Jason! Wake up! Don't you hurt my friend! *Te voy a matar*, you hear me! I'll fucking kill you if you hurt my friend! Jason, wake up!"

He isn't asking for help…

They strapped Alexei to the table as he screamed obscenities and threats and begged for the young Jason to wake up, but his friend remained peacefully asleep, the heart rate monitor beeping calm and steady.

The procedure proceeded as Jason had seen before, though, if possible, even more barbarically, with whatever was being extracted from Alexei flowing into some kind of device, then through the tubes and into Jason. Alexei's yells of defiance turned into screams of agony.

Jason watched the procedure, unable to look away until they inserted the final needle, and Alexei lay limp and lifeless on the table.

Only then did Jason turn away and violently vomit all of the content of his stomach onto the floor. His body convulsed again and again, emptying everything it could until only bile and spit were left. He fell to his knees, dry heaving and gagging, tears pouring down his face.

No…Alexei…no…I can't…I killed…

He sensed someone in the room, and he lifted his head and teary eyes to see a figure silhouetted in the doorway at the top of the stairs. They were tall and lean and seemed clad in torn rags. The dim light from the screen reflected briefly off their goggles in a flash of red.

Then he heard the rattling, raspy breathing.

The Bear stood at the top of the steps and descended towards Jason.

CHAPTER 25

Jason didn't move. Whatever The Bear was going to do, he deserved it. He killed his best friend. His best friend had died screaming and defiant, never asking for help, only concerned for Jason's safety.

The breathing grew closer, and Jason lowered his head. He waited for the first blow and wondered if he would feel it. Would he die screaming? Would it be quick? Would he know it was happening?

Did Alexei know it was happening? Did he wonder the same things?

Did Alexei hate me for doing this to him? For not waking up?

Jason felt something on his shoulder and winced, preparing for whatever came next...but nothing did.

He looked up. The Bear was kneeling next to him and had a gauntleted hand on his shoulder.

"Aren't you going to kill me?" Jason asked, his voice raw. "Didn't finish the job the first time."

The Bear stared at Jason through red-tinted, impenetrable goggles, and the cycler rattled with a breath.

"I showed you what you can do," The Bear said in an electronically mangled voice, with an accent that Jason couldn't place. "The doctor wanted you to know how."

"What I'm..." Jason flashed to flying through a window, being outside in the sun. "*This*? This is why I can be outside?"

Jason heard a thin chirping noise that sounded like it was coming from The Bear. Jason moved his head and saw that The Bear had an earpiece in. He was hearing whoever was talking to him.

"You are critical," The Bear said, or whoever was on the other end of the earpiece said through The Bear. "You are ready for your next evolution."

"What...what does that even mean?" Jason yelled, his throat raw from the effort. "That was my *friend*! You killed my friend! *I* killed my friend! For what? So I could *go outside*?"

"No, you are so much more than that. You are what we need to be."

Jason stood and lashed out at the only thing that was near him: the podium. He wrenched it from side to side, ripped it from the stage, and hurled it across the room at one of the windows. It hit and bounced off, leaving a spider web of cracks where it struck.

"He was my friend," Jason said, his words barely a whisper, choked out through his sobs.

The Bear cocked his head at the chirping in his ear. "He was worth more as parts than as a person."

The Bear's head snapped back so quickly from Jason's punch that the earpiece was flung across the room and clattered to the floor.

The Bear swung back, but Jason remembered his lesson from their first bout. He ducked under it and slipped to the side. He drilled The Bear's ribs with two quick shots and slipped away again, and the man...or whatever he was… grunted something garbled through the odd cycler.

The Bear quickly regained his composure and charged in, and Jason slipped to the side once more, but The Bear was still quicker than Jason had anticipated and landed a blow into the middle of Jason's chest that made his heart skip a beat.

Can't let him get his feet planted.

Jason didn't engage and instead rolled backward over one of the long tables in front of the audience chairs. The Bear leaped over the table and tried to stomp into Jason's gut, but he threw a chair in the way. The Bear's foot landed awkwardly, and he started to lose his balance, but not before bringing his foot to the ground, destroying the chair. He grabbed Jason by his jacket and swung him to the side, throwing him two rows back.

Jason hit another row of tables, his momentum carrying him over the smooth surface and into the chairs behind.

The rattling from the Bear's cycler gave Jason enough warning to roll out of the way before another blow crashed down where he was a moment before. Jason kicked straight into the front of The Bear's knee. He staggered but didn't go down.

Jason jumped to his feet, grabbed another chair, and swung it as hard as he could. The Bear tried to get an arm up to block, but Jason swung true, and The Bear was rocked to one side. The chair connected with The Bear's side and head, and the sound of metal hitting the floor followed as The Bear's cycler was ripped from his face.

What was underneath, Jason saw, was the lower half of a human face. Nothing monstrous or deformed, just a mouth, nose, and a square jaw, with some blood dribbling from the blow.

Jason swung the chair again to bring it down on The Bear's head, and The Bear raised his other arm to block it. Blow after blow landed, and he drove The Bear down to one knee, but the arm stayed up, blocking the worst of the damage. Finally, Jason brought the chair down as hard as he could, but this time the chair exploded over the limb. The rags had been torn away from the onslaught, and Jason saw metal where there should have been flesh and bone. No blood, no torn skin, just an exoskeleton arm.

The Bear used Jason's moment of shock to land a punch to his face with the unexposed arm. Jason expected the impact to feel like rebar, but instead, it felt like getting hit with a normal, organic appendage. Albeit an appendage that was attached to someone who knew how to throw a punch who did a ton of steroids.

Jason's cycler was torn from his face and flew across the room as he reeled from the blow. He was able to slip the next two swings thrown his direction and quickly scrambled out of the way.

Jason knew he couldn't win in a direct fight.

Or an unfair fight.

He looked at the prosthetic arm and dropped the scraps of the chair still in his hand.

This guy isn't even human.

The Bear wiped some blood from his face and pressed forward, tossing chairs and debris out of his way. His movements held the air of inevitability.

No, he is human, he just cheats. Need to find a way to cheat back. Jason slipped past another blow but didn't dodge the elbow that quickly followed in time. His vision exploded in stars, and he stumbled back, trying to keep his balance and maintain consciousness.

Jason felt himself sucking wind and forced himself to slow his breathing, to calm himself, to think. Breathe in, hold, breathe out…

Just breathe…

The Bear hurled a chair at Jason with a frustrated roar. Jason ducked, the chair collided with the already-cracked window, and the spider webs grew.

Just breathe…wait…

He glanced at the window and wasn't sure if he was actually hearing the whistle of air blowing through or just imagining it.

Outside is death.

Except for me.

Jason didn't realize that the roar that filled the auditorium was his until after he had collided with The Bear at full speed. He grabbed around The Bear's torso, pinning the mechanical arm to his side, and pushed forward. The Bear hammered down on Jason's back with his free arm, but Jason continued his charge toward the window.

Into the window.

Through the window.

And outside.

They rolled across the graveled terrace and into the scaffolding that bordered it. He heard something clatter off one of the metal supports and saw his phone spinning in space, plummeting down, down, down, becoming a small dot and then disappearing. Jason could feel the wind blowing in his hair and on his face; on the hazy horizon; he could see the beginnings of pink and red.

The wind whipped at The Bear's rags, and he kicked at Jason, forcing him onto the scaffolding itself, beyond which nothing would stop Jason from plummeting into the void. Jason instinctively grabbed whatever he could and felt his fingers clasp around one of the metal supports holding the scaffolding up.

The Bear wheezed noisily, pulled himself closer to Jason, and tried to push him. Jason grasped desperately at the support and tried to pull himself back onto the roof terrace. The Bear swung with his prosthetic arm, and Jason moved, the metal limb smashing into the scaffolding and leaving a dent. Jason felt the whole structure shudder and shift, and loose materials fell from a higher level. He heard the dull thud as pieces hit the gravel and saw some random tools and lengths of rebar.

The Bear continued to push and wheezed again as he tried to take a breath, and Jason felt the force trying to shove him into the nothingness behind him weaken.

Jason kicked twice into The Bear's face, his heels connecting squarely with the red-tinted goggles, and he felt something give. One of the lenses was cracked, and the goggles were hanging oddly on The Bear's face.

The Bear grabbed Jason by the ankle with his metal hand and yanked, and Jason was tossed back onto the terrace. A piece of metal rebar bashed into his ribs with the impact, and he sucked in a breath reflexively.

But his lungs didn't burn.

The doctor wanted me to know how.

Alexei was the how. Whatever they did, whatever they took from Alexei and forced him to die screaming and cursing them, they put into Jason. It fixed the Horkrim's Syndrome. It made it so he could go outside untethered, unencumbered, like people used to do decades ago.

The Bear marched forward, slower than before, and the wheezing sounded like it was intensifying. He tried to kick at Jason, but he blocked it. The Bear fell to one knee and clamped down on Jason's neck with the mechanical hand, and started to squeeze.

Jason tried to pry the fingers away but to no avail. The grip tightened. He knew it wouldn't matter if The Bear couldn't breathe outside if The Bear strangled the life out of him. Black spots started to dance at the edge of his vision. He knew he would be unconscious before The Bear finally succumbed to the environment.

Jason flailed about blindly and wildly for anything. His hand brushed the textured metal of rebar. He grasped it and swung at The Bear's head as hard as he could.

The Bear released his grip and fell over with a groan. Jason gasped, filling his lungs with air, still shocked and amazed that he was doing it *outside*.

The Bear started getting to his feet. Jason swung the rebar again, this time aiming for the prosthetic arm. Metal clashed on metal, and The Bear fell to the ground again as his arm was taken out from under him.

Jason dropped a knee into The Bear's back to hold him down. The Bear started pushing himself up again, coughing and wheezing, the metal arm's servos whirring as he slowly powered his way to his feet.

Jason jammed the rebar into the space between the exoskeleton's struts that formed the forearm and twisted. The limb squeaked, and the joint squealed, but The Bear continued to push himself up. Jason threw his leg over The Bear's head and rolled, flipping him onto his back. He pinned the man down with his legs, and Jason used his whole torso to twist the rebar.

The metal squealed as it twisted with the leverage. Jason smelled ozone as the servos in the joints continued to fire and fight against Jason. He pulled and twisted again, putting his entire body into his effort, and with a crackle and a high-pitched groan, the arm finally gave way. The elbow bent in the wrong direction with a *snap,* and he immediately felt the opposing force cease. Jason twisted the rebar again and rotated the arm at the shoulder in a full circle, and more crunches and sparks ensued as he disabled the unit.

The Bear stayed relatively silent, save for the rattling coming from his chest as he tried to breathe. His chest rose and fell in short intervals, unable to process the soup of pollution and whatever else permeated the outside air.

Jason took some deep breaths to calm himself. He grabbed The Bear by his coat and dragged him inside. The air smelled sweeter, and he could hear a ventilation system running that hadn't been running before, trying to repressurize the room. Jason figured that the air quality was probably enough to not outright kill The Bear.

He pulled some wires from the ruined podium and used them to secure The Bear to one of the tables. The Bear didn't fight, breathing shallowly, arm sparking at his side.

He gathered his headgear. As he picked up his goggles, he saw a small object under one of the tables. He investigated and saw it was the earwig The Bear had been using.

Jason inserted it in his ear. "You there?"

There was no response, and Jason thought the unit might have been damaged. Then an electronically scrambled voice came through. "Hello, Jason."

Hearing his name in that voice sent a chill down his spine. He didn't want that kind of familiarity with evil. "You did all of this?"

"You're emotional. It's understandable. It's one of our many failings as humans."

Jason felt a maelstrom of thoughts all trying to be voiced at once, and finally croaked out, "Why?"

"For the benefit of humanity. For our guaranteed survival." The voice sounded confident, but there was no condescension that Jason could detect. It sounded more like a parent explaining something to a child. "I know you don't understand, but I hope you will one day. You are my greatest work, my Patient Zero. You have helped humanity more than you can imagine."

"I'm coming for you." Jason felt nothing but cold fury in each word.

"I look forward to that day." There was a subtle *click*, and Jason knew the connection had been disconnected. He pulled the earwig out and shoved it in his pocket.

Jason's leg hurt, and he saw that his pants were soaked with blood. His ribs and head hurt. He wanted nothing more than to go to sleep for a week.

Instead, he walked up the auditorium steps, rebar dragging in his hand, and pushed into the hallway.

He wasn't done looking.

Chapter 26

An alarm sounded in the hallway, and an annoyingly pleasant voice was calling for evacuation. Emergency strobes flashed. Jason limped down the hallway, rebar dragging on the tile, and he searched.

More doors, more empty rooms.

He figured at some point, some kind of security would show up. He doubted that emergencies from the facility were routed through the usual channels. It would be hard to explain rooms of abducted kids to the firefighters.

He looked behind him and saw the bloody trail he was leaving. If private security did show up, he knew they wouldn't have difficulty finding him. And he didn't know if he was in any shape to fight anyone else.

He pushed it out of his mind. It was a "Future Jason" problem. "Right Now Jason" needed to find the surgical suites amid the maze of offices and labs. Some part of him marveled at how many people must work in the facility. Another part was horrified that not a single one had enough of a conscience to blow the whistle on the atrocities he saw committed here on what seemed like a nearly daily basis.

For the "good of humanity", Jason was sure all of them would say. He thought he had seen the extremes people would go to justify their behavior, but …this was at a level that he couldn't comprehend or wanted to.

What did that mean, that he was "Patient Zero"?

He fingered the earwig in his pocket. There were many questions, and he would need to answer them later.

For what felt like the hundredth time, Jason shoved a door open and expected to see yet another lab or communal work area. Instead, he found a hallway, windows on either side. He took a step inside.

He looked through the first set of windows on his right. There were cages stacked on each other, two high, the kind Jason had seen in veterinary clinics in Center City. He saw something inside them and was about to continue down the hall when one of the objects moved. He looked again and felt the last of his horror and ire and rage drain out of him, the tank spent.

In each cage, he saw an emaciated child in a surgical gown. He pushed open the door to the room. A few of the kids slowly raised their heads, hollow eyes looking at him but not registering any recognition or response.

Jason's hands shook as he unlocked the first cage. He opened the door and gently reached a hand in, palm up, in a gesture of aid.

At first, the kid didn't respond; she just stared at him with wide, blue eyes.

"Is this real?" She finally said, her voice tiny and barely above a whisper.

Jason knew if he said anything, he would start sobbing, so he just nodded. Tears overflowed onto her cheeks, and she took his hand. It was small and cold, and Jason wasn't sure she would be able to hold anything, it felt so weak. She pulled herself forward into his arms as he helped her and lowered her to the floor.

Jason moved on to the next cage, and the next, opening each one with shaky hands and helping each child out. With each cage, he hoped he would see Markus, but he did not.

He opened all of the cages except one; it was empty.

The kids all stood on unsteady legs, rocking back and forth like they would fall over in a stiff breeze.

Jason finally found his voice. "Ready to go home?"

The kids nodded, tears streaking down their faces. The first little girl took Jason's hand and squeezed, though not very hard. Jason led them out into the hall.

Across from him was another window that looked into an operating room. It looked identical to the one in the video: a table in the middle, a child strapped into it, and the familiar halo device being moved into position by one of two scrub-clad figures.

Jason caught sight of his reflection in the window, and what he saw would have scared him if he had any emotion left to feel. Blood stained his face, and his hair slicked to his scalp with sweat and more blood. He blinked, saw through the reflection, and finally saw the child strapped to the table: Markus.

Jason pushed the door open and stepped in, girl hanging on one hand, rebar grasped in his other. The room smelled of antiseptic and felt significantly colder than the hall.

Both figures froze when Jason entered, glancing between him, the kids, and each other.

"Get out." Jason's voice was little more than a whisper, but to his ears, it was a whisper of a winter storm that promised a cold end to whoever and whatever didn't seek shelter.

The two figures got the same impression. Both ran for an exit, slipping on the floor and knocking over trays of tools in their haste. Jason let them run past him, never taking his eyes off Markus.

He dropped his rebar and released the little girl's hand. He approached the table and started undoing the restraints.

"Hey, Markus," Jason said quietly. "Your mom's worried about you."

Markus wiped tears from his face and snot from his nose with his newly-freed hand. "She is?"

Jason continued undoing the restraints. "Yeah, she sent me to look for you. Let's go see her."

He helped Markus down from the table. He picked up his rebar, and the little girl immediately clamped onto his hand again. He looked around at all of the kids. He knew they would need years of therapy to get back to some semblance of "normal", if that was even a possibility. Some wounds went too deep, he knew. But at least these kids would get back to their families. And he had some answers for the other names on his list.

He led the kids back into the hall and out into the main complex. The strobes were still flashing but now were red instead of white. A moment later, he felt a vibration in the floor. Smoke started pouring out of some of the office doors, and he felt the temperature in the hallway increase. Flames began to lick at the walls.

Jason increased his pace as much as he dared and backtracked through the facility, now utterly silent save for the sound of bare feet padding on the tile floor. Smoke gathered near the ceiling, and it was now apparent that the facility was on fire. He felt another rumble in the floor, and a door blew off its hinges and slammed into the wall just in front of him.

If the kids were any more scared than they were already, he couldn't tell. He motioned for them to stay low and he crouched down as well, trying to keep out of the smoke. He led them past the labs and conference rooms, and into the lobby.

To his surprise, there was no security to greet him, nor was there any evidence of a fire suppression system kicking on. He filed the details away for later.

He took the kids to the elevator lobby and pushed the call button. They waited in silence until the doors slid open. They entered the car. The trip down was quick, and Jason again felt his ears pop with the sudden change in altitude. The temperature fell back down to something more comfortable as they descended.

The doors opened to a sea of bright lights and chaos. Jason held his hand in front of his face to shield his eyes until they could adjust, and he felt the kids crowd behind him. The glare finally died down, and he could see that on one side of the glass lobby, the entire street was lined with patrollers, lights flashing. On the other side were vans with media logos emblazoned on their sides, and a mix of police and journalist drones flitted about.

A tactical team in full gear stood at the ready in the lobby but were being held at bay by a line of what Jason guessed was private security who looked as well-armed as the police. Les stood in front of one of them, his face red with anger. Belford stood in between them and the line of security personnel.

"We need to get up there!" Les shouted, and from the sound of his voice, Jason guessed it wasn't the first time he had made the statement.

"You don't have a warrant," one of the security guards replied. "If you don't have a warrant-"

"I don't need a warrant if I have probable cause, asshole," Les growled.

"You don't have that either, detective," Belford said.

"I've got a recorded conversation admitting there are a dozen kids up there-"

"...from a discredited source and an illegal wiretap," Belford said. "Stand down. Now."

"So how about the giant fucking explosion on the 86th floor? How about that?"

"Not our problem," Belford said.

"Screw this," Les said and started pushing through. "Tac Team on me, we're going in."

The private security force readied their weapons, and Belford got in Les' face. "No, you are not. I'm in command here, and you are not authorized to do anything. Stand down." He shouted over Les' head towards the tactical team starting to form behind Les. "I'm in charge here, you will obey my orders. Stand down immediately..."

Belford's face became slack, and his words stuck in his throat as Jason pushed through the line of security guards with a dozen kids in tow.

One of the guards planted themself in front of Jason, weapon at the ready. Jason stared into the guard's eyes.

"Move." Jason said it so quietly that he doubted anyone else could hear him.

The security guard did, however, and a moment later, they lowered their weapon and moved aside. Jason continued escorting the kids into the lobby. EMTs rushed forward towards them, and when some of the security guards looked like they were going to interfere, several members of the tac team moved into a shielding position, and their body language said one thing: *Please. Try.*

Belford's face had gone gray, and his mouth opened and shut like a fish trying to breathe air. Finally, his voice returned. "Jason Thane…you…you are under arrest…"

Jason stopped before his former team member and held out his hands. "OK." Belford didn't move. "Go ahead," Jason said. Belford remained still, his usual smug look of entitled confidence wholly gone. "Forget your cuffs? Again?"

"Detective Caporelli, place Thane under arrest."

Les jammed his hands into his pockets. "Oops. Guess I forgot mine, too."

Belford began to look panicked. "Somebody here, place this man under arrest immediately!"

The other officers in the lobby turned their attention either to the kids being helped by the EMTs or to each other, keeping a wary eye on the security guards that still formed a line, preventing anyone from entering further into the building.

Belford wildly looked around the room, and when no one responded to him, he turned his glare onto Jason. "You're finished," he growled. "You're done as a cop."

Jason lowered his hands. "Derrick, I just led a task force that made the largest splice bust in history. I just saved a dozen kidnapped kids from a burning building. I exposed a human trafficking ring using children for medical experiments." He stepped closer to Belford. "So come at me."

Belford was shaking. "When Chief Swan gets done with you…"

"Hey, moron," Les said. "Do you think she's going to take the fall for ignoring Jason's warnings about the missing kids? Or do you think she will position herself on the right side of this and throw someone else under the bus?"

Belford's mouth opened and closed several times. "No, she wouldn't…I'm her right hand…" His voice trailed off.

"There you go," Les said. "I knew you'd get there. Eventually." Les turned and walked away, and Jason followed; Belford was left shaking and seething as reality crashed down on him.

When they were out of earshot, Les said, "You know you're screwed, right?"

"Yeah," Jason sighed. "This may have bought me a little grace," he said, gesturing to the pandemonium around them. Firefighters had arrived and were trying to get into the building, and they were being stonewalled as well. EMTs were checking out the kids, starting IVs, and taking vitals. Jason did not doubt that they would need a few days in the hospital, at least, to treat the physical symptoms of their confinement. "But yeah, it's me or her, and I don't know if I come out on top of that."

"Just lay low for a while," Les said and patted Jason on the shoulder. "Let things calm down. You'll be reinstated, and then you can figure out your next move."

Jason shook his head. "I don't even know if that's what I want anymore."

"You're done being police?"

Jason shook his head. "I don't know. Maybe. They don't want me. Honestly, I got more accomplished when I operated outside the system than from within it. And I've got to start from scratch investigating whatever was going on upstairs now that all of the evidence has gone up in smoke. Literally."

"But it's done," Les said. "Right? I mean, the facility is toast, the kids are safe…"

"They aren't done," Jason said. "There are at least two other sites, maybe more. And my gods, Les, they've murdered hundreds of kids…" Jason swallowed his grief. "All in the name of science or research or some bullshit. They've put too much money into this to walk away from whatever they're trying to accomplish."

Les looked concerned for his former partner. "OK, but remember…you made a difference today. This hurt them."

Jason looked over the kids, and the little girl with the blue eyes smiled a weak smile and waved a tiny wave at him. He felt a profound sadness at the pain they had endured, but he also felt a spark of hope for each of them. They would get to go home. Their loved ones would know what happened instead of living in the suffocating darkness of ignorance.

The ignorance that had driven Jordan to the edge. That had tortured Amira every day for twenty years.

The ignorance that he could no longer share with them. An ignorance supplanted by profound guilt.

Jason felt a new weight on his shoulders on top of the bone-weariness he already carried. A weight he had to bear on his own.

"It's not enough," he said. "This might have hurt them, but they need to hurt more. They aren't done yet. And neither am I."

Thank you for reading The Fall.

Could you take 30 seconds to leave a review?

Join The Fall mailing list to get updates on future projects at cb-books.com.

Join the discussion in The Fall Facebook group at facebook.com/groups/thefallseries.

About the Authors

Connor Stevens and Brian Wiggins are both from South Jersey. They also both hate writing about themselves, so that's all you're going to get.

Made in United States
North Haven, CT
06 January 2023

30685138R00186